going coastal

forge books by wendy french

Going Coastal
sMothering

going Coastal

wendy french

a tom doherty associates book
new york

This is a work of fiction. All the characters and events portrayed in this novel are either fictitious or are used fictitiously.

GOING COASTAL

Book design by Nicole de las Heras

A Forge Book
Published by Tom Doherty Associates, LLC
175 Fifth Avenue
New York, NY 10010

www.tor.com

ISBN 0-765-31349-9

EAN 978-0765-31349-2

First Edition: January 2005

Printed in the United States of America

0 9 8 7 6 5 4 3 2 1

For Kate Rappé,
my best friend since the first grade, an age
of ponytails and kneesocks.
Thank you for a lifetime of giggles, and for
introducing me to Dave.

And for Dave himself,
who not only tolerates our shenanigans,
but encourages them.

acknowledgments

I'd like to thank my agent, Sally Harding (New Zealand's greatest export), my editor, Paul Stevens (master of reassurance), and Natalia Aponte at Forge. Thanks to Edwin Fotheringham for two whiz-bang covers, and to Mike Hipple, Ryan Griffiths, Allison Kline, and Damon Brown for their efforts.

Huge thanks to the writing group who suffered through the first draft: Linda Kearney, Deanie Barbour, Kelly Hale, Diane Terhune, Anne Schmidt, and Georgia Conn. Also to the two we've lost, Gloria Bradford and Robert Gray.

For ongoing encouragement I'd like to thank Sally and Stuart McDonald, Tamarah Robinson, Sandy French, Peggy Campbell, Brenda Erickson, Jen Moss, Ray Bailey, Christine Love, Anita Murrin, Kim Kanakes, and the Queen Bee of getting the word out, Danielle Carpenter.

For day-to-day cheering on at the cube farm, thanks to Rana Anbe, Sue "The Hammer" Ashfield, Samantha Burt, Paula Burtch, Brian Cunnington, Matt Darcy, Dee Davis, Cindy Deane, Sylvia Dillon, Eva Dodd, Lisa Haas, Paul Halvorson, Deonna Hayes, Erika James, James Lawrence, Brandon Maldonado, Tammy Moore, Lorri Romie, and Diane Shimomura.

Special thanks to Jeane Robinson of The Tenth Muse bookstore in Seaside, Oregon, and Roberta Dyer of Broadway Books in Portland for being so supportive of a first-time author when *sMothering* was published.

And finally, thanks to the people and scenery of the Sunshine Coast of British Columbia, Canada, where this book was originally set, and to Willows Galley in Victoria, B.C., for being my favorite fish-and-chips shop on earth.

going coastal

one

Marty McDade's uneven fingernails gripped the flesh of my right buttock and I knew I should have spat in his gravy. I spun around to face him, prepared for our third confrontation in as many days, only to be mocked by a smile. His *sales* smile. The self-proclaimed Used Car King of Bent Harbor was more like the Lord of the Lemons, and my brother had the Yugo to prove it.

Slow drops of sweat dribbled from his receding hairline, down his forehead, and nestled in the lashes of his beady brown eyes. As usual, he had a mid-cardiac arrest look about him, and only the steady movement of his hands reaching for french fries, dipping them in thick beef gravy, and raising them to his waiting lips proved that he wasn't about to drop dead (at least until he'd finished eating).

His greasy fingers had no business on my ass.

I turned to see a glimmer of amusement in the eyes of Marty's top salesmen, Ed Banks and Tony Fletcher. They were paunchy, middle-aged sheep, who couldn't come up with their own opinions if their commissions depended on it, and I was sick of being their daily joke.

"Do you mind?" I snarled.

"Not a bit, Jody," Marty said, "you've got a sweet ass."

It wouldn't have been so bad if his son hadn't been sitting next to him, staring out the window, his lean face flushed with the rich red hue of Marty-fication.

Lucas McDade.

I hadn't seen much of him since we'd finished high school, and he'd left town along with most of our graduating class. As I cleared the older men's plates and tried to come up with a stinging retort for his father, I watched Lucas from the corner of my eye.

He was still on the scrawny side, lucky to have sidestepped his father's girth gene. His eyes, staring at Bent Harbor's midweek shuffle, were the same washed-out blue I remembered, framed by almost invisible blond lashes. His jawline was covered with a faint dusting of stubble while his lips were faded and dry, as though he'd spent the past ten years at sea.

I cringed slightly, wondering if he remembered groping me in the darkness of the Starscope Theater in ninth grade. His breath had been hot and reeked of red licorice, his hands clumsy with the wooden toggles on my cardigan. Things hadn't gone very far—a few sloppy kisses and a couple of wool-weakened squeezes when the toggles defeated him. I couldn't recall exactly what I'd seen in him and, since he hadn't acknowledged our acquaintance in the forty minutes he'd sat at table 11, I didn't give a rat's ass.

I piled plates and gathered cutlery, wishing Marty would find a new lunch destination, but he and his wingmen frequented Dean's Ocean Galley for every break their schedules allowed. They treated each visit as a unique opportunity to belittle me and giggle like a trio of twelve-year-olds with a stolen porn magazine. They were all single, no surprise, considering their toothpick-sucking and belching, not to mention the furtive reaches under the table to make groin adjustments, as though their intimate bits and pieces would take flight if left unattended.

I turned to pile the dishes into a bus pan and Marty pinched me again.

"Hands off!" I barked, glancing toward the kitchen to see if

Dean was a witness. He wasn't in the cook's window, which meant he was either having a smoke out back with the latest in a string of useless junior-high dishwashers, or he'd taken an issue of *Time* into the restroom for a bit of "system cleansing," as he liked to call it. Either way, I was on my own.

Of course, I'd told Dean about the lewd jokes and comments, but there was very little he could do. He'd asked them to tone it down, but he was a teddy bear, and they knew it. Besides, Bent Harbor was a small town with a weak-kneed economy and I couldn't really expect him to turn away customers.

In seven years, I'd gradually become immune to the crudeness, but the physical stuff was a different matter and my patience was wearing thinner than Marty's comb-over.

"Sorry, Jody," he smirked. "You're just too tempting in that getup."

"Ah, yes," I said, through gritted teeth, "the synthetic-fiber defense. I'm sure the irresistible lure of a poly-knit blend has been the downfall of men for centuries."

"Huh?" he grunted as I turned away.

I cursed my insipid sailor dress and moved to clear another table, certain I'd think of the ultimate zinger in three or four hours, when it was too damn late to use it.

I pocketed a two-dollar tip left by the fire chief, which brought the day's total to just short of sixty bucks, not bad considering it had been a slow shift. I carried my bus pan to the vacant kitchen, and returned to the dining room with a damp cloth. Relieved to see that Marty and company were absorbed in conversation (except Lucas, who was still staring out the window), I wiped ketchup and grease from the Formica and glanced around the restaurant, amazed I'd worked there so long.

A thick layer of dust covered the collection of seashells in the far corner, and the plank walls were lined with the same creased maps and old photographs of prize-winning fish (caught somewhere other than our shallow dip of coastline) that had been on display when I'd started the job. A ship's knobby steering wheel, rescued from the St. Peter's flea market and rummage sale five or six years earlier, leaned against the hostess station, apparently awaiting its unlikely return to sea. Old glass fishing floats, tangled in frayed nets, hung from the ceiling like some kind of mariner's chandelier.

Dean called it "ambiance."

Sixteen booths lined the rain-streaked windows, their torn turquoise seat covers depressing, at best, and each table was outfitted with ketchup, malt vinegar, salt and pepper. Laminated menus, boasting big meals for small budgets, were tucked behind chrome napkin dispensers, an absolute bitch to clean. I'd spent countless afternoons attempting to defy fingerprints with a bottle of Windex, a dishtowel, and a string of profanities.

Of course, my assessment of the restaurant wouldn't be complete if I didn't consider the thin layer of grease on the checkered tile floor, furniture, light fixtures, and, most importantly, all over my body. I never felt clean at work, and even when I showered at home under a scalding spray, it was nearly impossible to clear the glossy sheen from my pores and hair. And the smell! The entire city block was drenched in the odors of fish, fat, and french fries no matter how much bleach we used on the floors or how quickly our ceiling fans sliced through the air.

If heaven could be found on earth, it was nowhere near Dean's Ocean Galley, but that was the price I paid to live in Bent Harbor. I could have raced to Seattle like everyone else, but I'd chosen to stay. It wasn't a perfect town, but it was my home.

* * *

I walked to the counter, where Max and Jaundice were slurping coffee and shooting the shit, just as they had every afternoon since retirement from the electric company.

Jaundice wore the yellow golf hat and windbreaker that earned him the nickname years before I was born, and Max fiddled with the zipper on an Adidas track jacket designed to shelter a younger man's belly. They were best friends for life and my most tolerable regular customers.

If, in some parallel universe I could only fear, I had to choose between them, I'd say Jaundice was the better looking of the two. There was more substance to his wild spray of white hair and he was long and lean, like a lizard or insect. The thick lenses inside his square black frames reduced his eyes to dark specks. His teeth were his own and the envy of Max, who wore chipped dentures, discolored by tobacco, coffee, and foul language. Next to Jaundice's lanky build, Max looked even shorter and more bulbous than he actually was, so he liked to prop himself on the highest stool at the counter for the sake of aesthetics.

I caught Max's eye and he gave me a wink, the signal he was ready for dessert. I pulled a slice of blackberry crumble from the pie case. The sugar and oat topping was soggy and stained dark purple from sitting too long, but I placed it in front of him anyway, knowing he wouldn't care.

"Hot damn!" Max crooned. "I was just about to say I wouldn't mind some dessert and here it is. You're like some kind of mind-reading computer, Jody."

"Yeah, well . . . ," I murmured.

"I mean it! Goddamn high-speed technology!"

"Okay, Max."

"Click-click-buzz-buzz. A waitress with the brain power of a *computer*. This place should be called 'Megabites.' "

He dragged me through the same stale routine every day and didn't seem to notice I'd stopped laughing in 1998.

"So, what's the topic of the day, guys?" I asked, leaning against the counter to rotate my heels. Pain didn't care about the faux-leather, rubber-soled orthopedic horror shows I slipped my feet into every morning, and the varicose veins I predicted would be splattered across the backs of my legs by the time I was thirty were bubbling closer to the surface with every shift I worked. Age twenty-seven and my body was *already* betraying me.

"Let's see," Max mumbled, pudgy fingers stroking his bristled chin. "P.J's having another episode, so we dropped him off at Whispering Pines this morning." He polished his fork with the tail of his flannel shirt, and I couldn't fault him for doubting our latest dishwasher's dedication.

"He didn't want to go," Jaundice said, stirring his coffee. His entire chin moved when he spoke, like a ventriloquist's dummy.

"You got that right," Max agreed, scooping a mound of crumble into his mouth.

P.J. Hardison was the town's dominant nutcase, slightly overshadowing the runner-up, Dottie Maple, who was oblivious to the competition. He was about the same vintage as the men at the counter, though a childhood accident had left him slightly off center.

"What kind of episode?" I asked, starting to refill the salt and pepper shakers. I wasn't sure how his state of mind was measured, but as far as I could tell, his entire life seemed to be one weird, extended episode.

P.J.'s favorite pastime was rattling off a random and endless list of hockey players' names. He liked the sound of his own voice almost as much as he loved the NHL, and while his muttering alone was bearable, the rambling used to be accompanied by the rhythmic swinging of a rusted machete. He'd claimed to be keeping Old Marine Highway safe by hacking off overhanging branches and increasing visibility for drivers, but his fervor was enough to make more than a few people nervous. Back in 1993, the local police decided that while P.J. wasn't dangerous, the weapon was, and they'd confiscated it. He spent a couple of days down in the mouth until my brother, Josh, dug an old *Star Wars* light saber out of our basement as a replacement. Judging by the beaten bushes I'd seen in recent years, the force was still with him.

"Well, sometimes old P.J. gets to be like a broken record with those players," Max explained. "He gets stuck on one name and can't seem to get past it. Repeats it for days." He shoveled another forkful of crumble into his mouth and groaned with pleasure.

"This time it's Bobby Orr," Jaundice added. "Bobby Orr, Bobby Orr, Bobby Orr—"

"Cut it out, for Christ's sake!" Max snapped. "It's bad enough with just one of you doing it." He turned his attention back to me. "Orr's been on his mind for three or four days now. Hasn't been that bad since seventy-eight."

"Seventy-seven. The electrical storm was in seventy-seven." Jaundice added two spoonfuls of sugar to his coffee.

"It was seventy-eight."

"Seventy-seven. I was with Gert. That was the year she left." He looped a bony index finger through the handle of his mug.

"She left you four times," Max pointed out, unnecessarily.

"I *meant* that was the year she left for good." Jaundice frowned into his coffee and I couldn't tell if he was depressed by his wife's memory or the flavor.

I watched two elderly women squint at the menu in the front window for a full minute before stepping inside.

"Do you serve take-out fish and chips?" the taller of the two asked, gripping her white purse as though theft were the soup of the day.

"Absolutely," I said, offering her my cheesiest smile.

"We'd like a cod and a large chips to share, please." She started toward the counter with tiny, birdlike steps.

"I'm sorry, we only have halibut," I said, for what must have been the eight thousandth time in my waitressing career. The sign on the roof should have read "Dean's Ocean Galley. If you don't like halibut, fuck off."

"No cod?" she gasped, and Max smiled between bites. He'd been trying to talk Dean into adding it to the menu for years.

"No, ma'am. We've always served halibut," I told her.

"Always?"

"Always." I nodded, and muttered to myself, "Since the beginning of goddamn time."

The woman turned to her friend, who was still hovering near the front door. "Did you hear that, Phyllis? No cod."

"Eh?" The smaller one lifted a white-gloved hand to her ear.

"No cod," her friend repeated.

"What's theology got to do with my supper?"

"I said, *no cod*."

"Eh?"

"There is no cod!" My voice boomed toward her.

"May he strike you down!" she gasped.

"Oh, for goodness' sake." Her companion sighed. "We'll get hamburgers across the street."

The door slammed behind them and Max continued with his story as though there'd been no interruption. "So, P.J. was at his worst in nineteen seventy-seven." He looked to Jaundice, who reluctantly nodded his approval. "There was an electrical storm while he and his brother Dirk were out fishing."

"In an aluminum canoe," Jaundice interrupted.

"I'm getting to that."

"On Shiver Pond," Jaundice said.

"It doesn't matter where they were."

"Details make the story, Max."

It didn't matter whether I'd heard the tale before, or if I was listening to them at all. They could talk until their coffees were colder than a toilet seat at two A.M. without skipping a beat.

"Anyway, those two get caught in a downpour," Max continued, "so they head for shore. When they reach the safety of land, they take off across that meadow on the west side. You know the one, right, Jody?"

I nodded.

"*Of course* she knows the one. You can't go to Shiver Pond without seeing the meadow." Jaundice rolled his eyes.

"Can I *tell* the story?"

"Doesn't seem like it."

Max sighed and continued. "Okay, the rain's pouring down and they have to run across the meadow to get to their truck, so you know what they did?"

I shook my head.

"Those dumbasses ran across an open meadow in a lightning storm, using an *aluminum canoe* for cover!"

"The lightning killed Dirk," Jaundice explained.

"Yup, that's the kicker. The normal brother dies and old P.J. gets the charge of his life!"

"That's what stalled him on Guy Lafleur."

"Right." Max nodded. "The Lafleur kick lasted damn near a week. That was the first time we took him to Whispering Pines."

"God only knows what they did to him, but when we picked him up for Dirk's funeral, he was onto new players."

"Right. Gordie Howe and so on. Cured, I suppose," Max laughed. "Well, as cured as old Patrick James could get."

Patrick James. Along with the rest of town, I'd been calling him "Poor Judgment" for as long as I could remember.

"Now it's Bobby Orr," Max said, shaking his head.

"At least he's stalled on one of the greats," Jaundice added. "He'll be fine in a few days, I'm sure."

A loud burst of laughter erupted at Marty's table and Jaundice glanced over his shoulder. "What's with them?"

"The usual. They're being assholes again."

"So, ignore them," he suggested, as though the thought had never crossed my mind.

"I try, but it really pisses me off. I'm sick of coming in here, day after day, and taking crap from a bunch of car jockeys." I was just getting warmed up. "And the worst of it is—"

"You know, some folks say that sour grapes make whine," Max offered between mouthfuls.

"Great. I'll try to remember that."

"All I'm saying is, sometimes life is the shits. Deal with it."

"I appreciate your candor, Max. All *I'm* saying is, I can do better than this."

"I hope so," he said, "I've been drinking lukewarm coffee for fifteen minutes and you haven't even offered me a warm-up."

"That's not what I meant."

"I know." He smiled and handed me his mug.

"Can we get a total over here?" Marty called from across the dining room.

I gave both Max and Jaundice refills before moving toward the McDade table.

"Yessir," Marty taunted, as I handed him the bill. "She can fill out that uniform like nobody else."

I glared at him, my ideal zinger still out of reach.

"Come on, Jody." He leaned toward me, belly pressed against the tabletop. "We all know how you feel about me."

"You're like . . . bad sinus congestion." I grabbed his plate.

As I turned to walk away, Marty patted my backside with a warm palm. "Then I guess you wanna blow me."

While the three older men laughed hysterically, I turned to see Lucas wincing on my behalf and I felt something snap inside. I'd heard worse jokes and managed to walk away, but suddenly seven years seemed like too damn long to put up with Marty's bullshit. He would *never* stop harassing me, and his sneering smile would always be waiting at the corner table, pushing me to believe that Dean's Ocean Galley was as far as life would take me.

I froze, dropped his plate and cutlery onto the nearest table with a clatter, and stood dead still, hands on my hips.

Ed's face was flushed, and I saw tears of laughter glittering in the corners of Tony's eyes. They were laughing at me because they *could,* knowing I had to be polite and friendly for the sake of a few lousy bucks in tips. I was tired, sore, greasy, and it was never going to get any better than clearing tables and slinging fried fish. There was no ladder to climb, and no promotions to look forward to. I was a waitress. *Period.* Even though the money I put away was slowly building up in my savings account and I was inching closer to buying my dream house on Sitka Point, I loathed the feeling at the end of a shift that all I'd accomplished was feeding a bunch of losers too lazy to cook for themselves.

In a moment of defiance I made a big decision.

"That's it!"

"That's what?" Marty asked, running stubby fingers through what remained of his hair.

"*It.* I've had it with you guys, with this whole place." I untied my apron and tossed it on the nearest table, adrenaline pumping.

"What, you're *quitting*?" Marty asked, lips stretching toward a smile.

"Yes!" Saying the word was like releasing a held breath, or loosening a belt. I was ready for the next stage of my life. I could do anything, be anything! I could control my own destiny. *"I quit!"*

"Again?" Ed and Tony asked in unison.

"Yes, *again,*" I snapped, refusing to let them steal my thunder.

"For real this time?" Marty asked.

Of course, they'd seen me go through the motions of quitting, only to return to work the next morning with my tail between my legs, at least six times before. By the time I'd reached my doorstep, I realized that even if I found another job in town, which was about as likely as Marty having a low cholesterol count, nothing would pay as much as the Galley. Tips, large or small, had always reeled me back in.

But this time I'd had enough. *This time,* I really meant it.

"For real." I nodded briskly and headed for the kitchen, noting the slight smile on Lucas's face and the slack-jawed shock of Max and Jaundice.

With each step away from Marty I felt my confidence build, and by the time I reached the doorway next to the deep fryer I was ready to burst with a newfound sense of power.

"Where's Dean?"

From behind a pile of filthy pots and pans, a gloved hand pointed me in the direction of the office. It was actually a large supply cupboard, with no windows and little room for much in the way of furniture, but Dean didn't mind. I peered in the doorway, where receipts and check stubs were piled next to menu samples, paper place mats, and an overflowing ashtray on the wobbly card table he used as a desk. My boss sat on a folding chair, reading the *Bent Harbor Times.*

"Uh, Dean? I need to talk to you."

"Oh, hey, Jody. Come on in." He shuffled his chair to one side until I could step into the space. "What's going on?"

He smiled, his teeth bright white against the darkness of his skin. His broad cheekbones and lips were pure Makah, and I envied the density of the short, black hair he claimed was difficult to style. At well over two hundred pounds, but only five foot six, he was a low wall of a man, with thick, leathered hands resting patiently on his knees. Behind his glasses I could see a fine web of wrinkles, a reminder that he was nearing sixty.

Suddenly, I felt guilty about quitting.

Seven years earlier he'd given me the job, despite my lack of experience, and aside from his choice of asinine uniforms, he was a better boss than I'd ever hoped for. He was accommodating when it came to days off, and he fed me well, which probably accounted for the extra fifteen pounds I'd packed on.

"Dean, I—"

"Quit?" he asked quietly, catching me off guard.

"Well, yeah."

"I could see it in your face. For real this time?"

Why did everyone have to ask?

I thought about the classified ads I'd scanned during my coffee break that very day. Linda Larson's plea for Avon reps was outlined in bold next to listings for an experienced telemarketer and a part-time paper route on the east side of town. That was it. I had no chance for immediate employment, but I didn't want that to matter. It was time for a change.

"For real, Dean."

"You're sure?" At least he had the decency to keep a straight face. How many times had we exchanged those words?

"Pretty sure." There was no sense in burning my bridges.

"You know you can always come back if things don't work out."

"I appreciate that." Returning to the Galley was practically the dictionary definition of things not working out.

"Okay, then." He sighed. "Don't worry about covering any more shifts if you don't want to. Katie's starting in a couple of minutes, and Barb wants extra hours. One of my nieces has been asking about part-time work, too."

"Oh." I was disappointed to hear my absence wouldn't leave a glaring hole in the schedule, but I pushed the thought to the back of my mind and concentrated on the excitement of leaving instead.

"Jody?"

"Yeah?"

"It's been a pleasure." He stood and offered me a handshake, which turned into a tight bear hug.

"Well, thanks," I said, when he released me, unsure of what else to say. "Thanks for everything."

I felt the sting of tears as I turned away from him and lifted my knapsack from a coat hook on my way out the door, but I also felt good about taking a stand and finally making a move to change my life.

I should have known better.

two

The scent of salt air surrounded me as I walked Old Marine Highway, cut through the Bargain Foods parking lot and into the residential district. *No more Marty McDade.* No more Ocean Galley. No sides of gravy and soft drink spills, cashing out at the end of the day, mopping the floor, refilling ketchup bottles, or smiling, smiling, smiling like some kind of imbecile.

I absorbed the local color; pastel-painted war housing on streets lined with Japanese plum and oak trees, daffodils and crocuses making early appearances while other blooms were still tightly budded. I gave a cursory nod to the Sampson kids when they skateboarded past me, weighed down by lopsided helmets and enough protective padding to survive a firing squad.

Mrs. Blisky was rearranging her garden gnomes in a semicircle, like a miniature cult, and the Howards were preparing for an outdoor barbecue. They didn't care that summer was a couple of months off, dammit, their new patio needed to be christened by Oscar Meyer.

Everyone I passed was content, myself included.

I'd shoved opportunity's door wide open and couldn't wait to see where it led. Planning my future between footsteps, I tried to remember what I'd dreamed of in the past. I'd been a waitress for so long I had to dig deep.

My elementary school plan to take Hollywood by storm was only slightly more feasible than neurosurgery, considering I possessed average looks and no discernible talents. In high school, I gave up on the idea of being a vet when a botched rat dissection earned me a failing grade in biology. My interest in public speaking disappeared during a brutal debate-team battle over "squares versus circles," and the only musical instrument I could play was the triangle. Kind of. Nearing graduation, I was filled with a mixture of delight and trepidation.

Fortunately, the board of education was better prepared than I was, and aptitude tests were issued in early spring for the droves of students without a clue.

As I basked in my fresh and exciting state of unemployment, I couldn't believe that *ten years* had passed since my unfortunate meeting with the school guidance counselor, Mrs. Corbett, a raging alcoholic blessed with tenure.

"Well," she'd said, exhaling a breath tinged with spiced rum. Her auburn dye job was fading fast, the sickly undertow of gray taking over. Her tired eyes waltzed from the manila envelope in her hands to the silver flask peeking out of her straw handbag. As if the rum weren't enough, the Magic 8 Ball on her desk did little to inspire faith in her guidance.

"Jody Rogers." Her tone was bored, and I assumed she hoarded her enthusiasm like her booze.

"That's me," I said, smiling.

"I hold your future in this envelope."

Somehow I doubted it. Sure, I expected to hear I'd make a perfect something-or-other, or a fabulous this-or-that, but my only true ambition was to buy a house on Sitka Point. If I could have done it collecting pop cans, I would have.

Mrs. Corbett struggled to open the envelope, her peach fingernails clawing at the tape. I questioned whether she was actually *drunk* until she reached for a pair of scissors, knocking the 8 Ball to the floor.

The answer was "definitely."

Finally, after some haphazard snipping, she was prepared to enlighten me.

"Hmm." Her eyes scanned the computer printout. "It looks like you're an ideal candidate for two careers."

Two careers. *Not bad.*

"What are they?" I asked nonchalantly, although I had to admit my interest was piqued. I could practically see the headline: "Below-average Student Wins Nobel Prize."

Of course, that was fairly optimistic, but it would have been nice to have the potential for greatness, even if I never attained it. At age seventeen life had no boundaries and it was surreal to sit across from a middle-aged malcontent in an ill-fitting pantsuit, waiting to hear just how far I could go if I buckled down and applied myself.

Who was I? What could I be?

"A geriatric nurse or a cake decorator," Mrs. Corbett announced with a tight smile of satisfaction.

What?

Surely I had skipped a bubble on the multiple choice section and thrown the whole test out of whack!

"A *geriatric nurse*? I suck at science." Certification would take me so long, I'd be geriatric by the time I finished. And *cake decorating*? Something was very wrong.

"Yes, well . . . not everyone is built for success."

I felt the heat of embarrassment warm my cheeks. "But . . ."

"No *offense,* dear. It's just that some people don't have the talent or skills necessary to propel themselves along." She flipped through my file. "Judging by your grades, I think the cake decorating would be a stronger bet. That way you won't have to worry about college."

Her tone suggested that everything was settled.

"But—"

"Don't waste your time, Jody. Save yourself some grief and set some reasonable goals."

My hands shook with both anger and fear. "I thought you were supposed to encourage me to reach my potential," I murmured. What if I *had* no potential?

"I'm being realistic, dear. I'm a guidance counselor, not a fairy godmother. It wouldn't be in your best interest to count on being, er . . . how shall I put this . . . *an achiever.*"

The words crushed me. Just because I was ambivalent about success didn't mean I wanted to be banned from it. I'd left Mrs. Corbett's office feeling ill, afraid to graduate and be set loose in the world.

I was unnerved that, ten years after our meeting, I still didn't know what to do with my life. That evil woman was probably continuing to destroy lives between drinks.

"That was a long time ago," I mumbled. "You've got a fresh start, so take advantage of it."

I stepped onto Keller Avenue to see Dottie Maple, Bent Harbor's runner-up nutcase, watering her lawn in nothing more than a white blouse tucked into flesh-colored nylons. I was tempted to mention the omission of outerwear, but I figured she wouldn't care. Aside from the control tops, she was a very free spirit. I waved and she saluted in response before her attention returned to the garden.

Although the meeting with Mrs. Corbett still gnawed at me, at least the sight of Dottie Maple was reassuring. The existence of Chris in my life meant I'd never end up a crazy, lonely old spinster.

His freshly waxed Toyota Corolla was parked in our driveway, and I quickened my pace for the final block before home.

Wednesday was his day off from the lumber yard and I knew he would have washed the dishes and vacuumed while I was at work. There was probably a six-pack of amber ale in the fridge, next to some thick pork chops or chicken breasts.

Of course, he had no idea our income had just dropped by half and we'd be dining on mac and cheese by Monday.

Money was always tight in our house and in the heat of the moment I hadn't considered how my exit from Dean's would affect Chris. I crossed our lawn and climbed the front steps, suddenly dreading his reaction to my rather rash decision.

It had felt so right!

When I opened the door, I heard the shower running and breathed a sigh of relief. At least I could plan a strategy for breaking the news. My first instinct was to use some kind of distraction technique, and the most promising choice of action seemed to be seduction. He was guaranteed to be disoriented enough after a nice batch of sex to take the news lightly. It wasn't a matter of using intimacy as a weapon, but as a *tool.* A communication tool, much like the mute button on a TV remote.

I raced down the hallway and into our room, where he'd not only made the bed, but carefully folded the clean laundry I'd left piled on the floor the night before.

I didn't deserve him.

I yanked off my sailor dress, damning the fact that I wouldn't have a chance to shower before the main event. A few well-aimed squirts of perfume and a smear of deodorant under each arm seemed to rectify the situation, and I pulled the elastic out of my hair to run a brush through the curly brown masses I'd cursed since childhood. The result was more frizz than allure.

Bad news called for the big guns of lingerie, and my usual white cotton granny's would be about as effective as a powder musket. I glanced around the room, searching for ammunition.

I wiggled into a blue satin negligee and, taking a hint from the awkward fit, remembered I'd accidentally tossed it in the dryer. The unfortunate results were broadcast by the bedroom mirror. Fabric that should have covered my thighs rode my hips instead, barely covering my flat ass, the body part I was most self-conscious about.

Privately, I blamed Chris's futon for the plains of my backside, certain that sleeping on a picnic table for a decade wouldn't have deflated my butt as thoroughly as a year on that pseudomattress.

I tried a sheer floral gown, but my image disappointed once again.

For the first time ever, I was relieved that Chris enjoyed endless, steaming, bill-tripling showers. I pulled off the gown and assessed my naked self.

My pale reflection was all freckled shoulders, average breasts, and wide hips. Granted, I had nice skin, but too much of it, thanks to my Galley weight gain. My arms were slim and borderline elegant, which only accentuated legs that were neither of those things. They were stocky and failed to taper into delicate ankles—the effect a bit too Flintstone for my liking.

As I peered at my flawed form and wished for instant change, I was mollified by the fact that Chris wasn't concerned about my glaring faults. Instead, he was a virtual encyclopedia of compliments, affirmations, and sensitivity.

In a moment of tenderness, I decided to wear his first-anniversary gift; a hooker-red lace bustier with a short, translucent robe and, to my chagrin, garters. When I'd opened the package eighteen months earlier, I'd assumed it was a joke, but Chris's expression told me otherwise. He'd encouraged me to try it on, with a nuzzle here and a feather-light touch there, but I'd laughed hysterically (partly in fear) and set it aside, never to be worn.

I found it in the bottom of my lingerie drawer, wrinkled and, astonishingly, *shinier* than I remembered. Grimacing at the sight of it, I struggled into the bustier, garter belt, and silky underwear, cursing my uncooperative body and praying I didn't look as awful as I felt. The contraption had more snaps, clips, and buckles than a life jacket and felt almost as comfortable. Attaching red thigh-high nylons required more dexterity than my shaking fingers could muster, but five minutes of fiddling with fastenings was all I could afford. When I was finally underdressed, I slipped into some red heels I'd worn for Halloween the previous year.

With one terrified glance in the mirror I knew that if I was willing to debase myself entirely to make the man happy, I should probably marry him.

God knows, he'd asked often enough.

When the shower finally stopped, I darted down the hallway to wait outside the bathroom door. I stood facing his Dalí print, wondering for the umpteenth time what melting clocks were supposed to *mean.*

When our cohabitation began, I'd tried to ignore his odd little pleasures, convincing myself that his *Star Wars* action-figure collection was "cute," his refusal to part with chipped dinnerware "endearing." The Chia Pet on the kitchen windowsill was an affront I couldn't ignore, however, and I'd buried it in a cardboard box along with his Metallica CDs, *Sports Illustrated* swimsuit issues, and the white cotton briefs I'd talked him out of wearing in favor of boxers. I didn't know why he had the lava lamp, or the I FEAR NO BEER T-shirt, the beaded curtains in the closet doorway, or the etched Bud Light mirror over his dresser.

I waited for him to emerge from the bathroom, but patience had never been my strong suit. I took a deep breath and knocked on the door.

"Chris, I'm home! I have a little surprise for you!"

"Jody?" His deep baritone could still raise goose bumps on my arms.

"Yeah, it's me. Open the door."

"Just a sec, I'm drying off." He paused. "Why aren't you at work?"

I had to stick to my plan. It was imperative that I save the gory details until *after* the sex, when the gods of lethargy took over.

"Just a rotten day." Well, it wasn't a lie, anyway.

"I haven't even started dinner."

Shit. He was apologizing. Guilt spilled through me. "That's okay," I chirped.

"I thought you weren't off until seven. What happened?"

"I'll wait until you're done in there."

"Is something wrong?"

I leaned against the wall, exasperated. "You're ruining everything," I muttered.

"Jody?"

"I want to tell you face-to-face."

"What happened?"

I gave up. "Look, I had a run-in with Marty McDade."

"And?"

"And he pinched my butt again." I sighed.

"You must have been flattered," a husky female voice said.

My heart clogged my throat like a sponge in a drainpipe. "Who said that?"

"No one!" Chris said, too quickly, then tried to cover his tracks. "I mean, who said what?"

"Who's in there?" I nearly choked on the words.

"Uh, sorry, I can't hear you over the water!" he shouted, then hissed, "Turn on the water!"

After a moment of fumbling and whispers, the water was running, full blast. Shocked, I tried to convince myself that the woman's voice had come from the radio, but logic sank in soon enough. *There would be no reasonable explanation.* Nausea tainted my stomach while my mind flipped through a photo collage of faces. Was it an ex-girlfriend, and if so, which one? Living in a small town meant I knew all of them. The voice was too low to be Amber's, and Leslie had moved to Portland. Carmen and Janice were both married, but that wouldn't rule out those skanks entirely. What if it was someone I worked with? Katie always said how lucky I was to have Chris, but would she do that to me? I couldn't stand the speculation.

"Who's in there?" I yelled.

"Just me."

"Ouch!" The woman again.

"Open the door!" My shock turned to fury.

"Just a second!" His voice was laced with panic, and I could hear him trying to open the latch on the bathroom window.

It was painted shut, thanks to my ineptitude with a roller.

"Open the goddamn door, you son of a bitch!" I beat my fist against the wood, ready to kill him and his guest. How could I be living a nightmare I'd never even considered a possibility?

"Can you hold on for just a second?"

"Open it!" I screamed, certain the neighbors were dialing 911.

At the click of the lock, the door slowly opened and my teeth clenched in dreadful anticipation. Chris appeared in a cloud of steam and, aside from his cringing expression, he looked just as I'd left him that morning. In a painful flash of anger, I *hated* his floppy blond hair and angular face, the cheekbones and jawline I'd memorized with my fingers. I loathed his chest, that chiseled mass of sculpted muscle, the arms he'd used to cradle me, and the delicate pattern of moles on his back.

The line between love and hate might have been thin, but at least it wasn't blurry.

Chris attempted to block my view of his partner in crime, but even his broad shoulders couldn't hide her completely.

"Oh, my God," I murmured. The short red hair. The vibrant green contact lenses. *The permanent smirk.*

"Jody, this is—"

"I don't need an introduction, you bastard! She's my cousin!"

"Oh, shit. I forgot." He tightened the towel around his waist.

"You *forgot*? I introduced you two." I paused for emphasis. *"At my fucking family reunion."*

"You don't remember, honey?" my dear cousin Beth asked, stroking *my boyfriend*'s biceps.

I was stunned into temporary silence.

She tried to cover herself with a damp washcloth, but her breasts weren't cooperating. Implants, a Christmas gift from her own father, had raised more eyebrows over the turkey dinner than the marshmallows in Grannie's aspic.

As I scowled at her perfect hourglass shape, I remembered what I was wearing. As if the situation weren't humiliating enough, *I* looked like the Pillsbury Prostitute.

Panicked, I tried to divert attention from myself.

"That's incest," I said with a sneer.

"Not quite." Beth's fingertips strolled through Chris's chest hair while he stared at his hands. "It would be incest if you and I were sleeping together, Jody."

"What?" I snapped.

"She's right," Chris mumbled, eyes downcast.

"I don't care! Get her out of our house!"

"Jody, calm down," Beth said.

"Get out!"

"Don't you think we should talk about this?"

"No fucking way!"

"Chris, aren't you going to say anything?" Beth asked.

We both turned to look at him as he tried to cover his suddenly erect penis with the folds of his towel.

"What, is this a *turn-on*?" I gasped.

"Geez, I uh . . ." He shrugged awkwardly, gazing at my gartered lower body.

I could have strangled him.

"Jody," Beth tried again.

"For the last time, *get out*!"

At that moment, she dropped the washcloth, exposing her damp, shiny body. She was all sleek curves and flawless skin, aside from the scarred nipples, which were more than slightly uneven and, like a pair of wandering eyes, seemed to point everywhere at once.

"Can you blame him?" she whispered before bending to lift a pile of crumpled clothing from the floor. She looked me over with distaste. "Nice garters, Jody. Real classy."

"Fuck you." It took all I had to refrain from tackling her as she brushed past me. I grabbed my robe from its hook and crawled into the safety of terry cloth, cinching the belt for good measure.

Chris and I waited for Beth to return, without speaking.

"Listen," she began when she reappeared fully clothed.

"One more word and I'll tear your lips off," I warned her.

Wisely, she held her tongue, aside from a hasty, "Fine. Be that way." After blowing an air kiss to *my* boyfriend, she left the house with a slam of the door.

I leaned against the wall and waited, expecting a burst of apologetic pleading and begging forgiveness. I was already looking forward to turning him down, but the words failed to spill from his lips. Hell, they didn't even *drip.* We stood in silence and I wondered how he could be the same man who'd professed love on the fourth date.

"So?" I asked, growing impatient.

"You look really nice in those garters," he said, hopefully.

"Don't start with me."

"I'm serious."

"How long has this been going on?" I asked, afraid of the answer.

"It doesn't matter." He fiddled with his towel and refused to look at me.

"Uh, yes it does."

He shrugged. "A little while."

I tried a different tack. "Did you actually think you could hide her in that puny bathroom?"

"Not forever."

I let out a short bark of laughter. "What, did you think she'd eventually evaporate, or that I wouldn't see her through all the steam?"

"You weren't supposed to be home until later."

"That's your explanation?"

"Well, it's just that . . . like I said, you don't usually get home until, like, *seven,*" he reasoned, finally meeting my eyes.

I stared at him. "What?"

"Look, I still love you and I think we can make it work."

"Are you insane? You've been sleeping with my cousin!" A revolting thought occurred to me. "Oh, my god, it was in *our* bed. You had sex with her on that shitty mattress!"

"*Futon,* Jody. And she didn't complain about it the way you do."

"Can you actually hear what you're saying?"

"Look, honey, we never said we were exclusive." He pushed a lock of damp hair from his forehead.

"*Exclusive?* We've been living together for two years! You wanted to marry me."

"But you didn't want to get married and then, like I said, we never mentioned the word 'exclusive.'"

"It was understood, Chris. Just like I haven't called you an asshole yet, but it's understood."

His skin flushed a deep pink. "Well, that seems a bit harsh."

All I wanted from him was some display of emotion, but there was nothing. Remorse was nowhere to be seen, never mind an apology for wasting two and a half years of my life. Almost three years thrown away on a son of a bitch who didn't even have the decency to consider blood ties when it came to screwing around. Instead, he just swung from one branch of my family tree to another, like some horny chimp.

I had to hit him where it counted. If I were jobless, he would be homeless.

"Get out." I tried to control my voice, but couldn't hide the quiver.

"What?"

"It's over. Get out."

"This is my place."

"Not anymore." I would crush him like a goddamn bug. He'd be packing his crap in garbage bags if that's what it took, shuffling along Old Marine Highway dragging a couple of Heftys.

"You moved in with me, Jody. Your name isn't even on the lease."

Shit. He was right. The bastard was right.

"Fine," I snapped, with as much righteousness as I could muster. "I'm leaving."

Where could I go?

"You don't have to leave. I'm sure we can work this out."

"And I'm sure we can't."

"Okay." He sighed. "I can't stop you."

"You could try," I muttered, turning toward our room to get dressed.

"She doesn't mean anything to me," he called feebly from the hallway.

"Is that supposed to make me feel better?"

"No . . . I mean . . . well, you know what I mean."

"I'll pick up my stuff on the weekend," I shouted, kicking off the goddamn heels and pulling a pair of jeans and a T-shirt over my wasted lingerie.

I heard the slap of his bare feet against the hardwood.

"You're really leaving?" He stood in the doorway, eyebrows raised in surprise. Finally, a reaction of sorts, but it was too late. *Way too late.*

"Don't touch any of my stuff," I warned him.

"Jode, come on. Where are you going to go?" His worried look probably had more to do with making rent than my safety and comfort.

"None of your business."

There was only one place I could go with no income, only two people who could help me weather the storm. It wasn't the step toward a new life I'd hoped for when I walked out of the Galley, but my choices were limited. I knew they'd welcome me with open arms, baked goods, clean sheets, and adoration.

At age twenty-seven I found myself equally repelled and relieved at the prospect of moving back in with my parents.

three

Chris's offer of a ride was about as tempting as a kerosene enema, so I set out on foot to Mom and Dad's.

The sky darkened as I passed abandoned hopscotch grids and bicycles balanced on kickstands, awaiting the next day's ride. It was only a matter of weeks before the mosquitoes would be out in force, their high-pitched hum filling the air as they hovered over sunburned skin. In the meantime, the evening air was silent, apart from the occasional buzz of clumsy moths meeting bug zappers for the first and only time.

I tried to clear my mind of rage and betrayal, concentrating instead on sidewalk cracks, flickering street lamps, and the soft breeze from the harbor.

I reached my childhood home at exactly seven o'clock, the moment my shift should have ended, and stood at the end of the driveway, soaking up the view.

Bent Harbor had adopted vinyl siding in recent years, so the wood shakes were replaced by glorified plastic. "Less upkeep," my father informed me when the installation was complete. He'd stood on the stepladder, waiting for me to pass him the first of three garish yellow wooden butterflies, which he mounted next to the window box, diagonally, in order of size. They were hideous, but more important to Mom than the flattened-spoon wind chimes she'd made at a woman's retreat, or the terminally vacant hummingbird feeder she religiously filled with sticky red syrup.

"No one would know it was our house without those butterflies," she'd explained.

When I reminded her of the numbered address on the mailbox, the front door, and the curb, she told me no one likes a smart-ass.

Unfortunately for my mother, her neighbors were purebred followers and nearly every house on the block had adopted their own trio of butterflies in varying shades of obnoxious.

Through the kitchen shades, Mom's familiar shadow moved back and forth from sink to stove. I could almost smell the forever scent of Pine-Sol and potpourri, apple soap and a thousand loaves of banana bread.

Home.

I climbed the steps and opened the door, inhaling all that was familiar with a sense of relief. Before I could release the breath, my replacement—Dad's Shih Tzu, Ruby—hurtled toward me like an animated dust bunny, her growls and snaps bordering on ridiculous. If it weren't for the pink bow designating her as their new little girl, I *might* have thought she was cute. It was unlikely, but possible.

I clapped loudly and Ruby screeched to a halt, spun around and beat a hasty retreat toward the kitchen, whining like worn brakes; the security system that kept on giving.

"Mom? Dad? It's me." I followed the dog's trail and stepped into the heart of our home to find my parents preparing to eat.

"Hey, Peanut. Good to see you," Dad said, dropping onto a wooden stool, heaping plate of macaroni and cheese and a bottle of ketchup in hand. "You're just in time for dinner." He tucked a napkin under his T-shirt collar and rubbed his substantial belly.

"I'm not really hungry, Dad." Certainly not for mac and cheese, anyway. I'd be living on the stuff soon enough.

"Don't be silly. Gladys, can you grab a plate for our girl?"

"Absolutely," Mom chirped, reaching into the cupboard.

I watched Dad remove his Seahawks hat, amazed at the ring of hat-head it left behind, severe enough to have been made by a toilet plunger. Did he know about the adjustable snaps?

His mustache had grown since I'd last seen him and he was frighteningly close to his goal of a bushy handlebar. He looked like a fugitive. His beer belly rested under the stretched fabric of the Superdad shirt Josh and I had given him for Father's Day in 1988. Poor health meant retirement from the pulp mill at fifty-five and, almost six months later, he hadn't shed a pound.

Mom's auburn curls were wrapped into the same loose bun she'd worn for every kindergarten-class picture in her thirty years of teaching. The shade of her frosty lips screamed Mary Kay, and she'd bought it years before Mavis Holland sold enough mascara and eye shadow to win a pink Cadillac. Mom wore her Winter Mist lipstick with pride, somehow convinced her minuscule purchase had sealed the deal.

She'd been able to buy early retirement at the same time as Dad and God only knew how they filled their days. Judging by the orange allure of their dinner, I could rule out cooking classes.

I sighed and sat at the table, which was covered in the same floral cloth and place mats that had been there two months earlier, and ten years before that. In fact, *everything* was the same. I knew the contents of each cupboard and drawer, from the shelf of lidless Tupperware containers waiting for their lost mates, to the ice-cream bucket filled with Mom's matchbook collection, which no one was allowed to touch, even in the event of a blackout. The magnetized "to do" list was stuck to the fridge, along with a few mangled coupons that would have expired by the time she remembered to take them shopping.

I had no doubt that Dad's socks were still safety-pinned together before going in the wash, and his hand tools were undoubtedly still hanging on the wall by his workbench, each item fitting perfectly in its black marker outline.

In light of my newly disheveled life, the predictability was comforting.

Mom scooped a large serving of macaroni onto my plate. Some of the cheese flavoring hadn't dissolved completely and lay in soggy fluorescent clumps throughout the pasta elbows.

Dad opened the ketchup and squirted a steady stream onto his dinner, then stirred the mixture with a fork until the meal was rust colored and runny. Mom showered her plate with at least half a cup of pepper.

"How did I live with you for seventeen years?" I muttered.

"Ketchup, Peanut?" Dad tilted the bottle toward me.

"Uh, no, thanks."

"S and P?" Mom asked, prepared to relinquish her penguin shakers, if only for a moment.

"Just a little salt, I guess."

"Oh, honey, I ran into Muriel Sanders this week," she said. "Hannah's getting married this summer."

"Again?" I asked.

"Mmm-hmm."

"To *David*, again?"

"That's right," she said brightly. "I guess they worked things out."

I rolled my eyes. Hannah and David Baxter wed three days after our high school graduation and produced their first child two months later. They divorced and remarried each other two times in the following ten years, adding two more offspring in the process. The last time I'd seen Hannah she wasn't picking up the toys and junk in her front yard, but pushing it all into a pile at one end of her moss-covered lawn with a snow shovel. If they had any more kids, she'd need a bulldozer. Even sadder was the knowledge that once her kids outgrew Big Wheels and tricycles, her yard would be filled with rundown cars and rusty kitchen appliances. Too bad living in a beautiful town couldn't guarantee a pretty life.

"So, when's the wedding?" I asked.

"July. Muriel wanted to know why you and Hannah never pal around anymore."

It wasn't a statement, but an accusation.

"We never did." I shoved a forkful of macaroni past unwilling lips. I'd had a turn at playing bridesmaid for number three, when her real friends started boycotting. Desperation forced her to place an ad for a flower girl in the *Bent Harbor Times.* Apparently, her own children were bored with the recurring role.

What no one in town could believe was that the perennial bride and groom continued to register at the Target in Fillington. Even their parents were fed up and I'd heard a rumor that Hannah's father gave them a six-pack of marriage certificates at her last rehearsal dinner.

"It wouldn't hurt to send her an engagement card, or give her a call," Mom said, sipping her milk.

"Of course it wouldn't," I agreed, mainly because I intended to do neither.

Ruby wheezed at my right and I turned to see her standing on hind legs next to Dad's chair, begging for scraps.

"Isn't she the cutest thing?" Dad crooned, dropping limp macaroni into her waiting mouth. She dropped to all fours and licked her chops with a revolting sucking noise.

"Such a good girl," Dad whispered, rubbing her ears.

I took another bite of my dinner and ignored both of them.

"So, what's new with you, Jody?" Mom asked. "You haven't been by here in weeks."

Had it really been weeks? I felt the sudden release of guilt toxins in my bloodstream.

"New? Not a whole lot," I lied, shoving a mass of cardboard-flavored pasta into my mouth.

"Nothing new?" Dad asked.

"Well, actually, there is something I wanted to run by you two."

"What's that?" he asked, lifting Ruby onto his lap to give me a spectacular view of her drooling smile.

Since my parents had assumed "shacking up" with Chris would eventually lead to marriage, I wasn't sure how to break the news that he was not only history, but a cheating son of a bitch. Mom seemed especially fond of him, and I knew she was looking forward to donning the Mother of the Bride title, while Dad liked having someone to "talk shop" with, whatever that meant. The news was going to hit them hard.

"Well, actually, uh . . . Chris and I are breaking up."

I waited for a gasp of horror.

"Is that right?" Dad asked mildly, meeting my eyes briefly before returning his attention to my canine doppelgänger.

I turned to Mom for a reaction.

"That's a surprise," she murmured, unfazed.

Did they understand what I was saying?

"Yes, it certainly is," I agreed. "We were together a long time."

"Well, these things happen, honey." Mom sipped her milk.

"It was the longest relationship of my life," I said, through gritted teeth. Didn't they see the importance of what had happened? This wasn't just a summer fling that ran its course, after all. This was a full-fledged *partnership* going down the tubes.

"Them's the breaks." Dad shrugged.

"Them's the breaks?" I snapped. "I thought he was the one."

"You did?" Mom asked incredulously.

"Well . . ." Perhaps it was an overstatement. "Anyway, I was wondering if I could stay here for a while. Just until I get some money together for first and last month's rent on a new place."

I'd already imagined how the conversation would play out. Dad would offer to either loan or flat-out *give* me the money I needed, which I'd firmly decline until he eventually talked me into accepting it. Of course, nothing in life was guaranteed, so Plan B dictated Mom would invite me to camp out in my old bedroom for a month or so. It was a win-win situation, for sure.

Or so I thought.

"Do you mean move back here?" Mom asked, licking cheese globules from the corner of her lips and blinking rapidly, like some kind of frantic Morse code.

"Only temporarily," I rushed to assure her. "Just until I get myself together."

"I don't know if that's such a hot idea. Gord?" The singsong kindergarten tone was a bad sign.

"Nope." Dad shook his head. "No, it doesn't seem like a good idea at all."

Were they kidding? Running me through the parental wringer for not visiting them? If it was harmless teasing, I could handle it. After all, they were right. I didn't stop in often enough and I felt bad about it, but between Chris and the Galley I simply didn't have the time. Of course, my load had lightened considerably that afternoon.

I chuckled quietly, then grinned like a good sport until I saw that they weren't smiling. Even the damn dog just stared at me, a long drip of spittle hanging from her mouth. "You *really* aren't going to let me stay?"

"You understand, don't you, Jody?" Dad asked. "After that incident with Josh, we just wouldn't feel comfortable."

Shit. My younger brother had burned more bridges than he'd ever built.

"Is he still on the reefer, honey?" Mom's voice was as shaky as her grasp of slang.

"I have no idea. And even if I did, which I stress again that I *don't,* he has nothing to do with this conversation."

"It was such a chore to straighten everything out with the police." Mom closed her eyes, the Patron Saint of potheads.

"Mom, I'm not going to grow *dope* in the basement!"

"I didn't say you were. We just can't be too cautious these days."

"Why'd you let him move that hydroponic crap in here in the first place?"

"He said he was growing African violets," Dad muttered, twisting one end of his mustache between thumb and forefinger.

"Those plants were four feet tall."

"We aren't botanists, Jody." He lifted his fork and resumed eating while Ruby stared at me.

"But Dad, common sense—"

"I just kept waiting for those little purple flowers to appear . . ." Mom's chin quivered.

"It took a lot to get your brother out of that mess." Dad added a healthy and unnecessary squirt of ketchup to his plate. "I called in a lot of favors."

"That's right." Mom snapped back to attention. "Josh could have gone to jail!"

"He *should* have gone to jail. He was selling pot to half the high school population."

Mom's jaw dropped. "That's a rotten thing to say about your own flesh and blood! You make it sound like it was his idea, Jody. You know perfectly well he got in with a bad group of kids. They caused him nothing but trouble."

"Ah, the sweet sound of denial. Whatever you say, Mom."

"He was a first-time offender," she added.

"You mean it was the first time he got caught."

"What are you trying to say?"

"Never mind." I sighed. "It's in the past. Look, I promise you that I won't commit a felony in your home. Can I *please* just stay for a bit?"

"Listen, Peanut." Dad gave me his trademark shoulder squeeze of consolation and I could smell the Old Spice I gave him for Father's Day every year. "We care about you kids. I mean, we love you so goddamn much, it's crazy, but there comes a time when we can't help you anymore, when you become adults and get out in the world."

"But I have nowhere to go."

He smiled. "Maybe one of the gals at the restaurant needs a roommate."

"Actually, I quit my job."

"You quit your job while you're looking for a new place?"

"Not exactly."

"That wasn't a smart plan, Jody. Not smart at all."

"Look, I'm *desperate* and you have a ton of space."

"You know," he replied, carefully setting Ruby on the floor, "it's funny to think back on how worried your mom and I were about how we'd keep busy when you kids left the nest."

"What does that have to do with anything?"

"We wondered what we'd do with ourselves."

"We wondered whether we'd be happy," Mom added.

I wondered what the hell they were talking about.

"To our surprise, we discovered we like having the place to ourselves. In fact, we *love* it." Dad smiled at Mom like he'd just spotted her across the dance floor at a sock hop.

"Thoroughly enjoy it." Mom winked at him.

Three's a crowd when it comes to foreplay, but luckily, Dad came to his senses before things got ugly.

"Anyway"—he cleared his throat—"now that we've developed some hobbies and spread our wings a bit in here, there's no space left."

"But my room—"

"Not anymore, kiddo."

"What's that supposed to mean?"

"Gladys, why don't you show her some of the changes we've made around here."

"Absolutely, love. Come on, Jody."

Mom led me down the hallway and into the bathroom, which was painted a new dusty pink. She was careful to point out the addition of slipproof seashell decals in the tub and a brass-trimmed medicine cabinet before leading me back to the hall. The wall-length display of school pictures had been replaced by inconsequential floral prints. While Josh's and my disappearance from view was mildly offensive, none of the changes were earth-shattering.

The rude awakening occurred when we stepped into my room.

My mauve canopy bed, blessedly familiar yet utterly hideous, was nowhere to be seen. The cork bulletin board, knickknacks, and swimming ribbons were absent, along with the few stuffed animals that survived my adolescence and the scrapbooks I'd carefully filled with photos, clippings, and mementos.

Granted, I hadn't lived there for almost a decade, but I'd always *assumed* the room would be left alone. I didn't expect my parents to turn the space into a shrine, but I never dreamed they'd erase me from my own bedroom!

Replacing everything I'd known as a child were a large wooden desk, overhead lamp, and a collection of paints and brushes. On the floor were three piles of round, sea-smoothed rocks.

"What's going on here?"

"I'm starting my own business." Mom lifted her arms, and tilted her head, as if she were Vanna White, revealing a vowel.

"What kind of business?" Before she could answer the question, I spotted her merchandise, lined up on the windowsill. Somewhere between fifteen and twenty rocks had been painted to look like ladybugs.

I turned to see Mom grinning.

"Are you nuts?"

"No, dear. I'm an entrepreneur." She lifted a rock and handed it to me.

I had to admit, the detailing wasn't bad, but how hard was it to paint black dots? "You aren't planning to sell these."

"Yes I am."

"To who?"

"Tourists."

"What tourists? No one *vacations* in Bent Harbor."

She shook her head, the misunderstood genius. "People will buy them," she assured me. "These days, everyone loves artwork that comes from nature. There's a man in Port Angeles who's making a fortune from driftwood doll furniture."

"I'll bet." I couldn't have stopped my eyes from rolling, even if I'd tried.

"Why do you have to be so darn cynical?"

"Well, for starters, why are they all ladybugs?"

"That's all I can paint right now, but I'll gradually master other creatures. I'm already working on the catalog."

Jesus Christ!

"What, you're selling these by mail?"

"That's right. And on the Internet."

"Mom, you don't even have a computer. And no one will buy rocks through the mail. Do you have any idea what it'll cost to ship this stuff?"

"I haven't looked into that yet."

"This is insane." My head pounded. "The Internet?"

"It's the information superhighway." She left the room and I followed her into Josh's former sanctuary.

His bedroom was filled with cardboard boxes, overflowing with junk that included roller skates, dusty board games, and carpet remnants. His Phish posters had disappeared, along with his water bed, and the only sign he'd ever lived there was a galaxy of dart holes on the far wall. The wide circle of damage was glaring proof that Josh's claim of marijuana improving manual dexterity was nothing more than a puff of smoke.

"Why can't I stay in here?"

"Because your dad's sorting through this stuff from the basement."

"What for?" I snapped.

"Don't take that tone, Jody."

I took a breath and tried to sound calm. "Sorry, Mom. What for?"

"We've been watching *Antiques Roadshow* on Monday nights."

I waited for more, but she just smiled and tucked some stray hair behind her ear.

"And?" I finally prompted.

"Oh, right." She shook her head and her tidying efforts were undone. "Your dad thinks we might have some old treasures."

"You've got to be kidding." I groaned, and Mom shot me a dirty look.

"I'm not."

"Couldn't he move this stuff back to the basement for a couple of weeks?"

"It took an awfully long time to move it up here, and he's got it arranged just so. He's got some kind of a system."

"I'm having some kind of an aneurysm." I paused. "Look, I'll help him move it," I offered, through gritted teeth, spotting the old leather boxing gloves Dad used to force Josh and me to "duke it out" with. At that moment, I would've gladly taken on either parent in the backyard.

"We're happy with the way things are, honey." She twisted her wedding band and gave me a sympathetic smile. "So, what happened with you and Chris?"

It wasn't the smoothest subject change in history but, as her thirty-year dedication to hairbuns indicated, Mom wasn't one for transitions.

"He met someone else." The words felt new and strange, like a lie under pressure.

"Well, I never did like him." She pushed one of the boxes closer to the far wall with her foot.

Support! Exactly what I needed.

"He's been sleeping with Beth," I announced, replacing my burning fury with trembling bravado for effect.

"There was something about him that rubbed me the wrong way . . ." Her voice faded and I wasn't sure she'd heard me.

"My *cousin,* Beth." I paused, then added, "Your *niece,* Beth," for clarification.

"I think it was the jewelry." Her nose wrinkled with distaste.

"What are you talking about?"

"Chris. I don't like to see a man wearing jewelry. It's sleazy, like that John Travolta in *Saturday Night Fever.*"

I never had to worry about finding her on the cutting edge of pop culture.

"What jewelry?"

"You know, that gold necklace. It was trashy."

"Mom, it was a crucifix. He's Catholic."

"That's no excuse for poor taste," she said.

Desperation set in. "Mom, I *seriously* have nowhere to go."

"You're twenty-seven years old, love."

"I'm homeless!"

"I know, but what kind of parents would we be if we bailed you kids out of every mishap?"

"Good ones," I muttered. "You've got to help me out, here."

"Honey, I don't think you've even tried to help yourself. The most important thing a parent can teach their child is problem-solving."

"You've got to be—"

"And your father and I've had so little time alone together, Jody."

"I'm only talking about a couple of *weeks*."

"Joan Dawson's husband dropped dead of a heart attack at fifty-six. Do you think she saw that coming?"

"He was over three hundred pounds!"

"This time is very important to your father and me. Don't you think we've done enough for you kids?"

I couldn't argue the point, but it still didn't seem fair. Where was the woman who picked me up from school when it rained? What happened to the dedicated mother who packed my lunch and braided my hair? *Josh* was the one who couldn't be trusted, not me.

I'd never given my parents a second's worth of trouble and this was my reward? I'd never been kicked out of a class or sent to the principal's office, or . . . well, there had been one minor incident, but it could hardly be considered my fault.

Our family took a trip to Seattle to see the Ice Capades, and when we drove through the city after the show, Mom pointed out the prostitutes huddled on several street corners. In eight-year-old wonder, I admired the sparkle of their stiletto heels and the sheen of their leather skirts, patent handbags, and massive hair.

"Ladies of the evening," Mom murmured, as if it were the

name of an exotic fragrance or a Renaissance painting. Josh and I were too young for a job description, so we assumed they were exactly what they looked like; glamorous women waiting for a ride to the opera or a fancy restaurant.

When I returned to my second-grade classroom, it was time to make Mother's Day cards. I folded and stapled several pages together, determined to make mine the best Ms. Mosley had ever seen. My card soon became a booklet. The front page featured a carefully crayoned stethoscope around the neck of a blond woman. Underneath the illustration were the words "my mother is not a doctor." Similar drawings followed, announcing that she was neither a policewoman nor a truck driver; neither a ballet dancer nor a stewardess. Before the final page, which featured a damn good likeness of the woman who bore me and proclaimed her a supermom, was a colorful combination of dangling earrings, a minidress, crimson lips, and a wide smile. The simple phrase "my mother is not a lady of the evening" earned me an afternoon on the bench outside the principal's office and my mother a hasty parent-teacher conference, complete with horrified looks from Ms. Mosley and a reprimand from our principal.

Although Mom didn't let me off the hook, and the day ended with a lengthy dinner-table lecture on proper etiquette, she'd sat through that meeting with her head held high, defending my freedom of speech with ferocity, as though I were facing the death penalty instead of two days of recess detention.

Where had that woman gone?

"I'm sorry things didn't work out for you and Chris." Mom dug a spare bobby pin from her skirt pocket and secured her hair. "He doesn't know what he's lost."

"Thanks, Mom. You know, when I saw Beth standing there, looking like . . . well, like *Beth,* it didn't do much for my self-confidence." Images of her bulging fake breasts jiggled through my mind.

Mum shook her head. "Honestly, Jody, I don't know why you worry so much."

"She's gorgeous."

"And you're a perfectly lovely person."

"What's *that* supposed to mean?" Perfectly lovely person, my ass.

"You should feel sorry for Beth," Mom continued, warming to the topic. "Imagine going through life regarded only as beautiful."

"Uh, thanks, Mom."

"You've got . . . *spunk.* And that's—"

"Okay, Mom."

"Far more important than looks. After all—"

"Please stop. You've done quite enough."

"I'm glad to hear it," she said, giving me a quick but forceful hug.

I left her in the midst of Dad's junk mecca and returned to the kitchen, where I found a stack of three cardboard boxes next to the door. Each was labeled with my name in thick, black marker. While I tried to overcome my bewilderment, Dad added another box.

"What's that?"

"The rest of your things. Your mother packed them, so I'm not sure what's where." He scratched his head. "It's mostly stuffed animals and photo albums, I think."

"Why is it sitting here?" I asked, afraid of the answer.

"So you can take it with you."

It was one more devastating moment to add to the day's tally. My personal history, crammed into cardboard and awaiting ejection from the family fold. As an added bonus, Ruby was nestled in her own little fleece-lined bed, and I swear that salivating demon was sneering at me.

"Dad, I don't even have a car to move it, let alone a home to keep it in."

"We need the space." Dad shrugged apologetically.

"This is ridiculous."

"Look, Peanut. I'll keep it until the end of the week. Can you pick it up by then?"

"I guess I'll have to."

Frankly, I was a little more concerned with where *I* would live than finding a home for a bunch of toys. I had no desire to stay in the padlocked apartment of my pothead brother, and rooming with dear cousin Beth certainly seemed to be out of the question. My only other choice was to crash at Erin's house. My best friend was not a fan of sudden imposition, but I couldn't think of anyone else.

I opened the door to leave.

"Are you on your way, Jody?"

"Yeah." I felt a flicker of hope for a last-minute change of heart.

"Look, I know you'd like to come home and have us take care of you, but it just won't help matters."

"So I hear."

"We should have been harder on you kids when you were growing up. It's our own fault, really. We should have made you take out the garbage, or deliver newspapers."

"Okay, Dad. Enough with the tough love, already."

"Your mom made butterscotch pudding if you've got time for a bowl."

"No, thanks."

"She added raisins," he said, as if that would tip the scales of temptation.

"I'll see you around, Dad. Tell Mom goodbye for me."

"Will do."

four

I was in a state of shock.

A lousy boyfriend's betrayal was one thing, but to be abandoned by the people who'd brought me into the world? That was quite another. And to be displaced by a fucking Shih Tzu and a pile of painted rocks? The walls of my life were being knocked down so fast it was only a matter of time before the roof caved in.

I was on my own. A solo artist. An independent. *A loser.*

I'd never really considered how much I relied on Mom and Dad as a safety net, but didn't I have every right? Parenting was a lifetime commitment, wasn't it? They couldn't just . . . *quit.*

I walked toward Erin's house in near-darkness, kicking the sidewalk with every step. How had everything gone so wrong? As I cursed myself and my unprecedented stupidity, a long and unfamiliar car pulled up next to me.

I quickened my pace, heart racing, as the car kept up. The streetlight in the next block was out and I was tempted to turn down the back lane to my right, hoping the car passed right on by, but the lane was too dark.

I pulled the key chain from my pocket, to use as a weapon, if necessary. Somewhere between making plaster casts of my hands and roasting marshmallows at summer camp, I'd been taught to place one key between each finger, creating a metallic claw to slash an attacker's face. I never thought the grisly lesson would come in handy, but there I was, thanking Ranger Dan with every step.

I glanced over my shoulder to read the license plate, but only made out the letter *D.* It was a dark sedan, a "late model" as they said on cop shows, but the make and year were a mystery to me.

The car's horn sounded and I nearly collapsed in fear. My instincts told me to run for my life, but I couldn't decide which way to go. Through my panic, I heard a power window opening.

"Hey, need a ride?" It was a man.

"No, thank you," I said, voice jolted by the speed of my steps.

"Come on. It's not safe for you to be out walking alone."

Oh, he was slick. What next? Would he ask for my help locating a lost puppy, or offer me some drug-coated hard candy? *Sick bastard.*

"I'm fine," I said, picking up speed.

"I can take you anywhere you need to go, Jody."

He knows my name?

I turned to look at the driver, wondering how the creep knew who I was. Prepared to memorize whatever details of his face I could before sprinting into the darkness, I squinted into the shadows of the car.

Lucas McDade.

I was too pissed off to be relieved.

"What the hell are you doing?" I screeched.

"What?"

"Following me like that! You scared the shit out of me."

"I didn't mean to, Jody. I just wanted to . . . can I give you a lift?"

My hands found my hips and I started to tear into him, but the confusion in his face stopped me cold. Technically, he hadn't done anything wrong.

"Uh, yeah. Thanks," I mumbled, passing in front of the car and opening the passenger door. A Cadillac. It was a navy blue Cadillac, not that I needed the information anymore.

My exhausted senses were welcomed by a soft leather seat and the musky smell of aftershave.

"Thank you." I sighed, settling in.

"For scaring you? I really didn't mean to, Jody."

"I'll recover," I said, rubbing my hands together so he wouldn't see them shaking.

"Where to?"

"Erin Milne's place. You know where it is?"

He nodded and started driving through the darkened streets. Gradually, I relaxed, listening to the soft purr of the engine in an otherwise silent car. All I wanted from the world was a moment of peace.

"Listen, Jody, about today—"

"I don't really want to talk about it," I said softly.

He was quiet for a moment, concentrating on the road ahead, and I took the opportunity to look him over again. He wasn't quite as frail as he'd appeared at the Galley, probably because his father was no longer looming over him. His crew cut had darkened from the near albino shade of his youth to a dirty blond, but his skin was still as pale as the haze of his headlights.

He brushed the back of his hand against the stubble on his chin and cleared his throat before saying, "I'm sorry about my dad."

"So am I." I made a point of staring out the window to discourage further discussion.

"He didn't mean anything he said, you know. He was just kidding around."

"At my expense. And thanks for stepping in, by the way."

"I would have said something, but there aren't many jobs in town."

"Thanks for stating the obvious. What's that got to do with anything?"

"Dad hired me on when I got out of the army a couple of weeks ago and I don't want to rock the boat." His grip tightened on the steering wheel.

"*Come on.* As if your job would ever be at risk."

"Hey, there's a lot of pressure at the dealership to be one of the guys, and—"

"Give me a break," I scoffed. "That's bullshit."

"It's true! Dad keeps the place really competitive, so sometimes the only way to get ahead is—"

"To treat people like shit for a cheap laugh?"

He shook his head. "To go with the flow, Jody. I'm very concerned about job security right now."

"What could *possibly* threaten the employment of Marty McDade's very own son?"

"The return of his other son. Justin's coming back." His tone was defeated.

Marty's wife had left him and Bent Harbor when Lucas and I were in elementary school, taking Justin with her. Apparently a fifty-fifty divorce meant splitting the children, as well as the luxury cars and bone china. No one in town seemed to know what had happened to the disappearing half of the McDade family and, judging by Lucas's grimace, it wasn't the time to ask.

"What's he coming back for?" I could barely remember his older brother.

"That's what I'd like to know." He pulled a lighter from one pocket of his flannel shirt and patted the other for a pack of smokes, cursing under his breath when he realized it wasn't there.

"I haven't seen him since fifth grade or so," I said, hoping for more info.

"I bet he thinks he can cruise into town and cut into my share of the family business."

"Do you really think so?" It seemed a little far-fetched to me, but maybe I didn't find used cars as alluring as the McDade family did.

"Why else would he come back?"

"The same reason I never left. It's a great town."

Lucas shrugged in response. "*Whatever.* Anyway, I'm sorry you ended up quitting your job, but you *did* look pretty happy walking out."

I briefly explained why I was no longer happy and Lucas was kind enough to listen to me rant about Chris, my parents, and life in general. He even offered to ask about a secretarial position at the dealership, but backed off when I redirected my anger at him. As if I needed Marty McDade for a boss.

He parked the car in front of Erin's house and turned off the engine.

"Well, thanks for the lift," I said, reaching for the door handle.

"Jody, wait." He grabbed my arm.

"What?"

Before I really knew what was happening, his free hand cupped my chin and his lips bumped against my nose, searching for my mouth.

In a moment of confusion, I let him find it.

At first, his warm breath was more comforting than arousing, and my involvement was purely scientific. It had been so long since I'd kissed anyone but Chris, I couldn't help making comparisons. Lucas's lips were dry, whereas Chris's were lush and moist. Too moist, really. More often than not I had to secretly wipe my mouth when we broke apart.

Lucas's breathing was erratic, not that I needed any hint that he was nervous. His cheek was warm, but coarse, a sudden pleasure after Chris's lotion-softened skin.

I enjoyed the kiss as though I were watching it on a movie

screen until Lucas's tongue gently prodded my own and everything changed.

He tasted like spearmint, and washed my lips and tongue with the flavor in steady swirls of movement. He had learned a great deal about the art of the smooch since our junior-high encounter, and my temperature rose in response. I reached for the nape of his neck and moaned as his thumb stroked my face in slow circles.

His hands skimmed down my shoulders and across my ribs, alerting me to the forgotten fact that I was wearing raunchy lingerie under my T-shirt and jeans.

"Mmm, Jody," he whispered.

"Whoa, hold on," I gasped, pulling away. Breathing heavily, I tried to regain my composure by taking deep, measured gulps of air. Lingerie or not, kissing Lucas McDade was the last thing I should have been doing. My life was falling apart and I was busy slobbering all over a virtual stranger instead of concentrating on damage control.

"What's wrong?"

"This." I couldn't look at him.

"But I thought we could . . . I mean . . . do you remember when I took you to the movies?" He didn't wait for a response. "I liked you, Jody. *A lot.* I thought you felt the same way. I thought maybe we could—"

"That was years ago," I reminded him.

"I know, but I'm back in town now."

"I see that."

"And you're single."

"*Newly* single, Lucas. It's been a couple of hours, tops." I was ashamed to admit that part of me was tempted to ignore all logic and kiss him again, knowing nothing good could come of it. "I'm sorry. I shouldn't have let it happen."

He slumped back in his seat and stared out the window while I waited for him to say something. *Anything.* I focused on my hands, clasped in my lap, far too aware that mere moments earlier my tongue had been in his mouth. At least things hadn't gone any further, but if they had, I could have killed time refastening my bra, or buttoning my blouse, instead of sitting in numbed silence.

"Well," he finally said, sighing, "I guess you'd better go inside."

"Yeah, I guess so." I attempted a smile, but my dry lips clung to my teeth. "Thanks for the . . . uh, *ride.*"

"No problem," he mumbled, as I climbed out of the car.

He loudly revved the engine and sped down the street, screeching to a halt for a stop sign. I guessed it was his way of voicing an opinion. I waited until his taillights were gone before turning toward the house.

I climbed Erin's steps and rang the doorbell, utterly exhausted. When she didn't answer, I rang it again, and again. I checked my watch, amazed it was only eight-thirty.

"I'm coming!" she called from inside. "Jesus Christ, I'm coming!"

The door swung open and I offered my best friend a hopeful smile.

She was wrapped in a short, shiny black kimono, complete with embroidered gold dragons. She always wore slinky little numbers at home, regardless of the time of day. The moment she returned from her shift at the garden center, she threw off her overalls and slipped into something I certainly wouldn't have worn to answer the door. Her dark brown hair was unleashed from its usual waist-length braid, and her lips were clear of her standard crimson matte.

"Hey, there," I said.

"Hey, Jode." She smiled.

"Can I come in?"

"Sure." She stepped into the living room and lit a cigarette.

She'd been trying to quit smoking for years, using everything from patches to hypnosis, with no luck. Well aware of her industrious beginnings as a smoker of tightly rolled toilet paper, fern leaves, and all things flammable, I doubted she would ever break the habit.

We were an unlikely pair, having met in the cloakroom on the first day of second grade, when I caught her stealing my Hello Kitty lunch box (and its contents) and didn't tell the teacher. Erin decided that my silence was grounds for friendship and claimed me as her own.

She was raised by her grandmother, Gammy, but spent most of her childhood at my house, absorbing the family dynamic and eating anything my mother baked. We lived vicariously through each other, and while I watched her lift her shirt to flash high school boys her flat chest, she gazed at Mom's carefully labeled photo albums with jealous fascination, wishing she were part of something larger than her awkward family of two.

When Gammy died, the house, and what remained of the mortgage, was left to Erin.

"Thank God it's you," she said, perching on the arm of the couch. Gammy's brocade armchairs and cherry end tables looked uncomfortable in the company of Erin's big-screen television and multicolored rag rugs. "I was afraid you were Hannah Baxter."

"Why?"

"She's getting married again," she said with a groan.

"So I've heard."

"She asked me to be maid of honor."

"Really?" I planted myself in a leaky beanbag chair and a small stream of pellets spilled onto the hardwood floor.

"Yeah, and it's about fucking time!"

Erin cursed like it was punctuation.

"You aren't even friends."

"You aren't, either, but that didn't stop you from dyeing some satin pumps and planting a small garden in your hair for the last big day." She took a drag and exhaled slowly. "I've known her longer than you have, anyway. We were in Brownies together."

"Is that right?" Mom wouldn't let me join Brownies because I was already taking ballet and almost learning to play soccer. I would have given up both activities in favor of brown knee socks and a pencil clipped to my belt.

"We were in the same little group, Pixies, or Elves or some shit." She scratched her forehead with the jagged remains of her chewed fingernails. "We could have been fucking garden gnomes for all I care." She took another drag before continuing. "The point is, I've known her forever and she should have asked me before now."

I watched her exhale, surprised she cared. "Are you going to do it?"

"Hell, no!" She snorted. "I just wanted to be *asked*."

That was typical. As a kid, she collected stacks of Valentines but never sent any, hoarded birthday invitations and didn't attend the parties. Later on, she stopped returning phone calls, but saved messages on her answering machine, changing the tapes when they were full and storing them in a chest under her bed. She brought guys home from bars, slept with them, wrote their names in a tattered journal, and refused to see them again. While she feigned indifference to the opinions of others, she quietly measured herself with collections and lists. I blamed Gammy, who took a hands-off approach to grandparenting.

"So, what's going on?" Erin asked.

"I need a place to stay."

"Stay here." She closed her eyes and took a drag. The effort of inhalation only emphasized her high cheekbones.

"That's what I hoped you'd say." I smiled.

"You and Chris had a fight?"

I didn't want to rehash the whole evening, but knew she'd badger me for details until I gave her something to chew on.

"Marty McDade was such an asshole, I quit my job, and when I got home I discovered Chris and Beth, *as in my cousin,* were sharing a shower, since they've been screwing around. When I tried to stay with my parents, they turned me away because Josh is a total dumbshit." I skipped the Lucas McDade episode, barely able to grasp it myself. "So, here I am, jobless, homeless, and pissed off."

"I can't believe Chris and Beth were . . . what a bitch!" She paused. "More important, what a bastard!" She leaned closer, eager for more details.

"I don't really want to talk about this tonight."

"But you will, right?"

"Not tonight." I fidgeted in the beanbag chair, causing another pellet avalanche.

"You'll fill me in later?"

"Yeah." I sighed.

"I never liked that guy." She stood and walked across the room to hug me. "You can sleep in the spare room. I think the bed's made."

"Erin!" a male voice called from the back of the house.

"Just a minute!" she shouted as she released me from her embrace.

"Who's that?" I asked, surprised we weren't alone.

"Michael. I met him at the Sand Bar in Fillington a few days ago."

"And?"

"Erin!" he called again.

"And apparently he's scared of the dark." She rolled her eyes and shouted, "Just a second!"

"Sorry to, uh . . . interrupt," I said, blushing.

"No problem. He can wait. I'll see you in the morning and we'll get you all straightened out."

"Thanks, Erin." The words weren't enough to express my relief and gratitude.

It wasn't even nine o'clock, but I couldn't keep my eyes open. I washed my face, entered the spare room, and climbed into bed, fully clothed. Under the musty sheets, I prayed my life would look better by daylight.

I was awakened with a jolt followed by the sound of a muffled thud. A quick squint around the room, from the cedar chest of drawers in the corner to the papasan chair by the window, confirmed I was alone, and the thud sounded again, from down the hall. I slipped out from under the weight of a patchwork quilt and listened. If there'd been a consistent rhythm to the thudding, I would have assumed it was the age-old sound of sexual activity, but the noises were too loud, too erratic. I was tempted to call the police, but knew Erin only had one phone; an old portable in a constant state of recharging next to her bed.

My heart raced in response to visions from every horror movie I'd rented, and every murder mystery I'd read. I stepped onto the cold wood floor, trying not to make a sound, and pressed my ear against the door. Another thud. Despite the fact that I had no idea how to defend myself or the household against an intruder, I took a shaky breath and opened the door.

The windowless hallway was pitch-black, so I ran my hand along the wall to find my way toward Erin's room. When I reached the kitchen, the only room separating me from my best friend, goose bumps swarmed my arms and neck. Through the plaid tablecloth that acted as a curtain for the french doors of the master bedroom, a faint light moved from wall to wall.

He's in her room! Was he looking for jewelry? Did he want

money, electronics, or the thrill of the prowl? I'd heard about home invasions in big cities and the thought of some maniac standing over Erin's bed with a baseball bat and a violent streak was terrifying.

She slept like the dead, so I wasn't surprised the noise hadn't woken her, but it was only a matter of time before whoever had broken in fulfilled his desires, whatever they might be. I had to do something. *Fast.*

I crept farther into the kitchen, thankful for the pale sliver of moonlight illuminating the cutlery drawer. I tiptoed across the linoleum, wincing with every creak and groan of the floorboards, and grabbed the handle. The drawer was stiff, so I tugged hard, causing the utensils inside to jostle against one another with what seemed like a deafening crash.

"Shit!" I gasped. If the intruder hadn't restrained or injured her and her new boy toy already, I'd given him the incentive. I had to arm myself with whatever I could find. I reached into the drawer, scrambling through dull-edged table knives, wooden chopsticks stolen from the Peking Palace, an eggbeater, and two carrot peelers, desperate for a cleaver. Where were the knives? I saw no flash of metal in the moonlight, and the knowledge hit me with sickening speed; *she was a vegetarian.* There would be no steak knives, no serrated edges and polished blades of stainless steel. She favored the Cuisinart, and we would all die for her laziness! All I could hope for was a paring knife.

I knocked aside a rusted cheese grater and a boxed set of corncob handles. Never had useless gadgets seemed so sinister.

I froze as Erin's door opened behind me and I could barely breathe as my fingers closed around the handle of a marble rolling pin.

I swung around to strike my unseen enemy.

"Aaargh!" I yelled, leveling my weapon.

"Jody, no!"

I stopped in mid-swing and the rolling pin slipped from my grasp, marble cracking as it hit the floor. Erin stood in the doorway, alive and . . . *annoyed*?

"Holy shit! What the *hell* are you doing?" she asked, cinching the sash on her kimono.

"Someone's in your room!" I whispered, ready to lead her to safety.

"Michael."

"No, someone else. I think we have a . . ."

"He's the only person in there." She looked at me as though I were insane.

I watched the rolling pin spin across the floor, leaving crumbs of stone in its wake, until it struck the wall and cracked in half.

"He's the only person in there?" I repeated dumbly.

I'd saved the household from nothing. No intruder. No breach of security. No threat of a massacre.

So what was that flashing light?

"What were you doing, Jody?"

My brain was swept clear of logic as I tried to justify my behavior. "Nothing. I mean, I thought . . . I thought we had, that there was someone . . . I heard a noise and—"

"Never mind. Just go back to bed." She shook her head slowly, from side to side. "You've had a shitty day."

"I'm sorry, Erin."

"Don't worry about it. I'll see you in the morning."

It wasn't until I crawled back into bed that I realized the thudding had indeed been the one thing I'd been certain it wasn't. I'd interrupted Erin having sex.

I fell asleep, cringing in anticipation of what my tart-tongued best friend would say in the morning.

five

I awoke early, sheets twisted around my clothed body, somehow forgetting that my life had spiraled out of control mere hours before. When I finally recognized my surroundings and came to my senses, I knew I'd have to work quickly to put the pieces back together.

I undressed in the bathroom, pulling the wrinkled red satin nightmare away from my flesh, like a snake shedding skin. After a steaming shower, the highlight of which was trying to rinse the raspberry shampoo from my hair with the world's lowest water pressure, I dressed in the same clothing I'd not only arrived in, but *slept* in, and wandered into the kitchen for a bite of breakfast. I soon discovered that "a bite" was substantially more than Erin had to offer.

The refrigerator held a near-empty container of green cottage cheese, two small skim milk cartons, both well past their expiration dates, and a bag of leftover takeout from the Peking Palace. The idea of A.M. egg rolls wasn't entirely offensive until I saw the receipt, dated nearly two weeks earlier. An economy-sized tub of margarine and an even larger jar of mayonnaise were reminders that Erin layered her fats like winter clothing.

The antique tin breadbox on the counter was empty, with the exception of a small crowd of whole wheat crumbs from days gone by and several ketchup packets held together with an elastic band. The cupboards were filled with spices, syrups, and vegetable soup mix, but nothing of substance.

Since she'd put a roof over my head, the least I could do was buy Erin some groceries. Safeway was within walking distance, so I plucked a knapsack and a jacket from her hall closet and headed out.

The Japanese plum trees were in full bloom, spotting the street with splashes of pink, and while I knew the petals would drop to the ground and be trampled in a couple of weeks, they lifted my spirits.

"Despite the past twenty-four hours, life is good," I whispered. "Unemployment is an *adventure*." I'd earned a world of change by stripping away the old and all I had to do was welcome the new. Opportunity wouldn't pass me by.

The grocery store was almost empty and I quickly counted my cash before choosing a cart over a basket. I'd have to watch my finances a bit and avoid touching the savings account. One minor gap in employment wouldn't thwart my efforts to buy a house. *I wouldn't allow it.*

I had a week's worth of tips with me, and a check coming from the Galley for my final days of work. Not only that, the job hunt had the potential to be anything, including quick and painless.

My financial situation was indeed cartworthy.

I cruised the aisles, immensely satisfied as I tossed items into my rig, knowing I could buy whatever I wanted. With a smirk, I bypassed Chris's Cheerios in favor of Wheaties, grabbed sourdough bread instead of his usual rye, and added creamy french dressing, corn niblets, pork chops, and chicken wings. The power of singledom was incredible! I bought canned mandarin slices, pineapple chunks, and a big jar of maraschino cherries. *Fuck Chris and red dye number five!*

I scooped several cups of bulk trail mix into a bag for Erin, who was banned from the store for stealing handfuls straight from the bin to eat while she shopped. Her allergies had done her in, and guilt was impossible to deny when the store manager followed a trail of discarded almonds from the bulk section directly to Erin, who happened to be working on a mouthful of mix at that very moment. The Safeway in Fillington was a twenty-minute drive from her house, which explained her low food supply.

I totaled the groceries in my head as I filled the cart and, as the number climbed higher, I adjusted my mind-set, opting for generic brands and taking advantage of sale items, just like my mother. I bought mainly necessities, but threw in a few treats, as well. Chocolate cookies had cheered me in the past, so I bought two bags, in case the job hunt was less than stellar.

When I got to the checkout with a full load, the only cashier open was an anemic-looking woman in her mid-sixties. Her short, impossibly dark hair was plastered against her head with what I hoped was gel, although I couldn't rule out saliva. I stepped into her line and watched her slowly scan items.

It had been glaringly apparent since I'd entered the store and heard Kenny Rogers over the PA system that I didn't fit in with the other daytime shoppers. The woman in front of me was a young mother, clutching an envelope stuffed with clipped coupons, a drooling infant cradled in her free arm. Her cart was overflowing with Technicolor cereal boxes, chips, ice cream, and two more runny-nosed children intent on fighting over who got the prize in the already opened box of Lucky Charms. Behind me was an elderly man with a basket of vitamins and single-portion meats. Behind him, a middle-aged woman with several packages of beef jerky and a six-pack of Bud.

I wanted to distance myself from the rest of them, tell the cashier and anyone who would listen that under normal circumstances I was a working girl who shopped evenings and weekends, accompanied by soft rock. *My unemployed state is only temporary! I'm part of a totally different demographic. I am not one of you!*

As the cashier ran my items over the scanner, I watched the prices flash on her register, hoping I'd allotted enough for sales tax during my mental tally. My Visa was for emergencies only, and one measly day of unemployment didn't qualify.

"Hi, Jody," a voice called from behind me. I turned to see Lucas McDade at the end of the line.

I hadn't counted on seeing him again so soon, and if I'd spotted him shopping, I would have made a dash for the nearest exit. Apparently, while I avoided awkward encounters, Lucas sought them out.

"Hey," I called to him, hoping that would be enough, and turned my attention back to my rapidly increasing tab.

"It's my turn to buy doughnuts," Lucas continued.

I smiled weakly over my shoulder.

"Dad buys them most of the time, but today *I'm* doing the honors."

I silently willed him to stop talking and concentrated on the prices: $1.49, $2.79, $1.69. Were maraschino cherries really $4.59? I shouldn't have bought them.

"I can't stand the maple bars," Lucas said, "but Tony insists on having them. Dad likes the custard-filled ones, but they don't have any today . . ."

What in the *hell* was he talking about, and could I make it any more obvious that I wasn't interested?

The man behind me impatiently cleared his throat.

"I've always liked powdered donuts, the way the sugar tastes kind of cold on my tongue."

The cashier shot me a dirty look, as if I had any control over Lucas McDade's tongue. *Damn.* I winced. I *did* have control of it, a little more than twelve hours earlier.

"About last night, Jody . . ."

My palms were suddenly sweating. *Not here. Not now.* Couldn't the checker scan any faster? $1.99, $2.49.

"Excuse me," I heard him say, "would you mind if I went ahead of you? I need to talk to that young lady up there."

"Back off," the old man snarled.

"But I just have a few doughnuts," Lucas pleaded.

"You can wait in line like everybody else."

I silently thanked God for cranky old men.

$1.39, $.79, $4.29. *Come on, lady!*

"Just a dozen *doughnuts*, sir. And I'm paying cash."

"You want to take this outside?" The old guy meant business.

"Are you threatening me?" Lucas sounded shocked, but I didn't dare turn around for fear I'd encourage conversation.

"Everybody just calm down," the cashier said, punching in a code for red potatoes.

"Jody, I've been thinking about last night."

"Can we talk about this later?" I felt the heat rise in my cheeks and turned to see that he was a bright shade of red, despite the fact that *I* was the one being publicly humiliated.

"That kiss we shared was something I'd dreamed about for years."

"Kill me," I muttered.

The cashier dropped my jumbo jar of dill pickles and within seconds we were all inhaling the stench of brine.

"Aw, shit." She picked up the telephone. "Cleanup at checkstand four," boomed through the ceiling speakers. *"Bring a mop,"* she added, glaring at me.

"Sheesh." The old man sighed. "I thought I could get in and out of here in a couple of minutes at this hour."

"I'll be right with you, sir," the cashier politely informed him, then snapped at me, "Do you want more pickles?"

I shook my head and waited for the grand total, which turned out to be far more than I'd expected. I frantically counted out bills as she again requested a cleanup.

"Jody, I think I'm—"

"Not now, Lucas!" I shouted as I dug change from my pockets. How could I have been stupid enough to kiss him?

"But Jody—"

"I said, *not now*!" I threw the exact change on the counter and grabbed my cart, racing toward the door.

Just as I stepped on the automatic door pad, I made the mistake of glancing backward. The cashier's back was turned, and Lucas had made his way to the telephone. As the door closed behind me, I heard his voice calling through the speakers, "I'm in love with you, Jody!"

Shit.

"What's wrong with that guy?" I groaned. He'd been normal in the Galley and in the car, but apparently he was a total wingnut. *He's in love with me?*

I lifted plastic bags from the cart, looping their handles over my wrists and feeling the weight of the groceries cut grooves into my forearms. There was no way in hell I could carry it all, and that lunatic was going to rush through the door at any moment.

"Fuck it," I muttered, dropping the bags into the cart and pushing my load toward Erin's.

As I should have expected, one of the wheels refused to cooperate when I reached the sidewalk. I shoved with as much force as I could muster and, with a squeak of protest, the wheel was back in motion. I hustled toward Erin's place, the cart screeching with every step.

My tip money was almost entirely gone and I was broke until I could pick up my final check from the Galley, *in a week.* My personal nightmare was showing no signs of slowing down, and chances were good I'd run the risk of seeing Lucas McDade on every street corner for the rest of my life.

* * *

When I walked into the house, panting from speed and effort, Erin grinned at me from her seat at the kitchen table, then leaped from her chair to help me unload. Her smile faded when she saw what I'd brought home.

"You bought all *generic* stuff?" she said, scowling.

Her tone was enough to block Lucas from my mind.

"It's the same as the name brands." I sounded *exactly* like my mother.

"You've got to be kidding."

"It tastes the same," I insisted.

"Right." She rolled her eyes.

"It all comes from the same manufacturer."

She gave me a skeptical look and I had to refrain from yelling. "Do you actually think that Safeway has a *marshmallow factory*? Or a *light bulb plant*?"

"Whatever." She shook her head. "Your mom called."

As it turned out, Mom had wanted to make sure I was okay and requested that no one tell Dad she'd phoned. Twenty minutes later, Dad called for the same reason, also in secret. While Erin was talking to him, Mom appeared at the house with a tuna casserole to keep me from starving to death. So much for tough love.

"Can you help me bring the rest of this stuff in?" I asked.

Erin followed me to the front steps and whistled under her breath. "Nice wheels."

I ignored her and grabbed a couple of bags. Between us, we were able to unload the cart in two trips, then roll it into her basement, to be returned to Safeway at a later date.

"Now, about last night," she began as we shelved the canned goods.

"I thought we had a prowler," I mumbled.

"A *prowler*? You can't be that naïve, Jode. You must know what you heard."

"I guess so."

"We were getting it *on*."

"Yeah." I nodded, blushing.

"Having sex."

"Mmm-hmm."

"Loud sex, evidently."

"Okay, already! Look, I was thrown off by the light. I thought it was a prowler with a flashlight."

She disappeared into her room for a moment and returned with a large red flashlight. The bulb was covered with a layer of yellow cellophane and a cardboard cutout of a bat.

"It turns out Michael has a bit of a Batman fetish. He likes to play this little game while we're having sex." She flipped a switch and aimed the light at the darkest corner of the room. "I flash the Bat Signal on the walls and ceiling, alerting him to a Bat Emergency."

"I don't really need to hear this."

"And he gets going, all excited about saving Metropolis or wherever the hell Batman lives."

I cringed. "Didn't you just meet this guy?"

"In Fillington the other night."

"And he made this fetish known—"

"Right off the bat. Ha! Pardon the pun."

"Jesus."

"Men's silly fantasies have to be appeased from time to time, and if he wants to pretend he's a superhero, that's fine with me."

I broke eye contact.

"Come on," she said, laughing. "Don't be such a prude."

Erin had accused me of prudish behavior since we were little girls, citing as examples the fact that I didn't like carrying on conversations from the cubicles of public restrooms, and wouldn't sneak a peek at the *Playboy* magazines in the Dumpster on Coleman Avenue. Erin was the kind of person who talked to complete strangers about her menstrual cycle.

"I'm not a *prude.*" How many times had I said those words?

"Then say 'penis.' "

"What?" Could the day get any more bizarre?

"Just say the word 'penis.' "

"Why?"

"To prove you aren't a prude. Try it. Penis, penis, penis!"

"Cut it out!" I shouted, saliva pooling in the corners of my mouth. I'd gone from dissatisfied waitress to rabid nutjob in a single day.

"Fine!" Erin saw my volume and raised me ten decibels.

"Fine!" I snapped back, then burst into tears. I hated to cry in anyone's company, but it was hardest in front of her. I'd never seen my best friend shed a tear, even when Gammy died.

Erin reached over and hugged me, tightly. "I'm sorry, Jode."

"It's okay."

She held me for a few quiet moments. "You don't have to say 'penis.' "

"It's not *that,*" I sobbed.

"Well, I'm sure generic peanut butter is just as good as Skippy."

"That's not what I'm upset about!" I wailed.

"Do you want to tell me what's going on?"

"No."

"Please?" She rocked from one foot to the other, swaying with me. "I might be able to help."

"It's complicated."

"Then it's lucky I'm not a complete moron."

"It's embarrassing."

"For Christ's sake. *Everything*'s embarrassing to you. Start at the beginning."

I told her the whole story, beginning with Marty McDade and

ending with the love proclamation at Safeway. At first I was angry when she laughed, then I started to see the humor in it. A giggle escaped from my throat, followed by a hearty guffaw. "*Lucas McDade,* for fuck's sake!"

"Well, first things first," she said, when we'd regained our composure. "You need a job."

"I already checked the classifieds, and there's nothing." I sighed. "I don't want to be a twenty-seven-year-old with a paper route, Erin."

"Relax. There's a temp agency by the doughnut place on Beech Street. While you were shopping, I made you a two-o'clock appointment, assuming your schedule was pretty clear."

"Two o'clock *today*?"

"No time like the present." She shrugged.

"But I feel like hell. I *look* like hell."

Rather than reassuring me and tossing off a few of the compliments I was fishing for, she *nodded.* "We need to do something about your appearance. It won't do you any good to go to an interview looking nondescript."

"Nondescript?" My heart sank. "So much for support."

"I'm just telling it like it is. The way you look now, they'll forget you five minutes after you leave." She separated her damp hair into three sections and started braiding, piece over piece.

I was too shocked to speak. How could I possibly be *nondescript*? I had frizzy hair and a relatively clear complexion! At five foot eight, I was taller than the national average, and slightly pigeon-toed! I had an extremely flat ass and freckles blanketing my shoulders like a shawl. For crying out loud, nondescript was worse than hideous!

"Sensitivity isn't a disease, you know," I told her.

"Honesty's the best policy."

"Can you see I'm hurt, here?" I asked. "Sometimes I think you have etiquette Tourette's or something. God, the way things just fly out of your mouth!"

"Why are you getting so touchy?" She found a rubber band in her shirt pocket and secured the braid.

"In case you've already forgotten, I'm going through a few crises right now. What I need is *support.*"

She looked at me for a long moment before telling me she was sorry.

"Apology accepted."

"You know, you can't just look at the negative side of your situation. Think of this as an opportunity to change your life."

"Yesterday, I did. Hell, even this morning I still had hope, but—"

"You'll get through this," she assured me, but I had my doubts.

six

I put my wardrobe needs in Erin's capable hands with a sense of relief. If there was one thing she knew (aside from sex), it was job interviews. After handling the hiring and firing at Bent Harbor's premier nursery for almost five years, she was an expert on first impressions. Ongoing subscriptions to *Cosmo, Elle,* and *Vogue* meant that her knowledge of fashion far surpassed my own, which seemed to begin and end with the "don't wear white after Labor Day" rule.

I absently ran my fingers through the wiry depths of my curls, wishing for something a little more slick and sophisticated. Of course, it was going to take more than a new hairdo to jump-start my life.

Erin returned from her bedroom with an armload of skirts, slacks, and blazers, including enough twill to clothe corporate America. She placed the hangers on a doorknob and started riffling through the goods.

"Okay, what have we got here?" she mumbled. "We should probably get you into some bright colors, something to suit the season." She pulled out a fuchsia dress and I held my breath in fear until she dropped it onto the kitchen table. "Not professional enough," she muttered, reaching for a lime-green sweater I'd never seen before.

"That might be a bit warm," I said. *And a bit repulsive.* I tried my best to be tactful and asked, "Where did you get that?"

"Oh, it was Gammy's." Her tone was nonchalant, as though I shouldn't mind fashions from beyond the grave.

"Is all of this stuff hers?" I asked. I wasn't too keen on Gammy when she was alive, and the thought of slipping into her duds was enough to curl my toes.

"Most of it. That's the great thing about fashion, Jody. Styles just keep repeating themselves. Gammy was wearing some of this stuff in the seventies and now it's back in vogue."

If my senses didn't deceive me, along with "this stuff," Gammy was inclined toward dangerous amounts of flowery perfume. She'd been dead three years and the fragrance was as pungent as the cosmetic counter at a five-and-dime. And were those moth-balls I smelled? I could only hope clogs weren't back in vogue, recalling Gammy's extensive collection.

"I don't know how retro I want to be at this interview," I hinted. "How about we concentrate on the stuff that's yours?"

Erin smiled and continued her perusal of the clothing. She found a lavender short-sleeved blouse, held it under my chin and exclaimed, "Perfect! Now, what do we have to go with it?" She dropped it into my lap and the search resumed. "Pants are no good for an interview . . . this suit will wash you out . . . Aha! Here it is." She handed me a pale gray skirt and matching jacket with faint pinstripes.

I changed in the bathroom and, from what I could see in the medicine cabinet mirror, knew there was hope for me. Erin added some chunky-heeled gray shoes, earrings, and a small silver brooch before leading me to her bedroom. I ignored the sight of her newly rumpled satin sheets and the torn condom wrapper on the floor as she carefully applied my makeup, mixing Plum Night and Moon Sliver eye shadow together. She experimented with lipsticks and glosses until she found the right shade, then twirled my hair into a tight bun, leaving a few curls loose in the front to frame my face.

When I saw my reflection, I almost believed I could survive the interview, a mere two hours away.

"Now, the résumé." She led me into her den, where the computer was already running. She typed my name but used her address and phone number.

"Oh, yeah. I almost forgot I'm homeless."

She rolled her eyes. "Okay, you said you want an office job, so let's focus on related skills."

"Erin, I've been a *waitress* for seven years."

"We'll work around it."

"I have *no* office experience."

"Let's just think for a second." She tapped a fingertip against her front teeth, a sure sign her brain was slipping into overdrive. I'd seen the gesture every time she'd faced a problem, from choosing between grape and orange popsicles to creating the ultimate excuse to dump a guy. "Did you do payroll?"

"No, Dean does it. I was just *on* the payroll."

"Close enough." She started typing.

"Erin!" My stomach tightened. "Lying on my résumé is a crappy idea."

"Calm down. Did you order supplies?"

"Sometimes."

"There we go! Inventory control."

"*Erin,* I added tartar sauce to the order sheet when Dean told me to."

"Look, do you want a career change or not?"

I shut my mouth and let her rewrite my history. Pretty soon I wasn't a waitress, but assistant manager at the Galley (based on the fact that I'd been there the longest and had my own key to the restaurant), and director of marketing (I took care of seasonal coloring contests and I'd written two job listings for the *Bent Har-*

bor Times employment section). By the time she'd finished, I didn't recognize my own job. She printed her efforts on cream linen paper, and I was amazed by how professional it looked.

The final step of interview boot camp was an interrogation at the kitchen table.

"Where do you see yourself in five years?"

"*Come on.* They won't ask me that. And if I knew what I wanted to do, I wouldn't be wasting my time with a temp agency."

"Don't say I didn't warn you." She lit a cigarette and took a long drag. "What's your best quality?"

"Geez, I don't know."

"*Wrong!* It's organization. *Always organization.*" She shook her head at my naïveté.

"Fine. Organization."

"Good. What's your weakest trait in the workplace?"

"Not *having* a workplace," I said, trying to hold back a laugh.

"If you don't want to take this seriously . . ." She crushed her cigarette in a nearby saucer with unnecessary force.

"Okay, okay. Uh, weakest characteristic . . . maybe confidence?"

"Wrong! And that's a double whammy, too. First of all, never answer a question with a question, and second, don't say a word about low self-esteem. You tell them your weakest quality is that you're a perfectionist."

"Jesus Christ," I said.

"*Listen to me.* Bullshitting is the only way to survive. You either lie or embellish your way through this interview, or you're screwed."

"It just doesn't seem ethical."

"Well, you've got two choices. You can enjoy the rather limited perks of morally righteous unemployment, or you can get a job."

I nodded in defeat.

"Moving right along. You've got to make sure you find some common ground with your interviewer. If she's got a picture of a dog on her desk, you're a fucking canine fanatic. If there's a bunch of that New Age self-empowerment shit on her bookshelf, you tell her you're into the power of positive thinking. Are you with me?"

"If she has spinach in her teeth, I tell her I hate dental floss. Yeah, I get it."

"Good, because we've gotta move, here. I can give you a ride over there, but you'll have to find your own way home. I got stuck with the evening shift."

We climbed into Erin's 1977 Honda Civic and I was still buckling my seat belt when the gear grinding began. We whipped through minimal traffic, past Safeway, onto Old Marine Highway and all the way across town. A swarm of butterflies came to life in my near-empty stomach and a layer of moisture soon covered my palms.

"This isn't my only chance," I murmured. "There are plenty of jobs out there."

"Yeah." Erin smiled. "You could be a waitress at Dean's Ocean Galley."

"Erin."

"There's always the mill . . ."

"Bite me."

"That's the spirit!"

We pulled into the parking lot of a small brick building, and as soon as I saw the sign, I knew why she hadn't mentioned the agency's name.

"*Temp*tations, Inc.?" I winced.

"It's kinda cute." She shrugged. "Give it a try."

I stepped out of the car and held the door open between us. "It sounds like an escort service."

"I honestly don't think an escort service could survive here,

Jode. The men in this town are so cheap, finding someone to go dutch on a bowl of minestrone is like striking gold."

"But *Temp*tations?"

"Just walk right in there and give 'em hell."

I shut the car door and, with a tap on the horn, she abandoned me. I took a shaky breath and entered the building.

The office was empty of all life-forms, aside from some wilted ferns and a receptionist wearing a space-age headset. She was probably several years younger than me, but her black power suit made her look at least ten times more professional. I gave her my name and she handed me a clipboard with a stack of papers to fill out. The top two forms were an application and a request for employment history.

"I brought my résumé," I said brightly, attempting to hand the clipboard back to her, but she didn't look up.

"Please fill out all forms."

"But most of this information is already on my—"

"All forms." She glanced upward and gave me an apologetic smile.

I sat on a plush chair, balancing the clipboard on my knees. The office smelled like a combination of disinfectant and potpourri.

"Would you like some coffee?" the girl asked.

"No, thanks," The polite smile Erin and I had practiced was already coming in handy.

The girl pointed at her headset. "I'm talking to my boss."

"Oh. Sorry." I winced.

She shuffled papers while I transferred all of the information from my résumé into the tiny spaces on the agency forms. My writing was barely legible.

"Can I get you anything?" the receptionist asked.

I surreptitiously peered at the front desk and saw her staring at some files. Another headset conversation. I continued to list my Galley duties in the smallest print I could manage.

She cleared her throat and repeated the question.

"Are you talking to me?" I asked.

"Yes."

"No, I don't need anything." *Just an escape hatch.*

After another ten minutes of paperwork I was told my career counselor was ready to see me. I stood and straightened my skirt, then followed the receptionist down a long hallway to a door left slightly ajar. I could smell something else under the potpourri haze. Something sweet.

She pushed open the door and I froze in mid-step.

Son of a bitch!

Sitting behind a stack of color-coded files and a Magic 8 Ball was Mrs. Corbett, my high school guidance counselor.

"Have a seat." She directed me to a rickety metal folding chair.

She hadn't aged gracefully, that was for sure. Her dye job was clumsy and deep wrinkles creased her unnaturally dark skin, undoubtedly the result of a few trips to the Tan-o-rama salon on Bay Boulevard.

I sat down and grimaced as the chair creaked under my weight.

"Is this your first time using an agency?"

"Yes, it is." Did she recognize me as one of her teenage victims? *Apparently not.*

Mrs. Corbett explained that while she looked over my application, I'd take some standardized tests. After she'd seen the results, we could discuss employment opportunities.

She seated me in a windowless box of an office and left me with a battery of computer tests to assess my spelling, grammar, and typing skills

Forty minutes later, the printer produced my results, which she removed from the room before I had a chance to look at them. Next was a multiple-choice quiz, featuring questions like "When did you last assault a coworker" and "Does your drug habit affect your job performance?"

Everything went surprisingly well until I reached the math test. I could handle the basics, but I'd forgotten how to do much more than that. I struggled through word problems, not giving a rat's ass how long it took a train to travel from Portland, Oregon, to Portland, Maine, or how many pages Betty Bookworm could read in a given hour. By the time I reached the end of the third page of seven, I was tired and cranky. My stomach was growling louder than Dad's Shih Tzu, and I was sure the sound could be heard throughout the office.

After a full two hours of testing, I was back in Mrs. Corbett's office, waiting for the receptionist to tally my scores. I sat in silence, gazing at the Magic 8 Ball, until she dropped the stack of papers onto Mrs. Corbett's desk and cringed at me.

Was it that bad?

"Let's see now." Mrs. Corbett studied the pages. "Great job on the spelling and grammar."

I smiled and nodded, but she made no eye contact. Instead, she poured a cup of steaming coffee from the thermos on her desk. In addition to the mocha, I smelled the distinct odor of spiced rum.

In search of Erin's suggested "common ground," I scanned the office, but there were no photos on display, no books or plants. The only wall decoration was a macramé monstrosity of brown wool and wooden beads. I could find no words of praise, so I said nothing.

"Typing thirty words per minute meets our minimum requirement," she said, licking the rum from her lips. Her smile lasted until the final pages. "Oh, my. The math portion was a disaster."

I bit my lip. "Yes. I'm a little out of practice."

"You couldn't even handle the *fractions.*" Her frown threatened to slide right off her chin.

"Math was never my strong point." I tried to smile, but it felt like a grimace.

"Obviously." She took another sip from her tainted mug and it was like twelfth grade all over again. She was even more condescending than the last time we'd met *and* she was still drunk. Under the circumstances, giving me grief over a math test was ludicrous.

"Should I anticipate multiplying fractions on the job?" I asked, barely containing my sarcasm.

"That's not the point."

"May I ask what the point is?"

"As I mentioned before, these are *standardized* tests of basic knowledge, and your basic knowledge is far below—"

I didn't want to hear another word.

"Do you even remember me?"

"Should I?"

"You were my guidance counselor," I said, through gritted teeth.

"Hmm, I don't recall." She reached for the mug again.

"You actually told me I shouldn't count on being successful."

"Well," she said, looking over my résumé. "What have you been doing since you graduated?"

"Working as a waitress."

"I see." Her tone suggested I had proven her point.

I was livid. "Mrs. Corbett—"

"I built this agency from scratch because I got tired of selling pipe dreams to kids like you."

"Pipe dreams?" I gasped. "Telling me I was doomed to—"

"It's a tough world out there," she interrupted, "and you have to be prepared for it. Take this testing, for example. I have to make sure my employees are qualified to handle their placements because it's *my name* that goes down in flames if they can't do the job. I'm in a very stressful position."

"I understand that, but—"

"I don't think you *do* understand. I'm the gatekeeper around here. What I say, goes, and if I don't think you're qualified, *you aren't.*"

She shuffled through a bunch of folders and I just knew some fabulous job was in that stack. As much as I would have liked to give her a piece of my mind (a stinking, seething, angry piece), I bit my tongue. I needed a job too badly to let my emotions take control.

I took a breath before speaking. "What I'm looking for is the opportunity to move on to a new career," I told her. "I don't think poor results on one math test should come between me and a job."

I explained that I was willing to do anything but reception. I'd spent enough time pasting on a smile at the Galley, so grinning and bearing it didn't fit in with my new life plan. I also mentioned that I didn't have a car, so I'd need a job on a bus route. Considering the loss I'd take on tips, I told her I had to make fourteen dollars an hour.

She made no attempt to hide her amusement as she choked on a mouthful of caffeinated booze. "I have a secretarial position open at the mill."

"Isn't that the same as a receptionist?"

"I suppose."

"But I just told you—"

"It's all I've got." She shrugged, a cruel twinkle in her eye.

"What do you mean?" I stared pointedly at the stacks of paper all over her desk and the prominently displayed folders. "What are those?"

"Take-out menus. I'm having a late lunch."

I paused while the news sank in. "So, the position at the mill is my only choice?"

"Yes, and it pays . . . let's see here." She checked a sheet of paper. "After our fee, you'll be making eight dollars an hour."

"*Eight dollars?* You've got to be kidding."

"It's more than minimum wage. Take it or leave it."

"I guess I'll, uh . . . take it," I said, as something died inside me.

"Very well. I'll contact the office manager and tell him we've found someone. In the meantime, I want you to realize that you will be representing this agency. I want you to dress professionally and act accordingly. In light of Bent Harbor's job market, you should feel very lucky that I'm giving you this chance."

I held my tongue. *Barely.*

"Thank you, Mrs. Corbett."

"Oh, and one last thing. I have a little rule you'll have to live by, and it should be easy for anyone to remember." She sneered. "Even someone who's forgotten rudimentary math."

I didn't think I could hold back for another second.

"I firmly believe in the three *X*s. That's no excuses, no explanations, and no expletives."

I stared at her. "So, I guess calling you an alcoholic bitch is out of the question?"

My job offer was rescinded in two seconds flat.

seven

As soon as I reached the *Temp*tations parking lot, I attempted to kick my own ass with a chunky heel. *How could I have been so stupid?* There'd been a job at my fingertips, and I'd flicked it away like a piece of lint.

I walked toward the harbor, desperate for a little solitude.

City work crews were out in force, filling the street median with small clumps of flowers sure to double in size by early summer. Apparently, the only plants resilient enough to withstand the exhaust fumes of local traffic were also the ugliest. Even the bright orange optimism of marigolds couldn't save them from looking like something out of Mother Nature's bargain basement.

Along the sidewalk, colorful flags hung from the streetlights, a distraction from the bland storefronts of Hammerhead Hardware (advertising their annual Nail Sale), the Coastal Cafe (We Roast Our Own Beans!), and the rest of the floundering businesses in the commercial district. Bent Harbor always felt the dull ache of recession, like continuous jet lag.

Those who didn't move away from town found work at the pulp mill, scrabbled together a couple of part-time jobs, or collected unemployment. Some of us had spent our lives bragging that we'd never resort to mill work, but it seemed as if pulp were the only thing that always paid.

"I should have left with everybody else," I murmured, knowing perfectly well it wasn't true. The thought of city living turned my stomach.

I was in a full-blown funk, but all it took to lighten my mood was the sight of a deserted beach. I went barefoot, wiggling my toes in the sand for a few minutes before approaching the water. I waded in past my ankles, gasping at the temperature. It was the kind of cold that would have me shrieking if I'd jumped in, but I'd always been a slow mover, acclimatizing with every small step.

I felt the sand beneath my feet slip away with each pull of the tide and watched red and white buoys bob from side to side, creaking with each prompt of the ocean.

As usual, seagulls circled the sky, scavenging for fish and squawking over the tiniest scraps of food. A couple of mallards swam toward me, but I had no bread crusts for them. If I didn't find work quickly, I'd need them for myself.

I stepped back on shore and walked along the packed wet sand, watching light patches appear with the pressure of each footstep. I moved toward the tidal pools at the south side of the beach and, when I arrived at the natural rock pier, I climbed onto it, wincing as barnacles dug into the soles of my feet. I reached the top of the rocks, where small pools housed Bent Harbor's finest treasures.

I crouched and dipped my fingertips into the chilly water of a tidal pool, watching the ripples I'd created. My hand dipped deeper to touch the pink tendril of a sea anemone and I smiled as it stuck to me. Tadpoles darted between leaves of seaweed, and urchins lay at the bottom of the pool, their purple spikes all prickled allure. Patterned pointy shells were attached to the rock and I remembered how much time Josh and I had spent trying to pry them free so we could see what was inside, only to be disappointed by gooey flesh. I'd never expected to become one of those hats, but there I was, ripped from security and held, flesh side out to the world.

* * *

I eventually left the pier to return to the sandy beach and found a kelp bullwhip at least seven feet long. I couldn't resist picking it up and holding its bulb between two hands, lifting and cracking the tail down against the earth. I was surprised at how satisfied I felt when clumps of sand flew in all directions. I beat the ground again, and again, thrashing until I was out of breath and sweat was seeping into Erin's blouse.

"What the hell are you doing?"

I nearly jumped out of my skin, but turned to see Max and Jaundice sitting on a log. "How long have you been here?" I gasped.

"Long enough," Max said, with a snort. "Whatcha doing?"

"Nothing."

"It looks like you were beating the crap out of the beach," Jaundice said.

"No, I was just—"

"Lion taming?" Max asked. His legs dangled from the log, his feet barely grazing the sand. "Or is this some kind of S and M thing?"

"What do *you* know about S and M?" Jaundice asked.

"I watch the news, thank you very much." Max's eyes were fixed on me. "Seriously, what are you up to, kid?"

I settled next to them. "Taking out some aggression, I guess."

"Nothing wrong with that," Jaundice said, zipping his jacket. "Although you're hardly dressed for it."

I told them about my interview and the concern I felt about the direction of my life. As expected, Jaundice listened, offering some supportive grunts and nods while Max cut me off in mid-sentence to tell me things weren't the same at the Galley without me.

"It's been *one day,*" I reminded him.

"That Katie character's too slow with the refills," he grumbled.

"And she brought me a spoon for my fruit crumble. What kind of ninny eats crumble with a *spoon,* for crying out loud?"

"I'm sorry for your inconvenience," I muttered.

"When are you coming back?"

"I'm not."

"They need you."

"Dean's got plenty of help." It still stung to be so easily replaced.

"Not like you," Max said.

"Leave her alone," Jaundice interrupted quietly. "If you need a career change, make one."

"Shut your piehole!" Max barked. "No one's asking for your opinion." He turned back to face me. "When are you coming back, Jody?"

"I'm not."

"Why don't you drop off some résumés around town?" Jaundice suggested.

"No one's advertising. It seems like a waste of time, paper, and energy."

"No ad doesn't mean they aren't hiring."

"I guess." I stood up. "I better get going."

"Good luck with the job hunt," Jaundice said, extending a long, bony hand for me to shake. "Just remember, it's only been one day. You'll find something great in no time."

"Just come back to the Galley, for Christ's sake," Max whined. "Don't let pride get in the way of happiness."

"Whose happiness?" I asked, laughing as I walked away.

I slipped into Erin's shoes when I reached the pavement, wishing they were anything but high heels. As much as I appreciated the loan of her clothing, I wanted to get back into my own as soon as possible, which meant taking a trip to Chris's place. *My old place.* He wouldn't be off work for a couple of hours and, if I borrowed my brother's car, I could be in and out of there in about forty minutes, give or take. Josh lived in an apartment on Seabreeze Way, only a few blocks from where I stood.

When I arrived at Josh's building, I saw the rusted green Yugo in the lot and breathed a sigh of relief. I climbed two flights of stairs and found the door knocker hanging from one loose screw. The peephole had been removed, leaving a clear view into the apartment, which I wasn't quite prepared to face. I'd been there once before, but hadn't dared to step across the threshold. Three bags of garbage leaned against the exterior wall, waiting in vain for someone to put them in the bins downstairs.

I rapped my knuckles against the door and waited, then knocked again. I heard footsteps, followed by the release of two dead bolts and the shifting of several locks before the door opened. Standing in front of me was a dark-haired stranger in striped pajama bottoms and nothing else. It was almost four-thirty in the afternoon.

"Is Josh here?" I asked.

"He might be. Who are you?" He rubbed his eyes with one fist.

I wanted to ask him the same. Josh was the most industrious pothead I knew, meaning he had a part-time job at Video Nook, but his skinny paycheck wasn't enough to cover the rent. He was always sharing the place with mysterious, interchangeable roommates. It was no wonder I didn't drop by often, considering I had to negotiate visits with my own flesh and blood through a moron sentry at the front door.

"I'm his sister," I snapped.

"No shit? Josh has a sister?"

I nodded. Although I couldn't claim to keep my family ties in tight, responsible double knots, apparently Josh left his undone.

The roommate led me down a dark hallway, littered with chocolate-bar wrappers and fast-food packaging. Little Sicily pizza boxes were stacked waist high, trailing dead cheese and crusty pepperoni slices. The smell was pure decay. Shag carpeting was trampled bare in several places and matted with what looked like ketchup and grease in others. The roommate's feet were *bare.*

We arrived at a closed doorway with DANGER—HIGH VOLTAGE signs plastered across it.

"Josh?" He knocked on the door. "You have a visitor."

I heard frantic scurrying behind the door, followed by the sound of breaking glass.

"Who is it?" my brother's muffled voice asked.

"Says she's your sister."

"I *am* his sister," I hissed.

"What does she look like?"

"Shit, I don't know. Kinda frizzy brown hair and . . . brownish eyes." He looked me over before continuing. "She's got freckles and a scar on her forehead."

There was nothing like a first impression to boost my confidence.

"Uh-oh, and she looks pissed off," the roommate added.

"Thanks," I snapped.

"Yeah, she looks just like you, *but pissed.*"

"Listen, I hardly look—" I began, but before I could finish, several dead bolts clicked and the door opened.

"Hey, Jode. Come on in."

His blinds were drawn despite the hour and the room was lit by a single red light bulb, swaying from a cord attached to the ceiling. Clothing was either dumped on what little furniture he had, or scattered on the carpet, and antigovernment pamphlets were stacked on every available surface. His stereo speakers belched some low notes and indecipherable lyrics while stolen street signs leaned against graffiti-covered walls. The sound of breaking glass appeared to have been the demise of the green wine bottle lying in pieces on the floor. No attempt would be made to clean it up, I was sure. He would just step around it indefinitely.

"So, what's going on?" He flopped onto a bare mattress, spotted with suspicious stains. An underwire bra lay on the bedside table.

I had no idea what women saw in Josh or his shithole apartment, but he never had trouble attracting them. Granted, he was a relatively handsome guy, with wavy hair the same color as my frizz. His eyes were darker than mine and at times it was difficult to tell where his irises ended and his pupils began. The left eye was markedly larger than the right, giving his face a crooked appearance that matched his herd of cluttered teeth. Josh's scruffy goatee clung to his chin like wiry moss and always seemed to be in its first week of growth, never moving beyond the patchy stage. At five foot seven, he was a bit on the short side, but though he wasn't exactly what I would call muscular, he wasn't frail, either.

Perhaps the fact that he was double-jointed in one hand and spoke with a faint remainder of a childhood lisp was enough to boost him to the ranks of the exotic. Whatever the draw was, the ladies loved him.

When I spotted a Muffin Zone bag on the floor I figured he was still seeing Amy, surviving on a diet of day-old wheat-germ specials and six-grain surprises.

"What's going on?" I repeated. "Not much, I guess. What about you?"

"Pretty busy. I've got four shifts this week."

Dear God, my brother was officially working more than I was. "Great."

"Hey, if you're interested"—he dug under the filthy mattress—"I've got some two-for-one coupons."

"Uh, no, thanks."

He was generous with what little he had, and maybe that was what the girls liked about him. He may have been slow at times (he was convinced the thesaurus lived during the Paleozoic period), but he was kind, and when it came down to brass tacks in a relationship, kindness mattered.

"Mom and Dad said you got fired," he said, rubbing his nose with the back of his hand.

"They *what*?"

"They told me—"

"I wasn't fired. I quit! I can't believe they said that!"

"Oh, that's right. They did say you quit. I was half-asleep when they called."

"I'd had enough of the damn place, so I walked out." I thought my reckless act of insanity might impress him. He was always bugging me about playing by the rules.

"That was kind of crazy, Jode. There aren't too many jobs out there, you know." He stretched his arms and yawned. "And they said you broke up with Kevin."

"Chris." I tried not to take the blunder personally.

"Right, Chris."

"He was sleeping with Beth, if you can believe it."

"No shit? Well, she is pretty cute. If I wasn't related to her I'd—"

"Please don't finish that sentence."

"Do you have a place to stay?"

"I'm crashing at Erin's right now. I was barred from Mom and Dad's because of your bust."

"Yeah, I figured as much. Sorry, Jode." He paused for a moment. "You know, you could always stay here."

I coughed to hide the sound of my choking laughter, thanked him for the offer, and firmly declined. "There's something else you could do for me, though."

"What's that?"

"Loan me your car so I can clear my stuff out of Chris's place."

"No problem." He leaned over to grab the keys from the pocket of a discarded flannel and tossed them to me.

"Is it running okay?"

"Yeah, but it's low on gas."

I could use my gas card, if need be. "But everything else is okay, right?"

"Yup. I just put in a new battery. It's ready to roll."

I told him I'd return the car the following day and he said there was no rush since Amy had a car. My gratitude was immense.

"Hey, it's the least I can do. I'm your *brother,* Jody."

The Yugo took only two attempts to start and I peeled out of the parking lot, heading toward Chris's. I hoped I was right about his schedule. I wanted to move out alone, with a bit of dignity.

It turned out I didn't even need my house key; the door was not only unlocked, but ajar.

I had no suitcases, no boxes, and very little time, so I raced through the house, cramming my things into garbage bags. I mixed the dirty clothes with the clean, knowing I had the use of Erin's laundry facilities, and loaded the first round of bags into the car. I returned for my books, candles, and small appliances, packing whatever would fit into Tupperware containers and tossing the rest into waiting garbage bags.

I checked the hall closet and spotted the scuffed black leather motorcycle boots Chris bought at a garage sale for twenty dollars and wore daily for three out of four seasons. They were his prized possessions, his identity contained in a couple of pieces of cowhide. Before I thought better of it, I shoved them into my bag. He wouldn't miss them for months, but come fall, when he couldn't find them, he'd go nuts.

"Deals like those boots come along once in a lifetime," he always said.

"Easy come, easy go," I muttered, smiling with grim satisfaction.

I plucked my framed pictures from the walls and rolled my rugs off the hardwood.

"Chris, I'm home!"

I poked my head out into the hallway and spotted Beth in the doorway. She was carrying two Safeway bags and several hangers dangling clothing.

"You're already moving in?" I gasped.

She dropped the hangers in surprise. "What are *you* doing here?"

"Moving out. Are you going to answer me?"

"Yeah, I'm moving in." She marched past me, fake boobs bouncing with every step, and placed her groceries on the kitchen counter.

"Just like that?"

"Just like that." She smirked. "What did you expect, Jody? Was he supposed to come crawling after you?"

"I just thought that after two and a half years—"

"Two and a half or ten, it doesn't matter. He's with me now."

Her eyelids were at their usual half-mast, which she'd always claimed gave her sex appeal. I thought she looked like she had a concussion.

"Well, you can have him," I snapped.

"I already *do,* Jody." She smiled and pointed to the door. "Now get out of my house."

As much as I wanted to tear her apart, I kept my mouth shut, still chasing that elusive dream of leaving with dignity. I gathered the rest of my things, including the clock radio Chris relied on to wake him for work and the coffeemaker that only he used. I didn't drink the stuff, but I was damned if I was going to let him keep it.

I carried my load down the front steps, finding a scrap of pleasure in betting that if he cheated on me, he'd cheat on her.

* * *

Once the Yugo was packed, I nearly flooded the engine, but got it started and drove back to Erin's. I carried three bags to the door and rang the bell.

"Oh, Jody. You just missed Chris," my best friend said, opening the door and taking one of the bags. "And I just got screwed out of a shift. Dan thinks we need to cut down on staff, right before summer! Can you *believe* it?"

I was still stuck on item one.

"*Chris* was here?" My heart did a little jig.

She nodded. "Just give me a second to get off the phone and I'll help you unload."

She disappeared into the kitchen and I stood on the top step with a wicked smile. *He* had coming running back to *me*. Tracking me down at Erin's place was downright pathetic. I had no intention of taking him back, of course, but I was going to enjoy watching him try to win me over while Beth went ballistic. Sure, the gods had put me through the wringer, but it was all worth it. *Vindication was mine!*

I heard Erin hang up and waited for her to reappear.

"So, what did he say?" I asked, figuring he'd wanted her advice on getting me back.

"Not much. You know, it was kind of awkward."

Awkward was good, but *painful* was better. Was he going to beg for forgiveness? I'd have him on his knees, then refuse!

"I want his exact words." My eagerness was uncontrollable. If only I'd been there to see him squirm!

"I don't know if I remember them exactly." She absently fondled the tail of her braid.

"Well, try. Come on, I'm dying here."

"Let's see. He said 'Hi, Erin,' so I said 'Hi,' but with a really vicious tone and a shitty look for what he did to you."

"Excellent. I knew I could count on you."

"Then he handed me—"

Flowers? A love letter?

"—some envelopes and said 'I just wanted to drop off Jody's mail.' "

"What?" I couldn't have heard her correctly.

"He dropped off your mail." She shrugged.

"That's it?" My heart stopped dancing and plummeted into my stomach. No apology? No strategy to win my affection? *No begging?*

"Yeah. I'll grab it for you."

I thought I was going to cry. All I wanted was one small triumph!

"How did the interview go?" she called from the kitchen.

"Uh, not so hot," I said.

She returned with a small stack of flyers and bills.

Any split-second thought that he'd dropped off the mail as an excuse to see me was annihilated. Through the window on the telephone bill, I could see that he'd underlined my charges. His careful handwriting on the back of the envelope informed me that I owed him over two hundred dollars for phone, electricity, and credit card bills. In light of the circumstances of our breakup, he continued, he would cover the cost of the cable bill when it arrived.

"Oh, happy day," I snarled. "His affair with Beth is saving me a whopping seventeen bucks."

"He's an asshole," Erin said. "And a cheap little fucker, to boot." She pointed to a handwritten envelope with no return address. "What's that one?"

"A letter." I paused. "Who on earth would send me a letter?" The only person on the planet still choosing the post office over e-mail was my great-aunt Sylvia, but she only dropped a note at Christmas.

"Are you going to open it, or what?"

I tore the envelope and found a formal invitation, complete with gold italics and a response card.

"Ooh, nice." Erin peered over my shoulder. "Wedding?"

"I don't know," I murmured, scanning the text until I saw the fateful words. "Oh, shit!" It was migraine time.

"What?"

"This is the worst timing ever." No boyfriend. No job. A borrowed *Yugo,* for Christ's sake.

"What? What is it?"

"It's an invitation," I said with a sigh. "But it might as well be a death warrant."

"Will you just tell me what it's for?"

"It's an invitation," I repeated, wishing with all my heart it wasn't true.

"I got that part."

"To our ten-year high-school reunion."

Just when I thought life couldn't be any crueler, it hunkered down and gave me a wedgie.

eight

While I reeled from the shock that a reunion wasn't some laughable, distant concept but a hideous reality, Erin was enraged to find her name on the MIA list attached to the invitation.

"I'm living in the same goddamn house I was in high school!" she said, reaching for a cigarette and shaking her head. "It's the *exact same address.*"

"I'm sure you can straighten it out," I assured her. I would have gladly traded places with her, let my whereabouts remain a mystery, and skipped the whole damn event. "Who's organizing this nightmare, anyway?"

The telephone contact was none other than Hannah Baxter, bride of a thousand weddings.

"I should have known." Erin glared at the name. "She's out for revenge because I won't be her bridesmaid."

"She asked you yesterday," I said, checking the envelope. "This was mailed two, no, *three* days ago."

"She knew I wouldn't do it." She blew a cloud of smoke from her nose.

"Have you declined yet?"

"Well, no."

Rather than calling the MIA number and requesting her invitation, she stormed down the front steps, brimming with venom.

"Where are you going?" I called after her.

"Out."

I welcomed the solitude, feeling as if I'd aged five years in twenty-four hours.

I changed out of my borrowed outfit, carefully hanging it in Erin's closet, and slipped into a sweatshirt and jeans. As Mom's clandestine tuna casserole warmed in the oven, I finished unloading the Yugo and rounded up some hangers to put away my clothing. I suspected my stay at Erin's would be more than a couple of days, if the job hunt was as dismal as it looked. Even if I'd had money to burn, Bent Harbor's rental properties were few and far between, and suitable roommates were even harder to find.

Eventually bored by the limited wonders of folding sweaters and smoothing wrinkled blouses from the depths of my garbage bags, I took a break and checked the latest edition of the *Bent Harbor Times* for miraculous additions to the employment section. There were none.

I ate my dinner in front of the TV, but once the food was gone, somewhere between *Wheel of Fortune* and *Jeopardy,* I found myself bored, tired, and depressed.

I was in bed by nine-thirty, fully clothed and too defeated by life to consider a task as huge as locating my pajamas. I fell asleep immediately and probably didn't so much as change position in the hours before I was awakened by a slam of the door at 2:13 A.M.

In my groggy state, it took a moment to identify the noises coming from the hallway. Erin and a guest. A moaning, groaning, lip-smacking guest.

"Let's go back to my room," she said, between loud, juicy kisses.

"Mmm, let's just do it here."

"Dear God, no." I groaned.

"No, I've got a girlfriend in the spare room." Erin had better manners than I'd given her credit for.

"She's probably asleep," he said, between kisses. It sounded like he was chewing on a ham hock. "And if she isn't, maybe she'd like to join in."

I sat bolt upright, wishing there were a lock on my door. What kind of pervert had she picked up, anyway?

"Seriously," she said, laughing, "what if she wakes up?" She whispered, as though the wall separating us weren't as thin as the ice her partner was skating on.

"We'll be quiet. Don't worry about it."

Whatever he did next made her shriek with delight. "Stop that, Michael!"

"Who's Michael?" he asked.

I smiled in the darkness. *Finally* the endless testosterone parade had caught up with her. Michael was last night. I waited for her to talk her way out of it.

"Oops!" She giggled feverishly. "I mean, stop that, David!"

David? A new one. Considering her systematic sampling of most of the men around town, David must have been the freshest meat out there.

"Not David," he said, groaning with more than a trace of annoyance. "David Banner's the Incredible Hulk. Batman is *Bruce.* Bruce Wayne."

Batman again. I cringed in anticipation of things that go thud in the night and hoped his flashlight batteries were low.

"Sorry, Bruce." Erin laughed, then there was a moment of dead silence. "What's wrong?"

After a frustrated sigh, Batman whined, "Why is 'Bruce Wayne' so hard for you to remember?"

"Because I don't watch kiddie programming."

That was an absolute lie. She still curled up on the couch most Saturday mornings with a bowl of soggy cereal and a maturity level of age eight.

"What's that supposed to mean?"

"Nothing." She sighed. "Come here."

"Forget it. I'm not in the mood anymore."

Sweeter words were never spoken.

"Well, I'm sure I can fix that," she teased coyly and something banged against the wall.

"Oh, yeah. You sure can." He gasped.

Their panting was marginally entertaining until my bladder rebelled with the unmistakable twinge of urgency.

The last thing I wanted was to interrupt, but they were blocking the only route to the facilities. I waited as patiently as I could for them to move to the confines of Erin's room, but they seemed more than content where they were. I was treated to a symphony of racing zippers, huffing and puffing, despite my efforts to block the sound with a quilt pulled over my head.

Eventually, they bumped into the kitchen table and something landed on the floor with a bang.

"Oh, shit," Batman said.

"Please let property damage be enough to stop you," I whispered.

It wasn't.

"Don't worry about that," Erin said, gasping. "Worry about *this.*"

The groaning intensified, accompanied by a rhythmic crunching, and I hoped she wasn't using my brand-new box of Wheaties for her sexploits.

My parents' bedroom was next to mine when I was growing up, but I'd never been an earwitness to their sex life. In fact, I'd never overheard *anyone,* something I'd taken for granted until that night.

Judging by Batman's unbridled enthusiasm and the continuing cycle of shuffling, bumping, and crashing, Erin was proving to be a real dynamo. If I hadn't been sidetracked by my insistent bladder, I might have been jealous. Chris and I shared a good sex life, but it was nothing like the writhing passion outside my door. I couldn't recall a time I'd had him begging for mercy, and, unlike Batman, he had never reached orgasm while shouting "To the Batcave!" eight times.

When it finally ended, with the kind of emotional fervor I associated with Superbowl Sunday and childbirth, they retreated to Erin's room, gasping for breath and congratulating themselves on a job well done.

In addition to relieving my aching bladder, I suddenly felt an uncontrollable need to shower.

I let the steaming water pour over me as I lathered my skin with the fragrant soaps Erin liked to splurge on. I hummed softly under the spray, envisioning the career I would have soon enough, and the house on Sitka Point I'd someday own. I imagined Erin choosing a life of abstinence, my parents welcoming me home with open arms, loony Lucas McDade eloping with Hannah Baxter before she could marry her ex-husband again, Josh loaning out a Jetta instead of his Yugo, Marty McDade being sexually harassed by burly prison inmates, and finally, Beth and Chris tragically yet justifiably disfigured by a grisly accident of any kind. That shower was a piece of daydreaming heaven.

Toweling off, I realized I hadn't brought a change of clothing, and in my squeaky-clean state, I had no desire to crawl into the clothes I'd been wearing. Assuming the love machines were asleep or close to it, I decided to make the dash back to my bedroom in the buff.

Holding the bundle of dirty clothes against my chest, I turned off the bathroom light, opened the door, and stepped into the darkness. After the steamed heat of the shower, the air was as cool against my skin as the hardwood under my feet. I couldn't wait to curl up between the striped sheets of the guest bed and drift into oblivion, but when I turned to walk past the kitchen door, I almost collided with another body.

"Aack!" I shrieked, jumping aside and stubbing my toe against the wall. Excruciating pain hit and I reached for the injury, dropping my clothes in the process. Hopping frantically on one foot, eyes tightly closed, I tried to stop the tears from forming.

"Jody?" a male whispered.

Batman. I choked back a sob.

"Are you okay?" he asked, gripping my upper arm and steadying me.

"Fuck, no!" I whined.

"Do you think it's broken?"

"No . . . no, I'm okay, I guess."

"Good. You scared the shit out of me." He didn't sound remotely frightened and he reeked of beer.

When the tears stopped threatening to fall, I tentatively lowered my foot to the floor and felt only a dull ache. My heart had resumed a normal pace and my eyes were slowly adjusting to the darkness. I lifted my head to thank Batman for his help, and saw that he was buck naked.

"Oh!" I yelped. "I didn't know you were—"

"So are you," he reminded me.

"Shit!" I reached toward the floor, feeling for the clothing it was still too dark to see.

"Do you want me to turn the light on?"

"No!"

I found my sweatshirt and clutched it to my chest, then scrambled for my jeans, trying not to look at the pale glow of his skin. To my horror, he bent over to help, his skinny arms and frail form a tad unexpected. *This* was the guy Erin had been rolling around with for the past two nights? He was tiny!

It struck me that if I could make out the shadow of hair on his chest and, down a little further, the limp form of his exhausted genitalia, he could undoubtedly see the white brilliance of my flat butt and more. *Much more.*

"Uh, thanks," I stammered, wanting to flee the scene. "I can get it." I finally made contact with denim and snatched the jeans from the floor, attempting to cover any possible body parts. "Nice, uh, seeing you . . . I mean meeting you," I blurted, then ran to the safety of the guest room without waiting for a response.

In the morning, following a restless sleep, I groaned and rolled out of bed. Dreading the thought of facing Erin and her beau, I decided to act as though nothing had happened. What else could I do?

Erin was already dressed for work in overalls and a turtleneck. "Hey, Jode. I'm making waffles."

"Great, I'm starving," I chirped, casing the dining room for any sign of her cohort.

"If you're looking for Michael, he went home."

"Did he, uh . . ."

"He told me you had a close encounter of the nude kind." She laughed as she poured batter onto Gammy's waffle iron.

"I was just coming out of the shower, and—"

"Don't worry, Jode. We laughed about it."

Laughed about what, exactly? My flat ass? My breasts? The idea of the two of them giggling over me was unsettling.

"How's your foot?"

I wiggled my toes, surprised to feel no pain. "Fine, I think."

"Josh called this morning. You're supposed to call him back."

I dialed his number. "Do you need the car right away?" I asked, as soon as he answered.

"Hey, Jode. No, actually, you should hold on to it. I just heard about a job opening you might want to check out."

"Does it involve membership cards and late fees?" I wasn't desperate enough for Video Nook. *Yet.*

"No, a friend of mine saw a posting on the Internet. It's an administrative something-or-other for an electronics manufacturer."

"Here?" I couldn't think of any electronics places in town.

"Yeah, and today's the last day for interviews, so I got you the number."

"Today?" Not another interview. I needed some time to recover from the *Temp*tations fiasco, but I couldn't afford to miss the opportunity. I took down the number and asked if there was a job description included. If there was, he didn't have it.

"And Mom wants me to invite you to their place for dinner tonight," he said.

"Why didn't she just call me?"

"She didn't want Dad to know."

"Well, he'll be sitting at the head of the table, won't he?"

"I guess."

"So he'll know I'm there when I pass him the peas."

"Damn! Peas? She told me we're having green beans."

"It was a hypothetical vegetable, Josh."

"Huh?"

"Never mind."

I thanked him for the job tip and called for an appointment. I was given a waterfront address and told there was a slot open for an informal interview at eleven-thirty. The company was called

Wallace Enterprises, a name vague enough that I still had no idea what I was getting into.

"First off, it won't be informal," Erin said, when I told her the news. "They want to weed out the unprofessional candidates, so they trick you into thinking you don't have to dress up and wait to see what you wear."

"That doesn't seem fair," I muttered, amazed she could keep track of all of her conspiracy theories. Afraid she was right, I raced to her room in search of another suit.

Erin fed me blueberry waffles, then spent half an hour recreating the corporate winner she'd made of me the day before. Once again, I was amazed at the results. By the time I'd printed copies of my fraudulent résumé and jumped into the Yugo, I had only fifteen minutes to spare.

I arrived precisely on time and was welcomed by a middle-aged woman with a big smile I suspected had more to do with large teeth than enthusiasm. She introduced herself as Susan and left me with a glass of water while she delivered my résumé to her boss.

Alone in reception, I noticed the pastel prints on the walls matched not only the overstuffed chairs, but the carpeting, venetian blinds, and even the box of tissues on Susan's desk. Teal and mauve weren't my colors of choice, but at least they were soothing. I glanced through the pamphlets on the coffee table, but they highlighted company history instead of product information. Whatever Wallace Enterprises did, they'd been doing it for a good thirty years.

"Mrs. Wallace can see you now," Susan said, and I followed her to a lovely yellow office where a dark-haired woman about Mom's age sat behind a pine desk.

"Jody? Thanks for coming in on such short notice." She stood with her hand extended, so I shook it, hoping nervousness hadn't moistened my palms.

"Thank you for having me," I responded, settling onto a comfortably padded chair and admiring the watercolor print behind her.

"I hope you don't mind waiting for a moment while I go over your résumé. I was on the phone when Susan brought it in."

"That's fine," I said, smiling politely.

While Mrs. Wallace perused my typewritten pack of lies, I noted the gathered creases of laugh lines at the corners of her eyes and mouth, certain they were a good sign. Her mahogany barrette matched the streaks of color it held back from her face in a style that would suit Mom if she'd ever take a chance. Her nose was long and sleek with a surprising upward tip, like a ski jump, and underneath, her lips were smiling.

When she finally spoke, she complimented me on the longevity of my waitressing career.

I liked her immediately.

The interview was more like a conversation than the interrogation Erin had prepared me for. Mrs. Wallace said she wanted to learn about me as a person because it was a very small office, with a tight-knit staff, and compatible personalities were as important as work experience. I couldn't have dreamed up a better situation.

We talked about everything, from coastal weather to the effects of technology on daily life, from travel to education, family relationships to favorite pets and beyond. It was almost like a therapy session, or an extended lunch break with a good friend. I was having such a nice time, an hour slipped by unnoticed.

"I guess we should get to the subject at hand," Mrs. Wallace said, when we had covered practically everything.

She outlined the position for me, and it sounded like a perfect combination of tasks. The new hire would handle orders and help with brochure designs and printing. There wasn't much phone time involved, and almost no direct contact with clients. The hours were daytime, Monday through Friday, which meant evenings and weekends free for the first time in seven years. The salary was higher than what I made at the Galley with tips, and I was shaking by the time I'd heard it all.

"Our search for the right person has been very difficult," she said.

I nodded earnestly, the way I'd practiced in the bathroom mirror before I left Erin's.

"And I'm very pleased you called today, Jody."

"So am I."

"I have to tell you, you're the best candidate I've seen."

"Thank you," I gushed.

"You're very welcome. Unfortunately, as much as I'd like to expedite this process, I'm not the only person who handles the hiring."

"I see." I tried to keep my smile from wavering.

"What I'd like to do is look your résumé over again, with my partner, and see how he feels about calling you in for a second interview."

"That sounds great." Great, if waiting for an income was an option.

"Wonderful. Now, we wouldn't discuss benefits or holidays until that potential second interview, but is there anything you'd like to ask me in the meantime?"

"Uh, yes," I said, seizing the opportunity. "I was wondering what it is, exactly, that you manufacture."

She smiled and said that they normally saved the product details for the second interview, but she wouldn't mind making an exception for me.

I waited for her to say they built computer games or communication gadgets, but I was way off.

"We manufacture electric therapy equipment."

"I'm not sure I understand." I leaned forward in my chair.

"We work in the mental health field. Our products are used to administer small electric charges, much like static, for the benefit of patients with varying mental illnesses."

Shock therapy! I recoiled slightly, but she didn't appear to notice. Smiling benignly, I remembered Erin's advice to find some common ground with my interviewer. *If she has a picture of a dog on her desk, you're a fucking canine fanatic.*

"My aunt had shock therapy." It was a bald-faced lie, and Auntie Julia, the tax accountant, would have shit not only bricks, but whole city blocks if she'd heard me. I blurted the words so quickly, it hadn't crossed my mind that announcing a family history of mental illness might not be the best way to get the job.

"Is that right?" Mrs. Wallace asked, her face suddenly pinched.

Had I said something wrong?

"Yes, it was, uh, very helpful," I improvised.

"We prefer not to use the term shock therapy these days," she said coolly.

If that blunder wasn't enough to cost me the job, my departure from the office sealed the deal.

Flustered by the misguided efforts of my big mouth, I struggled to simultaneously rise from my seat, grab Erin's briefcase, and straighten my skirt. At the same time, Mrs. Wallace rose, walked to my side of the desk, and extended her hand for another shake. Somehow, in reaching for it, I lost my balance. It would take an instant replay for me to fully understand how I managed to fall on her, but I do know I didn't knock her to the floor. Instead, I righted myself by putting all of my weight on her left foot. As far as I could tell through the cloud of my babbling, she wasn't seriously hurt, but the look of disbelief I saw on her face convinced me it didn't matter.

Mortified, I was almost in tears (a state I was growing all too familiar with) when I left her office, so I raced past the receptionist and into the parking lot, hoping I could hold back the weeping until I'd reached the relative privacy of the car.

How had I sabotaged such a fabulous interview, so quickly?

I shoved the key into the ignition and gave it a savage twist.

The Yugo didn't start.

I tried again, but there was no response. I turned the radio knob and got no sound, then discovered the headlights weren't cooperating, either. Did Josh say he'd had the battery replaced, or that he'd replaced it *himself*? I was pretty sure I knew the answer.

Several more attempts with the key failed and I started to worry about how I was going to get home.

Humiliated beyond belief, I reentered Wallace Enterprises and asked for a most embarrassing favor.

While I opened the trunk and found Josh's rusty jumper cables, Mrs. Wallace parked a brand-new, shiny SUV in the space next to mine. She frowned at the sight of the cables and retrieved her own from under her passenger seat. They were perfectly coiled, still wrapped in plastic, and she looked at me as if tearing open the bag would cause a depreciation in the value of her vehicle.

I sat behind the wheel of the Yugo and stared at the floor mats, cursing Josh as Mrs. Wallace attached the clamps and boarded her vehicle.

My future seemed worse than bleak when the woman who would undoubtedly *not* be my new employer revved her engine and jump-started me, like one of her mental patients.

nine

During the drive back to Erin's place, I imagined the endless number of ways I could kill my brother. If he didn't know what he was doing, he shouldn't have felt compelled to replace the goddamn battery himself. He could have enlisted the help of a professional and *I* could have left Wallace Enterprises with a little grace.

An unfamiliar red Pinto was parked in front of Erin's house when I got there, and I prayed it wasn't Batman's. The last thing I needed was to face him in daylight while the memory of his flaccid penis was emblazoned on my brain.

I pulled into the driveway and saw that it wasn't Batman but Hannah Baxter sitting on the front steps with her three children. All I wanted to do was curl up in a ball on my bed.

"Hey, Hannah," I said, slamming the car door and gritting my teeth as I walked toward her. "Erin's at work."

Hopefully it would be easy to get rid of her and I could continue fuming at Josh in private. He was going to be damn sorry when I showed up at Mom's for dinner.

"I'm not here to see her." Hannah stood, exposing the bulge of pregnancy.

Another baby? Glancing at her grubby offspring, I couldn't imagine what made her want more. Her girls looked as if they'd spent the day not only making mud pies, but eating them. Two dirty blondes had awkward ponytails springing from various points on their heads, and the hair on the third was a scraggly, chin-length mess. Their cardigans ranged from misbuttoned to moth-eaten, with only filth in common, and the oldest one had a finger firmly planted up her right nostril, the skin of her nose stretched and strained from the digging within.

I knew it was entirely possible that Hannah was a wonderful mother, and that children were dirty creatures to begin with, but some attention to personal hygiene wouldn't have hurt.

"Well, if this is about the reunion, I just got the invitation yesterday. I haven't had the chance to RSVP yet." I hoped that would be enough to move the whole crowd off the steps and out of my way.

"Actually, it's about my wedding," she said with a smile.

Her blond hair was woven into some kind of french braid, leaving the glowing skin of her face exposed. I would have attributed the flush of her cheeks to her engagement if it hadn't been a fourth marriage. I would have held maternity responsible if it wasn't the fourth time for that, as well. Instead, as she grinned at me like a cherubic Barbie doll, I considered the fact that she was winding up for yet another go at life with David Baxter and decided that hers was the glow of stupidity.

"Can we come inside?" she asked.

"Look, Hannah, I'm having a really bad day, and—"

"It'll only take a minute." Her smile widened, flashing two rows of perfectly formed teeth.

Against my better judgment, I led the whole crew inside, determined to keep the visit as short and painless as possible.

Hannah pulled some stuffed animals from her bag to occupy the children, who immediately removed their shoes and made themselves at home, fingering Erin's CD's and books.

"Could you guys not touch that stuff, please?" I asked, suspecting they would turn into a miniature demolition crew if left unattended. Two of the girls sat on the floor, while the middle one leaned against the recliner, eyeing the knickknacks on the coffee table.

Hannah turned to face me and I was struck by her beauty for the hundredth time. She was flawless, aside from a small scar on her chin that added to her appearance rather than detracting from it. She had cool, gray eyes, like the harbor in late fall, framed by black lashes and delicately arched eyebrows. Even clothed in a man's flannel jacket and jeans, she was luminous. She'd been through a lot in the past ten years, but she looked better run-down and ragged than I would after a TV makeover.

With a face like hers, no one in town could understand what she was doing with David Baxter. He was short and stocky, with a greasy brown mullet and a permanent scowl, not to mention a missing incisor, a severe case of guttermouth, and a wardrobe of torn flannel shirts. The children definitely took after their father.

Hannah's adoration of her troll ex-husband/fiancé was enough to spark the interest of many local females, who assumed David must have some phenomenal qualities (or hidden physical characteristics) to keep the attention of the most beautiful woman in town. I knew better. David had been the only guy in school with enough unwarranted self-confidence to approach her. Convinced she wasn't good enough for anyone to take an interest in her, Hannah fell in love with David simply because he was the only boy who spoke to her. The revolting part was that once he had her, he treated Hannah like she should be *grateful* to him.

"Another wedding," I said, trying to hide my distaste. "I guess congratulations are in order."

"Yeah." She sighed. "This one's going to be perfect, like a fairy tale." She glanced at the kids on the floor and scowled. "Jacob, get your finger out of your nose."

The big one is a boy?

"So," Hannah continued, eyes glittering with excitement. "David proposed a couple of weeks ago, at the Marina restaurant. Naturally, I said yes."

"Naturally," I murmured, wondering if he gave her a new ring with each proposal. Did he get down on one knee, or toss the question at her between bites? Maybe he handed her a calendar and told her to pick a date. Did they celebrate each of their anniversaries, or only the most recent wedding? Knowing David, I doubted they celebrated at all.

"Are you sure you want to do this again?" I asked quietly.

"Don't be silly, Jody. I'm absolutely sure. David always says we're made for each other."

Before I could question her further, I heard a crash and saw the middle child pointing at the shattered remains of a vase on the floor. I recognized it as one of Gammy's favorites and knew I'd been foolish to let the Baxter clan inside.

"Oops," the kid said, stubby finger still pointing.

"Oh, darling," Hannah cooed. "Say you're sorry."

Bright blue eyes met mine and the single word was uttered with no emotion or comprehension.

"That's Erin's," I told Hannah.

"Tell her we're sorry." She didn't offer to clean it up, let alone replace it.

"It belonged to her grandmother."

"Kids will be kids." She sighed, shaking her head.

"Her *dead* grandmother."

"You should see our place. I'm lucky if I keep a set of dishes intact for longer than a week." She giggled and continued. "Anyway, the reason I'm here is to ask if you would do me the honor of being a bridesmaid."

The request caught me completely off guard.

"Geez, I don't know . . ." I hedged, but I knew very well the answer was a resounding *no fucking way*.

"It would mean a lot to me. We've known each other forever and I should have asked you to be in one of the others."

"I *was* in one of the others. Number three." *How insulting was that?* I had a fluffy, peacock-blue dress crammed into a garbage bag that very moment, waiting for the day I'd lose all of my mental faculties and wear it again.

"Oh, that's right. Number three." She grinned. "This is perfect! You'll know exactly what to do."

"I really don't have much time these days . . ." I let the sentence drift off, hoping she'd take the hint.

"But I ran into Erin this afternoon. She told me she was too busy with work to be in the bridal party, but you'd just quit your job."

"That's true." Erin and her big mouth! "But I'm working on a few leads right now and really need to concentrate on—"

"Jody, it would mean the world to me." She turned and shouted, "Jacob! Finger out! *Now!*"

"Hannah," I began, preparing to be tough. "No offense, but it seems like you're only asking me to be a bridesmaid because Erin said no."

"That's not true! And besides, I only asked Erin out of pity, since I'd known her so long. I didn't really want her involved." She paused. "So, it's going to be an afternoon ceremony on June fourteenth."

"Oh, *darn.* I'm going to be out of town that week," I lied.

"Well, that date's not set in stone. When would be a good time for you?"

She was going to plan her wedding around *my* schedule? "I don't think I'm the girl for the job," I said firmly.

"Not so fast, Jody. I have some swatches that are guaranteed to blow your mind." She pulled some scraps of fabric from her purse and laid them on the table. Silver and gold lamé. My mind was already blown. "The bridesmaids will wear two-tone dresses. I've got a picture here somewhere. You're going to love this."

She produced a ten-year-old *Seventeen* magazine, flipped to a page marked with a Hello Kitty bookmark, and pointed out a tight, floor-length monstrosity with a mesh train.

"It's the exact dress I wore to the prom!" she shrieked. "Great idea, huh? You know, *ten years later*."

If I hadn't seen her delighted expression, I would have thought it was a joke. There was no way in hell I was going to wear that dress, and it appeared the only way out of the whole mess was to be ruthless.

I took a quick gulp of air and blurted, "Hannah, I don't want to do it."

"What do you mean?" She closed the magazine and stared at me.

"I don't think I can be more clear. I don't want to do it."

"But Jody, I'm counting on you," she whined.

"I'm sorry."

"Do you think it's easy . . ." She took a shaky breath and choked on a sob. "Easy to plan four weddings?"

I had to remain distant. It was my only hope. "No, but I also don't know why you've done it."

"Because I love him!" she bawled. "I want everything to be perfect this time. I want a perfect day, followed by a perfect marriage." She sobbed into her trembling hands.

"Why is Mommy crying?"

Because she's a fool, I wanted to tell the kids. "She's not crying, she's laughing," I said. "Laughing really hard."

"Can't you understand, Jody?" Hannah asked, lifting a tear-stained face.

On some level, I *could* understand. But that didn't mean I wanted to support her impending mistake. "I don't know what to say."

"Say yes," she whispered, then caught sight of her son. "Jacob!

I'm not going to tell you again. Quit picking!" As soon as the words left her mouth, she was crying again.

All I wanted was a little peace and quiet.

"You were one of my closest friends." She took my hand and tightly gripped it.

When? I wanted to ask, but it didn't seem like the right moment. We'd never been close. Sure, she'd unfairly traded stickers with me in the third grade, and weaseled a few minor loans from me over the years. Yes, she'd talked me into chauffeuring David and his cronies around for the last bachelor party, a night of high-speed vomiting I wasn't likely to forget, but *close*? No, we were never close.

As I watched her cry on Erin's couch, unable to determine whether they were real tears or a sampling of the crocodile variety, I started to think maybe she and David actually deserved each other. I was desperate for her to leave, but knew she wouldn't let me off the hook.

"I'll do it," I said, already planning to talk my way out of it later.

"Oh, Jody! I'm so glad!" She reached over to hug me and I felt a twinge of guilt. "You don't know what this means to me. Thank you so much!"

"You're welcome," I told her.

"So," Hannah said, wiping the remaining moisture from her eyes. "When's the shower?"

"What?"

"The shower." Her eyebrows lifted in surprise. "Aren't you going to throw a bridal shower for me?"

My stomach tightened. "I guess so."

By the time Hannah Baxter marched her army of miscreants out the front door several hours later, I had a list of shower guests, potential themes, games and decorations in my hand. We had plans to look at fabric later in the week and I was expected to help her with the invitations and registry at two department stores in Fillington.

As I closed the door after them and leaned against it with exhaustion, I remembered my dinner date Chez Parentals.

"Shit," I muttered, racing to my room to find something presentable to wear. My black cords were immune to wrinkles and I found a navy blue T-shirt with only one minor stain. Good enough. I didn't want to arrive empty-handed, so I searched the kitchen for anything that could pass for wine and found nothing suitable. After briefly considering slapping a bow on the maraschino cherries, I checked the back garden for flowers to cut, but only the crocuses were showing. In a moment of weakness, I decided to take a loan from my sacred cow; the house savings. Considering I "owed" Chris two hundred dollars, I'd be digging into it anyway. A little bit extra wouldn't hurt.

That fucking Yugo started on the first attempt, and my anger at Josh was fueled by the surge of the engine.

I bit my lip to keep from crying out as I made my bank withdrawal. I stuffed Chris's money in a deposit envelope, drove to his place and shoved it through the mail slot in the front door.

I had to admit, it felt good to have some cash in my pocket. Two days without it had been depressing enough. I picked up a bottle of white and a small bouquet so my parents would see what a good-hearted daughter I was and regret their rash decision to close their doors.

When I arrived at the house, Dad was pulling into the driveway, Josh in the passenger seat.

"Hey, Dad!" I called when we'd all climbed out of our vehicles. I didn't bother acknowledging Josh.

"Jody." Dad's voice was gruff. "Why didn't you pick up your brother?"

"I didn't know I was supposed to."

"I told you this morning," Josh said.

"No you didn't."

"Yes I did."

"You did not," I growled. He could take us both down to age six in a matter of seconds.

"Yes, I did!"

"Enough!" Dad barked, looking at me as though it were all my fault.

"He's a liar," I said.

"What?" Josh's mouth hung open.

"Let me get this straight. I was *supposed* to pick you up, and your car was *supposed* to work. You told me it was in good running condition!"

"It is!"

"It broke down at my job interview. The president of the company had to jump-start me! Do you have any idea how embarrassing that was?"

"Did you leave the lights on?" Dad asked.

"No! Josh put the battery in wrong."

"How do you know?" Josh asked, hands on his nonexistent hips.

"Because it wouldn't start, you moron!"

"You should be grateful I loaned it to you."

"You should be grateful you're still standing."

"That's it!" Dad shouted. "Not another word from either of you. We're going to settle this my way."

Josh's eyes met mine and we both flinched. Dad's way only meant one thing, and I hoped he was kidding.

"Let's go," he said.

"Oh, God," I moaned. "We aren't kids anymore, Dad."

"You could have fooled me. Josh, get the gloves. They're in your old room."

"I don't think this is necessary," my brother mumbled.

"Oh, it's necessary, all right." Dad straightened his baseball cap with a quick jerk.

"Dad, I'm twenty-seven years old," I reasoned.

"If you act like children, you'll be treated like children."

I turned to Josh with some inspiration. "I'm sorry, I shouldn't have yelled at you. It was very kind of you to lend me the car." My smile was as false as the words.

"Me too, Jode. I should have double-checked the battery."

"Too late now," Dad said. "I'll get the gloves."

We followed him toward the house, dreading what was to come. In the Rogers household, fights between Josh and me had always been resolved in the backyard sandbox with two pairs of worn leather boxing gloves and Dad as referee. Our parents would stop whatever they were doing to lace us up and, by the time they were finished and we were standing in the sand like a couple of idiots, the anger had already drained out of us. Dad would make us start swinging anyway, hoping the shame of neighborhood kids watching our domestic battles would teach us a lesson.

"I can't believe this," Josh whispered as Dad disappeared through the doorway.

"We could make a run for it," I suggested.

"He'll only force us to do it the next time we're here."

"He can't *force* us, can he? We're technically adults, after all."

"Did he let us off the hook after that Jell-O incident?"

"No," I said.

"What about the broken VCR?"

"That was fourteen years ago, at least."

"You think Dad's changed?"

"Maybe we could convince him his heart can't handle the excitement . . ."

"There's no way." Josh groaned. "We're doomed."

We entered the house and smelled the mouthwatering aroma of roast pork. Macaroni and cheese aside, when Mom wanted to cook, she worked wonders. I inhaled deeply. I was starving and our stupid argument was only delaying dinner.

"You never told me I was supposed to pick you up," I said, wanting to be sure we were both clear about who was right.

"Yes I did."

"No you *didn't.*"

"How else was I supposed to get here?"

"I don't know, but I would remember if you'd told me."

"I did tell you!" His nostrils flared.

"No you didn't!"

"Save it for the ring, you two!" Dad yelled as he approached us, gloves dangling from his thick hands.

ten

Even when the three of us traipsed out the back door, I still didn't believe Dad would force a fight. For some reason, I thought Mom would interfere and point out that we were, indeed, adults. I hoped she'd call us to the dinner table and end the fiasco before it began, but Mom was nowhere to be seen.

Dad seated us on the back steps and, through my protests and Josh's pleading, set to work lacing me up. I watched him suck on the frayed ends of the shoelaces that had replaced the original strings long ago in an effort to mold the stray tufts into points. As he worked, he gave tips and warnings to both of us.

"Same rules as always," he said. "Nothing above the neck or below the belt."

He seemed to have forgotten that I'd sprouted breasts since my last foray into the ring.

"Dad, can I say *one more time* that this is totally ridiculous?" I gritted my teeth as he tied the laces at my wrists with unnecessary force.

"What's ridiculous is two grown people fighting like a couple of second-graders."

"Exactly my point."

"No," he said, steel in his tone. "It's exactly *my* point." His eyes dared me to argue, but I backed down and he turned his attention to Josh's gloves.

When he'd finished suiting us up and led us to the sandbox, I noticed two little heads peering over the fence separating our yard from the Hendersons'. Their whispers and giggles were barely audible, but I was unnerved to have an audience.

"Okay, Dad. You made your point," Josh said, as he was directed into a corner.

Soon, I was in a corner of my own, facing my younger brother across the sand, hesitant to put up my dukes.

I was about to make one last plea to stop the madness when all hell broke loose.

"Fight!" the bigger Henderson shouted, cutting me off in mid-thought.

His cry was immediately echoed by Little Henderson, then another boy, and another, until all of Greentree Avenue seemed to be shouting the word. "Fight! Fight! Fight!"

It might as well have been the tinkling song of an ice-cream truck, the way the kids came running. They appeared between the slats of the fence, on the balcony next door, and some of the pesky rodents actually had the gall to walk around the front of the house and stand in our yard! Unlike the boxing days of my youth, and adding to the humiliation of the moment, the spectators were about half my size.

"Do you guys want a three-round match or a fight to the finish?" Dad asked, over the excited yammering of every kid in an eight-block radius.

"Three rounds," Josh answered before I had a chance to speak.

"Three rounds it is." Dad nodded, twisting the ends of his mustache.

"Surely you aren't going to make us go through with this," I whined.

"Fight! Fight! Fight!" came the chants from the sidelines.

"I'm going to count you down. Three . . ."

"I think this has gone far enough." I tried to keep the desperation from my voice. "Where's Mom?"

"Two . . ."

"Get on with it!" Big Henderson shouted.

I made the fateful mistake of turning my head to tell him to shut up just as Dad counted "one." I had no idea what caused the sudden surge of cheering until it was too late.

With remarkable force for a petite pothead, Josh sucker punched me in the jaw.

My neck snapped to the left and I thought my head was going to break free of my body. I almost fell over, but regained my balance by twisting my ankle into an incredibly painful and unnatural position. I furiously waved my arms at the swarm of bees circling me, only to realize the buzzing was internal.

I'd forgotten what a mean left hook that ambidextrous little bastard had!

"You son of a bitch!"

"Come on, now," Dad said. "This has to be a fair fight. Keep it below the neck, son."

"Sorry."

"Don't apologize to *me.* Say it to your sister."

Josh offered me the word, solemnly.

"What the hell did you do that for?" I asked, running my tongue along my teeth to make sure they were still intact.

"I said I was sorry."

"Two penalty punches for Jody," Dad announced.

"Can't we just end this?" I sighed.

"Wimp!" Little Henderson jeered.

I was ready to throttle that kid.

"Wimp! Wimp! Wimp!" the crowd chanted.

"Take a swing, Jody," Dad ordered.

"No."

Josh stood in the middle of the sandbox, gloved hands hanging limply at his sides. "Come on, Jody. Don't you want to take out some frustration on me?"

"No."

"Don't you want to take a swing?" he taunted.

"What are you doing?" I snapped.

"Trying to get this whole thing over with." He spoke quietly enough that only I could hear him over the volume of the crowd. "I'm *starving.*"

"Hit her again!" Little Henderson shouted.

"I don't want to fight you," I whispered.

"He's not going to let us inside until we do this. Mom's got pork in the oven and we're going to be stuck out here until it's a dried-up, tasteless brick."

"Just forget it," I moaned, turning to walk out of the ring.

"Tackle her!" one of the kids shouted.

"Fight! Fight! Fight!"

"Come on, Jody!" Josh called after me.

"Just give it up." I started to step out of the sandbox.

"So, how are Chris and Beth doing?" he taunted.

"For fuck's sake!" I growled. "You stinking little shit!"

Josh didn't even have a chance to lift his gloves before I was pummeling his stomach and ribs. Each blow was greeted by raucous cheers from the audience and grunts from between my lips.

I'd never considered myself a violent person, but the satisfaction of pounding flesh with leather was a surprising delight.

With every punch I was well aware that our backyard brawl wasn't the sort of activity condoned by the general public. Each time my glove connected with Josh's body, I became less refined and feminine, and while I felt like a one-woman offensive, I was probably closer to *one offensive woman.* I didn't care. I heard the cries from the crowd and felt the release of pent-up negative energy, reveling in the sensation.

Pretty soon, Josh was able to regain an edge with a couple of well-aimed hits, but he lacked my adrenaline. I won the first round and we took a break for a moment.

"You sure you want to continue, Jode?" he asked, bent double and struggling for breath.

"I'm game if you are."

"If you want to call it quits, I'll understand."

I had no intention of being the one to back down. "Do *you* want to quit?"

"Round two!" Dad bellowed, drowning out Josh's answer.

We met at the center of the sandbox in a hurricane of movement, our limbs twisting together then unfurling amid groans and gasps. We made eye contact between swings and I knew the iron will I saw in the dark centers of his eyes matched my own. What began as a battle for brisket became a real match as we each realized how badly the other wanted to win. Josh jabbed my stomach and I felt my organs recoil. I pounded his shoulder and he squeezed me into a headlock, then laid a solid blow against my rib cage. I nailed him in the kidneys, regained my upright stance, and we were at it again.

Round two went to Josh, but I knew I could take him in the third. We were covered with sand and sweat, stalking each other like animals, and loving every minute of it.

"Useless pothead," I muttered, belting him.

"Family favorite," he barked, clobbering me in return.

He was dead wrong there, and I punched him for it. More kids gathered around the yard, yelling and screaming, while Dad paced the lawn, coaching both of us.

I hadn't felt so alive in ages.

We swung, hit, missed, connected, winced, thumped, swatted,

slammed, and banged for a good six minutes, until Dad saw that neither of us was willing to give in.

He finally called a draw, to the disappointment of our pint-sized crowd, who vanished almost as quickly as they'd appeared.

Josh and I slumped in the sand, drained of energy.

"Good fight, huh?" he asked, punching me lightly on the arm.

"It was, wasn't it?" I grinned, physical exhaustion in direct contrast to my mental state. I felt cleansed and oddly euphoric, ready to take on whatever life was planning to shove down my throat next.

"Sorry if I hurt you." His crooked smile met mine.

"Hurt *me*? Yeah, right," I lied, envisioning a bag of frozen vegetables parked on every inch of my aching body. "I hope I didn't hurt *you*."

"Not a bit." Josh rolled his shoulder and winced. "I'm sorry about the car, Jode."

"Aren't you kids glad you got all of that out of your system?" Dad asked.

We both nodded and handed him our gloves. He chuckled and thumbprint-sized dimples appeared on either side of his mustache. "So, the old man still has a few tricks up his sleeve."

"Okay, already." I rolled my eyes. "You were right."

"Could you repeat that last bit?" He cupped a hand next to his ear. "I didn't quite catch it."

"You were right," we called in unison.

It was nice to sit with the two of them, technically the only men in my life. We hadn't had a moment together in a long time.

I looked at Dad and thought of all the times he'd taken us fishing in a dented aluminum boat he'd borrowed from one of the guys at the mill. Josh and I fought over everything; worms, rods, sunscreen, and seating arrangements until the first fish was caught. After that sleek and slippery body was pulled from the harbor, any ill feelings we had for each other vanished.

When Mom attended a teachers' conference in Seattle for a week, Dad looked after us by packing our lunches with peanut butter and margarine sandwiches, beef jerky and chocolate pudding. He let me wear jeans and a skirt simultaneously, while Josh wore most of his clothes inside out. He took us to Ice Cream Village one night, where we split the Avalanche; fourteen scoops of any favor we desired, covered in a flood of syrups, nuts, and whipped cream. Dad spooned chocolate syrup into his mouth and pushed it through the gaps in his teeth with his tongue while we shrieked with delight, cramming our faces with maple walnut, bubble gum, and mint chocolate chip. We managed to eat almost the whole damn thing and the vomiting that came later only strengthened the memory.

I'd missed that sense of camaraderie in recent years. We never saw each other anymore.

"Dinner!" Mom called from the back door.

"We'll be right there," Dad called up to her, apparently unwilling to lose the moment.

I wasn't sure I could cross the lawn, never mind climb the steps.

"Well . . . Jody's surprise is here," Mom said.

"Just two seconds, Gladys."

"What surprise?" I asked.

"Just wait until you get inside," Mom said, then looked me over with a frown. "Oh, dear. Have you been fighting?"

"We'll be there in two shakes, honey," Dad told her.

My mind raced from one possibility to the next. Maybe they'd decided to let me stay at the house after all, and there was a freshly made, lemon-scented bed waiting for me. Maybe they were loaning me some money to see me through my crisis.

Jody's surprise.

* * *

I led Dad and Josh into the house to find Mom standing next to the fridge with an open bottle of beer in her hand. A beer, casually held by the queen of the wine spritzers and girly drinks that made her "tee-hee."

"Take this into the living room, honey." She lifted the bottle toward me.

"No, thanks. I'll grab some juice or something after I shower." I tried to slip past her, hoping a cold beer wasn't my big surprise.

"There's no time for that," she said, with a firmness reminiscent of Chris's futon.

"Mom, I don't want to eat dinner covered in—"

"Take it."

Bewildered, I grabbed the bottle and walked down the hall.

The large, unevenly cut remnants, left over from the carpet installation and positioned by Mom in high-traffic areas, were missing. I stepped onto the real carpeting, which looked brand-new, even after nine years, and I instinctively knew we had company for dinner.

As I neared the living room, I saw the familiar yellow spines of *National Geographic*s piled on the coffee table. On the chest of drawers Dad inherited from his parents, Mom's Hummel figurines were displayed next to a vase of dried hydrangeas.

When I reached the doorway, a complete stranger came into view, sitting in Dad's recliner and cleaning his glasses with a handkerchief.

He looked close to my age, with reddish hair combed a little too carefully to one side and a freckle collection that rivaled my own. I didn't know *who* he was, but there was no question about *what* he was. If the overwhelming scent of stale coffee wasn't enough to clue me in, the necktie-and-jeans combination, topped off with a brown corduroy blazer, filled in the blanks. If I'd seen one, I'd seen them all. He had to be a teacher.

The stranger didn't see me hovering, so I cleared my throat to get his attention. He squinted at me before slipping his glasses on, and once his vision was clear, he stared at me with a look of dismay. I realized my tousled appearance wasn't exactly runway material, either.

"I think this is for you." I handed him the beer, hoping he wasn't really staying for dinner. The last thing I needed was a stray educator.

"Thanks. You must be Jody." His eyes wandered from what I assumed was the wild stampede of my hair to the sand adhered to all visible flesh. "Looks like you've been busy."

He even *sounded* like a teacher. He shared a neutral tone, capable of killing interest in a single syllable, with both my fourth-grade science teacher and the head of my high school history department.

"Yeah, I've been busy." I was too irritated to offer any further explanation. "And you are?"

"Russell." He stared expectantly.

"Russell . . . ?"

"McAllister."

If he was playing some kind of mind game, I was losing. I'd never seen the man before, and his name wasn't ringing any bells, but his expression indicated I should know who he was.

"Are you . . ." I began, uncertain of where to go from there.

"Your date."

"My what?" I bleated.

"Oh, good." Mom entered the room with a tray of hors d'oeuvres. "I see you two are getting acquainted." She extended the food toward our guest and gave me a broad wink. "Miniquiche, Russell?"

He took a napkin and selected one, handling it as delicately as glass.

I watched as he nibbled on the pastry, *like a woman.* He chewed timidly and swallowed with a small gulp of pleasure, *like an old woman,* then patted his lips. *An old woman at a tea party.* He took another tentative bite, catching the minuscule crumbs that fell in his napkin. *A tea party hosted by the fucking Queen of England.*

"Mom, can I speak to you in the kitchen?" I asked.

"Well, I don't think we should leave our guest unattended." She smiled sweetly at Russell and ignored my burning gaze.

"It'll only take a minute." I grabbed her elbow and propelled her from the room, as she tucked some loose hair behind her ear. When we arrived in the kitchen, I closed the door and whirled around to face her.

"I dropped by the school yesterday to see some old friends," she explained. "Russell's a new teacher." She twisted her wedding band as she spoke.

"What is he doing *here*?"

"History, geography, and shop, I think."

"What?"

"He replaced Mr. Johnson."

"Fascinating news, Mom, but that doesn't answer my question."

Josh appeared in a clean shirt and brushed past us on his way to the living room. I could smell the trail of soap behind him, from what must have been the world's shortest shower, and wished I'd had a chance at the sink, at least.

"I invited him to dinner, to help you out," Mom said.

"Help me out of what?"

"He seemed like such a nice fellow, and since you're looking for love—"

"I'm not looking for love." I threw in air quotes, for good measure.

She patted me on the shoulder. "Of course you aren't, dear."

"I'm not." Chris had been out of the picture for what, *two days*?

"If you say so, honey."

"Even if I was looking, he's not a suitable candidate."

"Why not?"

"Who's the goober in Dad's chair?" Josh asked, returning to the kitchen and opening the fridge door.

"That's why not." I rolled my eyes.

"What's wrong with him? He's a perfectly nice man."

"How do you know? You just said you met him *yesterday*. You might as well have picked up a derelict for me."

Josh smirked as he grabbed a beer.

"He's hardly a derelict," Mom assured me.

"He's hardly my type."

"And what, pray tell, is your *type*?"

"Let's just say my criteria are a little different from yours, Mom."

"What are you looking for?"

"Sex appeal, for starters," I said, more to shock her than anything.

"Good grief." She raised her hand to stop me from going any further.

"Aww, give him a chance, Jody." Josh snickered, twisting off his bottle cap.

"I'll give him until dessert," I muttered.

Josh decided to keep Russell company and left us alone once again.

"You could have warned me, so I'd have had a chance to clean up before meeting him."

"Aha!" Mom waggled her index finger at me, eyes sparkling with triumph. "You *are* interested."

eleven

When my parents joined us in the living room, Dad looked peeved to see an interloper in his favorite chair and he watched closely as Russell and I attempted to make conversation.

I asked most of the questions, knowing I'd rather pretend to listen to him blather on about the politics of the school system than try to explain and justify my unemployed and homeless state.

I hated to admit it, but he turned out to be a fairly interesting guy, which made chatting in front of an audience easier than it could have been. He'd traveled all over South America after he got his degree and, after four years in Portland high schools, decided he'd had enough of city life and decided to move to a small town. When he told us he'd landed the job in Bent Harbor because no one else wanted to work in a piddly little town, Josh and I exchanged looks and waited for the "no offense" that never came.

I was entertained by his tales of being raised the third child in a family of seven, and Mom beamed between sips of her gin and tonic. Dad sat back, silent, watchful, and mildly amused. Did they actually think sparks were flying? The fact that he was *interesting* didn't mean that I was *interested.*

"So, where do you work, Jody?" Russell asked, once he'd summed up his life in a tidy and palatable package.

I'd forgotten that blind dates were a two-way street, and it was suddenly my turn to be judged. Although it was obvious to me that there was nothing between us, I didn't want it to be quite so obvious to him. I wasn't about to be let down gently by a shop teacher.

"I'm kind of between jobs at the moment," I said, hoping he wouldn't pursue it.

"Oh." He frowned.

It was the reaction I expected, but I mustered up some pride and looked him straight in the eye. He was awfully picky for an average-looking man in a corduroy blazer. *Who does he think he is, anyway?*

"What she means," Mom interjected, "is that she's been working in human relations."

"Relating to humans as a *waitress,*" I corrected. It was one thing for me to be dissatisfied with my life, but Mom lying about it was downright depressing.

"Right," Mom continued. "And now she's setting her sights on a new career. Something entirely different."

She smiled at me and I stared blankly in return, unwilling to play along.

"What's the new career?" Russell asked, tilting his head in my direction with interest.

"I don't know," I said, smiling sweetly at Mom. She made the bed, she could lie in it.

"Jody's been considering a partnership in my new business venture," Mom countered.

My jaw dropped.

"I didn't know you had a business," Russell said, turning his attention to Mom.

"Neither did I," Josh mumbled from his perch on the ottoman. "No one asked *me* to be a partner."

Mom explained her painted-rocks-by-mail brainstorm and I watched Russell's smile fade with with every word. Apparently I wasn't the only one to spot the glaring faults in her plan. She led him back to her "studio," and gave him the ten-minute version of a two-minute tour. When he returned to the living room, he looked distinctly uncomfortable.

"I'm going to call it 'Arocknids,'" Mom said, settling on the couch like a nesting hen. "Get it? It's a pun."

There was a lengthy pause.

"It's going to be just bug art, honey? No animals?" Dad finally asked.

"For the time being. I think animals are a touch out of my league at the moment, so I'll stick to ladybugs, butterflies, that sort of thing."

Russell cleared his throat. "Actually, Mrs. Rogers, the term 'arachnid' applies only to eight-legged insects."

"So what?" Josh asked.

"So, the name won't work for butterflies," he sniffed.

"Her average customer won't know that," Josh said. "Only a bug scientist—"

"Entomologist," Russell corrected.

Josh gave him a dirty look and it seemed the familial wagons were circling my potentially wounded mother. "Only a *bug scientist* would care. I think it's a great name, Mom."

If Russell thought I was a blind-date dud, I hated to think how the Rogers family was faring as a group. We hadn't even sat down to dinner and he already looked poised to leave.

"Thanks, dear," Mom said, leaving her seat and moving toward the kitchen.

I followed her and swung the door open. She was pouring rich brown gravy from a saucepan to the gravy boat. Evidently, Russell's presence warranted the good china, normally reserved for birthdays, holidays, and real dinner parties.

"It smells excellent, Mom."

"Thank you, Jody." She sighed. "I realize how difficult it must be for you to say that."

"What?"

"Well, you certainly didn't rush to the defense of Arocknids, and my choice of a date for you obviously isn't good enough." She scraped the remaining gravy out of the saucepan with a rubber spatula. "I'm amazed you can find it in your heart to compliment *anything* I've done."

"Mom—"

"Could you try, for my sake, to make a good impression?" She dumped the saucepan into the sink with a crash, clearly agitated.

"I think it's too late for that. Besides, he's looking down his nose at all of us."

"He's shy."

"He's a *snob.* You just watch his reaction when you place the final bowl on the table."

"He'll eat it."

"I wouldn't bet on it." I was guaranteed the last laugh.

"I'm telling him you made the dinner. You just watch how he reacts when he sees what a good cook you are."

"Seems like false advertising to me."

I hoped we could regain some family dignity by the end of what I could only hope was a short evening, but we weren't likely to score big points at the dinner table.

Like any family, we had our own little quirks and tastes. I'd spent my childhood happily oblivious to them, until Erin's first meal at my house in the third grade. I'd never considered my household to be different from others, but Erin told me we were not only different, but *weird.* At her insistence, I'd taken a closer look at our rituals and observed a less than pretty sight.

While I'd once assumed that every family ate "Hodgepodge" and "Triple-Decker dinner," I learned that the rest of the world, meaning the students at Bent Harbor Elementary, had no idea what these dishes were. I thought everyone's father referred to the blood drippings from beef as "the juice," poured it into a bowl and set it next to the gravy. And that he cut the tight knots from cooked roasts and asked "Who wants string?", distributing the meat-crusted twine for his children's chewing pleasure and saving at least one strand for himself to suck while he sliced and served.

I thought everyone used a "bone bowl" when they ate chicken, dropping the skeletal remnants of wings, breasts, and drumsticks into a communal dish to keep their plates from becoming cluttered, that every mother picked through the discards, muttering "There's still meat on here. *Look at all that meat!*", and gnawed on the cartilage, amazed to have raised such wasteful children. I was certain every family fought over turkey skin during Christmas dinner, tearing strips of golden greasiness from the bird before it even reached the table, and begged to eat the "parson's nose" or "the last thing over the fence."

Erin showed me that we were the only family laying claim to these habits, and from that moment onward, I dreaded anyone's initiation to our dinner table, Russell included.

I popped my head into the living room and told the men that dinner was ready, crossing my fingers behind my back to ward off bizarre behavior, knowing full well the effort was futile.

I felt a powerful surge of discomfort as we sat at the table, waiting for Mom to appear and smooth the rough edges of our conversation.

"Voilà!" she announced, pushing the swinging door open with her backside and turning toward us with a perfectly browned roast. Soon came applesauce, gravy, rolls and butter, garlic mashed potatoes, and Brussels sprouts, but when she brought out the final item, I knew I was about to witness the downfall of Russell McAllister.

In a large, ceramic bowl was the Rogers family's guest test. Ability to eat the contents would determine whether an outsider had the potential to be accepted as one of us. Even Mom would have to concede dating-game defeat if Russell didn't eat her grandmother's creation. After all, *rules were rules.*

I watched his eyebrows rise in response to the bowl and exchanged a smirk with Josh. I gazed at the mixture of mashed turnip and carrot, which we all referred to as "the orange stuff," and marveled at its garish coloring. The best part of the guest test was that the orange stuff was delicious, but very few people were willing to take the chance.

"So," Mom asked, breaking the silence. "Would you like some potatoes, Russell?"

"Yes, please." He passed her his plate, confirming, when asked, that he'd like sprouts, as well.

Mom heaped an enormous scoop of each vegetable onto his plate, then a spoonful of applesauce and not one roll, but *two.* I was on to her scheme. Filling up the plate so there was no space left for orange stuff was a violation, and she knew it. Like evil twins, Josh and I simultaneously reached for the bowl. He got to it first.

"*Orange stuff,* Russell?"

"What is it?" He winced at the lumpy pile.

"Do you *really* want to know?" I dared him.

"It's turnip and carrot," Mom snapped.

"Oh . . . turnip and carrot." He didn't sound convinced.

"Give it a try," Mom urged.

"I guess it couldn't hurt." He shrugged.

Underneath the table, my fingernails dug into my palms. Taking it was one thing, but *eating* it was quite another. Dad hacked away at the roast. "Crackling, Jody?" he asked, offering me a piece of crunchy, golden fat impaled on a fork.

For the sake of appearances, I shook my head. Dinner would be enough of a horror show without our guest learning that my family's favorite ingredient was vitamin G. Grease.

"More for the rest of us." Dad smiled, popping the chunk in his mouth. As he chewed, a fatty gloss shone on his lips.

I watched Russell's Adam's apple plunge as he swallowed hard.

"Jody's quite a cook," Mom announced.

"Did *you* make all of this?" Russell asked.

I smiled weakly.

"Of course not." Josh laughed, unaware of Mom's plan. "She was too busy boxing."

"Watching boxing?"

"No, we were going at it in the backyard," Josh explained, ignoring my feverish attempts to kick him under the table. "It was some fight!"

"She's got one hell of a right hook," Dad bragged, as though that were the kind of information a blind date wanted to hear.

Russell didn't comment, but concentrated on spreading his napkin on his lap, sneaking a peek at his watch in the process.

"Okay, Russell," Dad said, "just pass your plate this way and I'll load it up with some pork. Don't worry," he said, winking, "the guest always gets the crispy end pieces."

"Uh, no, thank you."

"Oh, you like it juicy." Dad winked again. "Good man. I'll give you a little something from the middle."

Russell tossed him a condescending smile. "I meant no pork, thank you."

Mom's knife clattered on her plate and Dad stared at Russell with a look of utter astonishment. *"No pork?"*

"I'm a vegetarian."

It was over. The table couldn't have been more stunned if he announced he was a hermaphrodite, and Dad probably would have been more accepting of that situation. Unlike a meatless lifestyle, double genitals wouldn't technically be Russell's fault.

I relaxed in my chair, delighted with the turn of events. Mom and Josh considered the herbivore route to be merely unsavory, but Dad thought vegetarianism was a vile disease. Russell could eat orange stuff with a shovel and it wouldn't change a thing.

A few idle jabs at conversation over the meal were uninspired at best, and while Ruby temporarily lightened the mood by rolling around on her back and begging for scraps, even a slobbering Shih Tzu had limited entertainment value.

Russell stayed for dessert, but not a moment longer, making some excuse about having mysterious "things" to do at home. He shook hands with each of us at the door and I was sure the relief was mutual.

"Well, *that* was a disaster," I said cheerfully, when the door had closed behind him.

"No meat." Dad shook his head in disbelief. *"No meat."*

Josh and I cleared the table in companionable silence, then loaded the dishwasher while Mom and Dad scarfed down a couple of stiff drinks. When we finished cleaning up, I tossed Josh his car keys so he could attend a party in Fillington and Dad offered me a lift back to Erin's place. I suspected it was a ploy to get rid of my stack of childhood possessions, but accepted nonetheless.

I poured myself a gin and tonic and the three of us sat down for a drink before departing.

"Rough night, huh?" I settled next to Mom on the couch.

"It wasn't so bad," she murmured.

"Until he played the vegetarian card," Dad scoffed. "How could anyone survive without *meat,* for crying out loud?"

"Erin's a vegetarian," I reminded him.

"Erin's a weirdo. Just like that kid tonight. Gladys, how could you even consider welcoming someone like that into the family? He'd weaken our bloodlines."

"I'm not so sure our bloodlines are anything to brag about," I mumbled. "I should be single for a while, anyway."

Dad asked how the job hunt was going and I gave him a run-through of my two disastrous interviews. Someday, I knew I'd be able to laugh about them, but they were still too fresh in my mind. He asked if I wanted to go back to school, but I had no desire to return to the classroom after such a long hiatus. "Mature student" was an epithet I could do without.

"You know you can help me with Arocknids," Mom said.

"I don't think so."

"I'm sure you could, honey. It'll take some time and practice, but don't sell yourself short."

"I meant, no, thanks."

"I see." She sniffed.

"Why don't you go back to the restaurant?" Dad asked.

"I don't really want to."

He laughed and slapped his knee. "You don't *really want to*? Hell, kiddo, do you think I *wanted* to spend most of my life in a pulp mill?"

"Well, no, but—"

"There's no buts about it." He reached for his glass and took a long drink. "I *had* to work there. Sometimes you've got to pay your dues, bite the bullet, and take what life dishes out."

"Including generous helpings of platitudes, apparently," I said, rolling my eyes.

"Pardon me?"

"Nothing," I assured him. "Look, I don't feel like I've got to settle yet, Dad. I'm only twenty-seven."

"I had two kids when I was twenty-seven."

"But I'm not you, Dad. I haven't made the same mistakes." Of course, I'd made a whole set of my own, but that was beside the point.

"Oh," Dad said quietly. "I see what you're saying." He very carefully placed his glass on the moist ring of his coaster, and I knew I'd hurt his feelings.

"I didn't mean it in a bad way . . ." *Why couldn't I keep my mouth shut?*

"Hey, don't worry about it. I used to think my father was a fool, as well. It wasn't until later that I realized he'd given up his own dreams to give me a better life."

"I never said . . . I never thought you were a fool! Mom, can you help me out here?"

She sipped her drink and refused to look at me.

"If you think you're too good for the Galley, don't go back," Dad said, rising from his chair. "Come on, I'll give you a ride home."

I wasn't ready to leave, but I approached Mom and kissed her cheek, thanking her for dinner. There was no response.

Dad loaded my boxes into his car without a word and drove me to Erin's house.

"Dad, I'm sorry if I hurt your feelings. I didn't mean anything," I said, holding the door open when I'd stepped out of the car. *What were the magic words?*

"Nothing to feel sorry for," he said gruffly.

"But Dad, I was just—"

"Never mind. It doesn't matter."

But of course it did.

twelve

After a restless sleep, packed with bad dreams and worse guilt, I awoke cranky and sore from my boxing escapade. It was already past noon, not exactly prime job-hunting time. Since I had no one to impress, and I'd showered the night before, I skipped the hygiene routine entirely and rolled straight from bed into some moderately clean clothes. I considered calling my parents to apologize, but didn't know what words could make the difference.

The money I'd taken from the bank the night before was gone, so I walked to the corner store and bought a newspaper with change I dug out of Erin's couch, relieved the wait for my final paycheck was only five more days.

As expected, no new jobs were listed, but an announcement for the reunion I'd rather die than attend mocked me from the bottom corner of the classifieds.

I made some breakfast and thought about what Dad had said. Maybe I was doomed to be a waitress and should get my job back while I had the chance. Maybe beggars really *couldn't* be choosers and I was lucky to have had a job with decent pay and pleasant coworkers.

Visions of Marty McDade danced in my head.

Returning to the Galley wouldn't be a *choice,* it would be a defeat. I could feel a headache coming on and all I wanted to do was crawl back into bed, but before I could slip under the covers, the phone rang.

"Hey, Jody. It's me," Erin said. "Did you get my message?"

"I haven't listened to the machine."

"I'm getting off work at about two. I thought you might want to go for a walk."

While not quite as tempting as sulking in bed, exercise would be good for me.

"Sounds perfect."

"Great, because we need to talk."

Dread lurched in my stomach as I hung up the phone. *We need to talk?* Wasn't that the prologue to being dumped? Whatever it was, it had to be bad. Was it money? I'd planned on contributing to her mortgage payment, but I couldn't do that until I got a job. Was it something I'd said? No, offending Erin was virtually impossible. *We need to talk?*

I sat on the beanbag chair for over an hour and a half, worrying. I should have spent the time trying to figure out the next step, making lists and all that bunk, but I simply didn't have the energy. By the time Erin arrived at the house, my stomach was in knots.

We walked to Porter Lighthouse, one of the oldest in the area, a beacon for passing ships and boats in distress. It was surrounded by parklands, accessible by gravel roads and well-worn footpaths, winding around boulders and tree trunks, leading the way to the ocean. It was the destination for family picnics, make-out sessions, and school field trips.

As we walked, we stepped over exposed roots and I brushed my fingertips against the reaching branches of salal bushes, a favorite of Mom's for filling the gaps in floral arrangements.

We reached the lighthouse and I settled on a driftwood log, picking at its splintering edges. The sun was warm and bright, a promise summer was on the way.

"Did you bring anything to eat?" Erin asked.

"Nah, did you?"

She produced two granola bars and handed me one. "Nice to get out of town." Her hands fiddled with the zipper on her fleece jacket.

"Yeah, it is," I agreed. "Funny how we never come down here anymore. It's so close." I couldn't remember the last time we'd been there together. Usually she was worn out from the lifting, digging, and watering at work. "Too bad we spend our free time indoors."

"I come here a couple of times a week," she replied.

"Okay." I laughed. "So much for my couch potato theory. What for?"

"To think, I guess."

I hoped the thinking had nothing to do with my presence in her house, but in recent days so much had been about me, I couldn't imagine what else it could be. Other than frequent, enthusiastic sex, I had no idea what was going on in her life. Suddenly I felt selfish and guilty.

"I don't know what to do about Michael," she finally said, and relief blew through me.

Michael was the problem, and that was a problem I could handle. I didn't even have to ask what she meant. Once she'd had enough of whoever she was briefly seeing, she always had trouble ending the relationship. I supposed that was why she started leaning toward the quick fling and no-phone-numbers route most of the time.

As usual, I was ready to offer a number of suggestions for the breakup.

"I can't seem to shake him," she said with a groan.

"I'm sure there's a way."

She'd dumped guys over candlelit dinners, by phone, and by e-mail. She'd had screaming fights in front of the drugstore, and dished out the silent treatment until men had walked away. She'd spoken with brutal civility in a coffee shop, and dropped the bomb on one poor guy at Hannah Baxter's second wedding. She'd even made *me* end a relationship for her when she had the flu and was too tired to deal with it. There was no doubt in my mind that she could shake Michael, and I was glad he was on his way out the door. I'd never have to face him again after our nude introduction *and* I could look forward to spending time with my best friend.

"I can't stop thinking about it," Erin murmured.

Planning the dump was hell for her, but once she'd decided to do it, she became obsessed.

While I geared up to brainstorm with her, she said something that abruptly stopped my train of thought.

"I mean, I never thought I'd fall in love."

"What?" I gasped. "Did you say *love*?" I stared at her fidgeting hands, then up at her uncertain smile. "Hold on a second, here. Are you saying you're in *love* with him?"

"Yes." She blushed. *She actually blushed.*

"With him? Michael?" I paused for dramatic effect. *"Batman?"*

"Yes, Jody." She sighed with exasperation.

"Since when? Didn't you meet him this week?"

"I don't know." She smiled. "It just kind of . . . *happened.*"

I was caught between sorrow, jealousy, and guilt for not being happy for her. I tried to smile. "Wow," was all I could muster, no great shakes under the circumstances.

"I know. I feel giddy about it, but scared, too."

Scared was good. Maybe there was a chance to end this thing after all. "For Christ's sake, *love*?" I asked. "It's an awfully big step," I added, trying to hint at danger and heartbreak.

"That's why I wanted to ask how you handled it."

"Handled what?"

"Telling Chris you loved him for the first time."

The question was unexpectedly blunt. "Well, I . . . uh . . ."

"I need your help, Jody. I've never felt this way before and you're the only person I can talk to."

I frowned. "Actually, it never happened. I never, uh . . . I never said it."

Her eyes bulged in disbelief. "You've *got* to be kidding."

"Nope."

"You were together almost three years and you never said you loved each other?"

"Well, not exactly. *He* said it to *me.* I just never really said it back."

"But I thought you loved him."

"I don't know . . ." I shook my head. "Everything's changed, anyway."

"Oh, that's right. He's an asshole. Well, never mind Chris. You must have said it to one of your other boyfriends." Her tone was hopeful.

"Uh . . ." I shook my head.

"Robert Lewis?"

"No. We were in *seventh grade,* Erin."

"What about Bruce Alvers?"

"No." Despite my obvious discomfort, she showed no sign of letting up.

"Oh, I thought for sure you had. Wasn't he the first guy you . . . you know, slept with?"

"What happened to 'fucked' or 'screwed'?" I asked.

"Michael doesn't like to refer to lovemaking like that." She almost looked demure. *Almost.*

Less than a week and he'd tamed her tongue?

"No, I never said it to Bruce Alvers, either."

"Todd Robinson?"

"No. Don't you get it?" I snapped. "I've never said it to anyone."

"Jesus," she muttered. "I thought *I* was the one with the commitment problem." She pulled a cigarette from her pocket and lit it.

"It's not a commitment problem."

"Guess again, Jode." She took a drag and slowly exhaled. "How many people have said it to you?"

"I don't know," I hedged.

"I'll bet you do."

"Okay, maybe five."

"*Five?* And you never said it back?"

I shook my head.

"What did you say?"

"I have to go."

"What?" She snorted. "You suddenly have a job I don't know about?"

"Very funny. No, I mean that's what I said. *I have to go.*"

"And?"

"And I left."

I didn't want to detail my cowardice, but the truth was that I'd darted out of movie theaters, restaurants, and even made barely clothed escapes not only from bedrooms, but from the beds themselves when the word "love" rose its prickly, confusing, and scary head. "Every time they said it, I left. It's a highly effective technique. Eventually, they stopped saying it."

Erin gave me a pitying look. I knew it wasn't entirely "normal" to feel such striking reticence toward love but, until that moment, I hadn't thought it was *bad.*

"No one's *ever* said it to me." She bent and ground her cigarette butt into the rock.

Hell, she never gave anyone the chance to say it. She booted them out the door as soon as the sheets cooled off.

"It's no big deal," I told her.

"No big deal? Are you a complete moron?"

I stared at the glistening water without a word.

She cleared her throat and attempted to change the subject. "Hey, remember when we used to come down here for Brownie campfires and marshmallow roasts?"

"I wasn't in Brownies." Along with gushing over the thrill of being in love, Brownie memories were one more thing I couldn't share with her.

"Oh, yeah. That's right." She paused. "We used to make s'mores, and we had these little pads we made out of woven newspaper and plastic to sit on so we wouldn't get wet. Know what we called them?"

"Nope."

" 'Sit-upons.' You know, because we sat upon them." She laughed. "That's Brownies for you."

"I don't want to talk about Brownies, Erin."

"Sorry." She stared into the distance for a moment before continuing. "I guess I shouldn't have brought up all of this Michael stuff right now."

Her lips unconsciously formed a smile when she said his name, and I felt a sting of jealousy. Where was the trucker-mouthed, do'em-and-leave'em girl I knew so well?

"It's just a bit hard to hear right now," I confessed. "But I want us to be able to talk about anything."

"That's what I want, too." She glanced at me, then away again. "You know, I wasn't going to mention this, but I saw Chris and Beth at Dairy Queen last night."

"Ooh, an ice-cream treat?" I sneered. "It must be serious." My voice cracked, shattering the illusion of indifference I was aiming for.

"Jody."

"*Dairy Queen,* now there's a fucking dream date. He's really pulling out all the stops."

"Come on, Jody. Give it up."

"Hey, aren't you supposed to be my emotional cheerleader?" I asked. "I think you're off the squad."

"Well, sorry, but considering what you've just told me about your love phobia, I'm looking at things a little differently."

"So now you're on *his* side. Great, Erin. That's just what I need to hear."

"Don't you think it's possible that *you* had something to do with your breakup?"

"Well, as far as I can recall, *I* wasn't in the shower having sex with my cousin, although my memory hasn't been what it should be lately." Nor was my judgment, considering I'd chosen a traitor for a best friend.

"I'm not talking about that. The thing with Beth is a symptom of a larger problem. A deeper issue."

"Thank you, Ann Landers."

"I'm trying to help."

"You're failing," I snapped.

"You're just mad right now."

"No shit."

"Look, you're just jealous because I've fallen in love and you're alone, unemployed, and miserable."

"My, my. Aren't we gracious?"

"Someone has to set you straight. Would you rather I lied to you?"

"Yes."

"Jody."

"Okay, already. Maybe I'm jealous because my life is going down the tubes."

"Apology accepted. Let's walk."

Before I could tell her that it wasn't an apology, she was heading toward the beach.

We climbed down the rocks toward the sandy cove and my brain pulsed with all kinds of emotions. All I wanted to do was go home and sleep for a couple of weeks.

As we were nearing the beach, we spotted Lucas McDade and, unfortunately, he saw us, as well. Still baffled by his Safeway love proclamation, I was in no mood to deal with him.

"Hey, Jody!" he shouted. He was covered with clinging, wet sand and looked exhausted, although his eyes darted with excitement. "This is *perfect*! I was on my way to find you. The timing is perfect. It's like fate or . . . *something*."

"Something like bad luck," I muttered.

"Why were you looking for her?" Erin asked.

"I've got to show you this thing I made, Jody," he said, ignoring her. "You're going to love it."

"Actually, I need to head home, Lucas. We've got stuff to do."

"Come on, it'll only take a minute," he pleaded.

We followed his beckoning arm farther down the beach and I scanned the horizon, seeing nothing out of the ordinary.

"It's right over here! Come on, you guys." He led us closer to the water's edge, where a huge pile of wet sand was waiting for us.

"Oh, no!" he cried.

"What are we looking at?" Erin asked.

"*It's gone.* It was right here a few minutes ago and now it's gone." The dark circles under his eyes made me wonder if the guy ever slept.

"What was it?" Erin asked.

"A message in the sand," he whined.

"SOS?" I asked. Given the opportunity, it's what I would have written.

"No, it was a poem." He gave me a sappy look and I half expected cartoon hearts to appear in the air around him. "A love poem for you."

I cringed.

"Oh, that's so sweet," Erin gushed. Normally I could have counted on her for outright mockery, but being anointed with the juices of love had rendered her useless.

"You don't love me," I told him.

"Yes I do, Jody."

"No you don't."

"Yes I do," he insisted.

"You don't even *know* me." How could he have possibly fallen in love with me in the *two days* since I'd seen him at the Galley? It had to be the same bug Erin had caught.

"I've known you your whole life!"

"You haven't seen me for *ten years*!"

"I've seen you with my heart," he said with a sigh.

I glanced to my right. Apparently even *that* statement wasn't enough to trigger Erin's gag reflex.

"Listen to me." I tried to remain calm, but I was ready to slap him silly. "You do *not* love me." I spoke slowly, so there would be no confusion.

"Yes, I—"

"Stop it!"

"Sorry, Jody," he murmured. "I just wanted to show you how much I care. Even though my brother's going to steal my job, I'll still have you."

"You don't *have* me. Jesus! What's wrong with you?"

"I'm sorry you missed the poem." He scratched his forehead. "I can't believe it's gone."

I couldn't contain myself any longer. "What did you expect, Lucas? You wrote it in the goddamn *sand,* for crying out loud! Right next to the tide line!"

"Jody," Erin warned, but I wasn't finished.

"*Of course* it was washed away. Writing in the sand isn't permanent, Lucas. Just like these ludicrous feelings you think you have for me aren't permanent."

"Are you referring to my undying love?" he asked, hand dropping to his side.

"Am I on *Candid Camera*? Is this an impractical joke?" I paused. "Uh, *yes,* I'm referring to the *undying love.*"

"Then I beg to differ."

I was exhausted. "These feelings will go away, Lucas," I said quietly. "They'll be washed away in no time at all."

"That's not true. What's between us is very special."

"For fuck's sake!" I screeched, causing him to blanch and take a step back. "There's *nothing* between us. In fact, there's no us at all, and there never will be."

He watched me, utterly silent.

"Come on, Erin. Let's go home," I said.

I saw her give my tormentor a sympathetic smile and a pat on the back before she turned to follow me. Somehow, I didn't maim her.

I stomped up the beach, hoping I'd nipped the infatuation in the bud. Sometimes cutting to the chase was the only way to communicate with people. I glanced over my shoulder and saw that Lucas was standing in the exact position we'd left him in; hands limp at his sides, staring after us. I continued walking. After all, emotions *were* as fleeting as writing in the sand, and I'd done Lucas McDade a favor by being brutally honest.

It goes without saying that I would have chosen my words more carefully if I'd known he had access to a cement mixer.

thirteen

During the walk home, Erin admitted that Lucas's behavior had been strange, but insisted it was oddly sweet.

"He'd better leave me alone from now on," I told her.

"I'm sure he's harmless."

"That doesn't mean he isn't annoying."

"You should be *flattered*."

The words struck the wrong chord, but it took a moment to figure out why. "Fuck! That's *exactly* what Beth said to me about Marty McDade pinching my ass."

"A little déjà vu never hurt anyone. Anyway, I think you're pretty hard on poor old Lucas. As Gammy used to say, don't make a mountain out of a molehill."

"And as she also used to say, a stitch in time saves nine. So I chose to end this thing now instead of waiting for it to fester," I told her.

"You're forgetting Gammy's immortal words: 'eat your broccoli or you'll grow up to be a waste, like your mother.' "

"I don't think that one applies to this situation." I snickered.

"You may be right," Erin said, laughing. "So what was Lucas saying about losing his job?"

"Oh, I don't know what he's worried about. Justin's supposedly coming back to town and Lucas thinks he'll get bumped out of the dealership."

"Justin, huh? Do you remember how cute he was?"

"No. We were eight when he left, Erin."

"He was my first crush."

"I'm amazed you held out until second grade." I laughed. "So you'll dump Batman the second Justin appears on the scene?"

"Of course not! I just want to see how he turned out."

When we got back to her place, Erin made a nice veggie casserole. It would have been nicer with meat, but that was the least of my worries. We drove to Video Nook for a movie, and since Josh wasn't working, I didn't have to listen to his version of Mom's version of my argument with Dad.

Batman was working the night shift, which meant Erin and I had the house to ourselves. We changed into our pajamas, made popcorn, and watched a chick flick of Erin's choosing. As she swooned on the opposite end of the couch and sighed at all the sappiest moments, I damned the disappearance of my cursing counterpart.

We were in bed by midnight and I was fast asleep when the doorbell rang. We met in the hallway, equally disheveled.

"Who the hell is that?" I asked.

"I don't know." She wiped the sleep from her eyes and ran her fingers through her matted mane of hair.

"Do you think it's Michael?"

"No, he has a key."

"He does?" I grimaced, unnerved that a virtual stranger had access to the house. "Open the door," I urged her.

"You open it," she said.

"Wimp."

"Chicken."

The bell sounded again, so I opened the door to find two cops on the front step.

They flashed their badges in a manner that rivaled the action on "CHiPs", despite the fact that they were both in uniform. The taller one even looked a little like Erik Estrada, aside from the acne clusters on his cheeks and a nametag identifying him as Wilson. Of course, Bent Harbor would never be mistaken for Hollywood.

"Evening, ma'am," he said.

I recognized him from the restaurant, but I'd never seen his partner before. I was suddenly conscious of the dancing-fruit pattern of my pajamas.

"Hi." My brain rattled with possible reasons for their appearance on Erin's doorstep.

"Are you Miss Rogers?" Wilson asked.

I nodded, shocked they were there to see *me.* Had Josh been busted again? Had something happened to my parents?

"Are you acquainted with a Mr. Lucas McDade?"

Was he hurt or killed? In my fit of annoyance, had I *wished him dead*? "Yes, I am."

"Intimately acquainted?"

"Intimately acquainted?" I repeated, slightly confused.

"They're friends from high school," Erin said, peering over my shoulder.

"Oh, I get it," the shorter cop, O'Connor, said. "You two ladies are—"

"No," I gulped as soon as I saw the twinkle in his eye. "We're just friends, as well."

"Will you let me ask the questions?" Wilson snapped.

"Sorry, I just thought that if this was a love triangle—"

"Believe me, it's not," I assured him.

"Well, it would have explained Mr. McDade's, uh, behavior."

"Am I handling this, or are you?" Wilson asked, and O'Connor's lips clamped together.

"What behavior?" Erin asked, nudging me out of the way.

"It seems that Mr. McDade wanted to leave a love letter for Miss Rogers."

"Terrific, another poem." I groaned.

"Isn't that more of a . . . *postal* issue?" Erin asked.

"A love letter in cement," O'Connor explained.

They told us a Mrs. Patterson on Flat Pine Road had reported a sighting of a cement mixer crossing her front lawn and turning onto Old Marine Highway. Her house had been struck by a wayward ice-cream truck two years earlier and she felt the vehicle posed a similar threat to the neighborhood.

A swerving cement truck proved easy to track and the police found Lucas at the wheel. During questioning it became apparent that he'd intended to blanket Erin's street with mix and carve a poem into it, *for my pleasure,* presumably. He'd firmly believed he wouldn't be detected, despite the volume of the truck's powerful motor, and was certain I'd be delighted with the results. What he hadn't realized was that there was no cement in the truck.

"He's crazy," I told Wilson.

"Clinically?"

"No!" I said hurriedly. "Just a little weird."

"So he's not your boyfriend?"

"No."

"And you had no idea about his plan?"

"Hell, no!"

"Okay, now." Wilson raised his hands. "He hadn't actually done anything by the time we found him."

"Except steal a cement mixer," Erin interjected.

"He works at the dealership he took it from. He had a key, so we let him off with a warning."

"Then what are you doing here?"

"We just wanted to make sure you knew the guy and he isn't a stalker or something."

I wasn't ready to rule out the possibility, but told the police I didn't consider him a threat. They left the doorstep and Erin and I were alone again.

"This is really starting to creep me out," I muttered.

"Maybe you should talk to his dad."

"I'm not talking to Marty. First of all, I can't stand the guy, and second, if Marty fires him, he'll have an extra eight hours a day to harass me."

"I wonder why he's targeting *you,*" Erin murmured, tossing her hair over her shoulder.

"Thanks a lot."

"You know what I mean."

We returned to our respective bedrooms and I had a terrible sleep, worrying about the next time I'd see Lucas.

As it turned out, my fretting was in vain. He disappeared from my life for the next three days, days I spent shuffling around Erin's house in a robe and slippers, feeling sorry for myself. I drank hot chocolate and ate the entire jar of maraschino cherries, a feat that had me peeing red.

I knew I was driving Erin nuts, but I couldn't concentrate on the mundane details of day-to-day living. Even dropping bread in the toaster was pushing the limits of what I could handle. Wallace Enterprises never called me back for that second interview, and while I wasn't surprised, it still struck a blow. My parents made no attempt to reach me, and Erin was so busy with Michael, she had no time for me. I decided to lie low and do nothing. Life was the shits and my meddling would only make it worse.

On the third day, I felt a glimmer of hope, knowing the Galley's payday was a mere twenty-four hours away and I'd have some cash in my pocket.

I picked up a newspaper, feeling slightly more buoyant, and found an ad for a job at the Saltwater Taffy House on Barclay Drive. They wanted someone with two years' experience to work flexible hours. Hell, I had *seven* years of customer service under my belt, and my empty schedule made me as flexible as a yoga instructor. I was practically *overqualified.*

Finally feeling capable of something more demanding than handling the remote, I showered for the first time in days and grabbed a copy of my résumé

The shop was within walking distance and I took my time, breathing fresh air and enjoying a day of minimal clouds and the soft glow of sunshine. I'd been foolish to stay inside for so long when I could have been reveling in the days of freedom temporary unemployment gave me. Once I was working at the Taffy House, I'd be full of regret for the time I'd squandered on talk shows and cartoons.

I stepped inside the sweet-smelling shop with a contented sigh.

The red and white striped walls gave me an immediate claustrophobic sensation I wasn't entirely comfortable with, and the color combination dominated the entire space; white shelving housed boxes of candy, and huge bins full of paper-wrapped taffy bites were covered with gaudy red bows and flowing white ribbons.

The woman behind the counter sported a red and white getup à la Mrs. Claus, and looked rotund enough to have spent more time sampling then selling.

"Excuse me," I said. "I'm here about your ad."

"Fabulous!" Her rosy cheeks bulged as she smiled. "The cashiering job?"

"Yes." I smiled like all I'd ever wanted from life was a career in taffy.

"You're the only applicant we've had and that ad's been running for the past two days."

If only I'd picked up the damn paper! My three-day sofa sabbatical could have been avoided entirely.

"Did you bring a résumé?" she asked.

I pulled a linen page from my folder and handed it to her, certain I could blow away the nonexistent competition.

She made a strange clucking sound and shook her head. "Honey, the ad said two years' experience."

"Yes." I nodded. *Is she blind?* "I worked at Dean's Ocean Galley, up the road, for seven years. I have plenty of cashier and customer service experience."

"Oh, you've misunderstood." She smiled sympathetically. "We need someone with two years of *taffy* experience."

I was too stunned to laugh.

I thanked her for her time (all forty-five seconds of it) and trudged back to Erin's house, where I slipped back into my pajamas, my fleeting zest for life obliterated.

On the fourth day, I didn't even bother with a newspaper. It was too depressing. Instead, I planned to swing by the Galley and pick up my paycheck. Of course, I was reluctant to enter the restaurant, since I had no newfound success to report to Dean, my coworkers, or my ever-inquisitive customers, and the last thing I wanted to do was field questions about my shitty new life.

I killed time by watching several talk shows and marveling at how much worse my life could be. At least I wasn't sitting on a stage with a bunch of losers as an example of a sex change gone bad, or a porn addict. Then again, I was a solitary loser, sitting on someone else's couch, clutching a remote control.

Eleven o'clock came and went, but I was too engrossed in a battle between two burly women for one tiny man to care. Next up was a show about brothers fighting for a romantic relationship with their sixteen-year-old cousin, followed by a housewife makeover special. Before each show ended, there was a preview of the next hour; a juicy tidbit to pique my interest and keep me in my seat. I didn't want to miss a second.

Erin arrived home from work at four, looking annoyed to find me on the couch in my pajamas. My cereal bowl sat on the coffee table, filled with some remnants of quickly decaying oatmeal and an empty mandarin can.

"Busy day?" she asked, with unmistakable sarcasm.

"Very funny. I was on my way down to the Galley to pick up my check and . . ." Well, the rest was obvious.

"And?" she prompted.

What does she want me to say? "And I didn't quite get there."

The phone rang and she saw that I'd moved the portable from her nightstand to the living room. She reached past my garbage and yanked it off the table. I could tell by the sudden upswing in her voice that it was Michael. "No, she hasn't found one yet," Erin said, glancing at me and smiling hopefully. "I'm sure it's only a matter of days, right, Jody?"

I nodded and tore open a Snickers bar. "Don't you have anything better to talk about?" I muttered.

"Yeah, she's looking. She had a couple of interviews this week."

"Three," I said, adding the Taffy House to my tally and shooting her a dirty look.

"No, no callbacks yet, but we're crossing our fingers."

I took a bite of chocolate, wishing she'd shut up, or move to another room. I could barely hear the television.

"You're kidding!" she suddenly shrieked. "That's crazy, but it might be crazy enough to work." She grinned and gave me a thumbs-up.

I pressed the mute button. "What?"

She covered the mouthpiece with her hand. "Michael knows someone, who knows someone, whose brother will run you over for two hundred bucks!"

Jesus Christ.

"*Run me over?* Am I supposed to be happy about that?"

She listened for a moment before speaking again. "Oh, it's a cash-only deal." She sounded disappointed.

"Am I missing something?"

"Just a second." She listened again.

"Why would I pay somebody two hundred dollars to *run me over*?"

"For the insurance," she whispered.

"What insurance?"

"Just a second, Michael." She covered the mouthpiece and sighed with exasperation. "*Car insurance,* dummy. If someone hits you, you can sue for all kinds of stuff: injury, emotional distress, loss of income." She paused. "No, I guess income wouldn't apply."

"Thanks for the reminder," I snapped.

"Michael says it'll solve all your money problems."

What exactly did Michael know about my money problems? "Pardon my stupidity, but won't I get hurt?"

"No, no. He'll just knock you over. You'll have a sprain or, at worst, a broken limb. Nothing major."

"Very tempting," I scoffed. "Are you honestly suggesting I do this?"

"Let me get his number, Michael."

"Why would anyone offer to be sued?" I asked. The scheme didn't make sense. "His premiums will skyrocket if I take him to court. Two hundred bucks won't cover his expenses."

"Just a second, babe." She turned to me. "I don't know every last detail, Jody."

"Wouldn't there be a police investigation of the accident?"

"I don't know," she hissed.

"That's *fraud,* Erin."

"He's just trying to help."

"Some help. I don't think the Superfriends would be too impressed with his plan."

"Jody!" She clamped her hand over the phone.

"That kind of scandal could rock the Halls of Justice."

"Shh!"

"What if they take away his Bat Signal?"

Her knuckles whitened as her grip tightened on the receiver. "Shh! He doesn't know!"

"What? That he's Batman?"

"No." Her jaw clenched. "He doesn't know *you know* he's Batman."

"Just tell him thanks a lot for thinking of me. I mean, it's not every day that someone offers to do me bodily harm for profit."

She ended the call and stood in front of me, hands on hips. "Why did you have to say all that shit?"

"Why did you tell him the details of my finances?"

"Jody."

"And since you're so concerned about my income, I'll have you know I was already planning to pay you *rent.*"

"Don't worry about paying me. I just want to see you get on your feet."

"By knocking me off them with some asshole's car? Don't worry, I'll get you your cash."

"Look, I know money is tight. You don't have to pay rent."

"It's okay, Erin. I'm picking up my check today." I pressed the mute button and the sound returned. A harried mother was about to confront her out-of-control daughter. I'd missed the backstory but figured I could catch up.

Erin moved in front of the TV, blocking my view. "Jody."

"Could you move over to the right a bit? This is about to get good."

She didn't move, but glared at me.

"What?" I shrugged.

"When are you going to pick up the check?" Hostility filled the room.

"Today." I tried to peer around her, but she moved to obstruct my view.

"*When* today?"

"Now, I guess," I muttered, rising from the couch for the first time in hours. I tried not to wince at the pain of my leg cramps.

"You might consider showering before you go down there," she said, as though unemployment had drained my common sense. *Of course* I was planning to shower. I just hadn't gotten around to it.

When I stepped out of the washroom, clean and refreshed, I could hear her on the phone again.

"I can't wait to see you tonight, Bruce Wayne."

"Great, another night of Bat Sex," I mumbled.

"No," she continued, "Jody didn't say anything about it. I hid your flashlight and the mask. She doesn't know."

I dressed quickly and grabbed my knapsack, heading for the door. As I crossed the living room, Erin scowled and pointed at the mess I'd left on the coffee table.

"I'll clean it up later," I whispered as I made a fast exit, wondering who would turn against me next.

fourteen

I entered the Galley expecting everyone to turn and stare, to point their fingers at failure and laugh their asses off. Instead, Katie gave me a quick wave as she poured coffee for a couple of guys at table nine and Max and Jaundice gave me a joint salute from the counter.

I made my way through a jumbled maze of chairs, amazed at how busy the place was. There was no sign of Dean, and I didn't feel quite right about going back into the kitchen as an ex-employee, so I sat on a stool beside Max to wait. The sounds and smells of the Galley were all the same, but it was strange to view the restaurant from a customer's perspective. I felt like an alien.

"I didn't think you'd ever come back," Max said with a smile.

"I'm just here for my check."

"Hey, you don't owe us an explanation," Jaundice said. "It's just nice to see you."

"Thanks, I—"

"I've had the worst service of my life in the past week," Max barked. "When do you start?"

"I just told you, I'm here for my check."

He frowned. "That's just like your generation. All you punks care about is the money." He stirred his coffee with a fork handle. "Look at this. I don't even have a goddamn *spoon.*"

"Last time I saw you, you were complaining that you had no fork."

"You wait and see what it's like when you're old and feeble."

"Some great mind once told me that sour grapes make whine," I said pointedly. "Have you guys seen Dean?"

"He's talking to the fire chief in the back office." Jaundice slurped his coffee.

"What happened?"

"That dishwasher kid was on fry duty," he explained.

"You can bet your ass it won't happen again." Max chuckled. "Nothing like a grease fire to perk things up."

"Everyone's fine," Jaundice assured me.

Katie was busy taking an order and I couldn't see any other employees.

"Is anyone else back there?" I asked, hoping someone could snag the check for me.

"*Everyone*'s in the back, dammit," Max grumbled. "And my coffee's colder than a witch's tit."

"Watch your mouth," Jaundice said, cringing. "And how cold is that, anyway?"

"You tell me. You were married to one."

"Are you trying to start something?"

"If I was, you wouldn't be able to finish it."

"Try me," Jaundice growled.

"Hey, guys. Calm down," I said, leaving my stool and stepping behind the counter for the coffeepot.

The napkin dispensers looked like they hadn't been cleaned since I left, and all the sugar and sweetener packets were dumped in one bucket. *Sheesh.* Someone would have to waste time sorting and separating them. Malt vinegar was spilled on the shelves below the counter in a wide, dark puddle that reached toward the coffee filters. It was a small-scale disaster area.

I scanned the chaos of the dining room as a girl I assumed was

Dean's niece emerged from the kitchen with a full tray of chowders. The place was understaffed with only two on the floor, and while almost all of the tables were filled, the empty ones needed clearing.

As soon as I refilled Max's coffee, Melanie Walker lifted her cup to indicate she needed more, as well. I warmed her mug and made a quick trip around the room to take care of anyone else in need. It was the least I could do to help out.

"Thanks, Jody," Katie said. "This rush started about two hours ago and hasn't let up."

When I returned the pot to the coffee machine, I saw the empty decaf sitting on the burner, violating the most explosive rule of waitressing. I cleaned it out, started a new batch, wiped the front counter with a wet cloth, and attempted to return to my seat.

"Hey," Max said. "Could you grab me a—"

"Fruit crumble? Hold on."

"Hot damn! You're like a computer—" He began his stale routine.

"Not anymore, Max," I warned him. After cutting a slice, I snatched an order pad from the second shelf and wrote a receipt, knowing how picky Dean was about keeping track of everything. I wrote the item and price on the first line, initialing the box on the bottom corner as I'd always done.

"Jody, can we get some napkins over here?" Jake Miller called from the corner booth. "This thing's empty." He waved the dispenser in the air, as if I needed proof.

"Just a second." I found a package under the counter, then filled Jake's and a couple of others that looked to be nearing their ends.

"Miss?" an elderly woman said. "I ordered a fish sandwich with no mayonnaise, but look what I got." She lifted her sesame bun, exposing an ocean of mayo.

"I'm sorry about that, ma'am." I took her plate. "I'll be right back with a fresh one."

When I walked into the kitchen, I collided with Katie, and her small bowl of gravy coated my pants in a hot, brown smear.

"Shit. I'm sorry, Jode."

"No problem." I sighed, handing the plate to Todd, my favorite cook. "Nix the mayo."

There was no sign of the dishwasher, and I could see that Dean's microscopic office was crowded with people. My check would have to wait.

"I haven't seen you for a few days," Todd said. "Been on vacation?"

"No, I—"

"Because this whole fucking place fell apart without you." Hired four years earlier, Todd had seen his fair share of busy shifts.

"It did?" I felt a twinge of pride.

"Yeah. You should have seen it last night."

"Bad?"

"The worst. Man, I'm glad you're back." He dropped a wire basket in the vat, where it began to sizzle.

I didn't bother telling him I'd quit, but tied a clean apron around my waist instead. It wouldn't kill me to help them through a rush, and the tips were more than welcome.

Rather than taking over tables immediately, I cleared and cleaned, wiping the booths down with a warm cloth and refilling every condiment bottle I could get my hands on. Several people welcomed me back, thinking I'd been sick or on vacation. For some reason, I didn't tell them the truth, either.

I overheard Kevin Fielder dumping Carrie Holt over a couple of chocolate shakes, then watched her leave in tears. Barbara

Philips told me that Hannah and David Baxter had been in a huge fight at Mallard Park that morning and a couple of tourists had stopped to watch. Convinced the argument was a performance piece, they'd tossed spare change and a couple of bills at the couple, who, for an encore, fought over how to split the money. Katie informed me that Dean had fired the last fry cook for eating frozen peas and carrots straight from the freezer, mostly because it gave the rest of the staff the creeps. That explained why the dishwasher was pulled from the pit to cook and almost burned the place down.

As I listened to the news, I felt like I'd been gone for months. I didn't know there'd been a motorcycle accident on Old Marine Highway two days earlier, or that Jack Hanlow won over twelve thousand dollars on a slot machine in Reno. I hadn't heard a breath of gossip for days, and it filled my ears like a sweet symphony. I couldn't believe it, but I'd kind of *missed* the Galley.

When the dining room was relatively clean, I started serving tables. I'd missed the sound of clinking coins and the feel of crumpled bills in my hand. The two other girls and I worked like a real team, dodging around each other with hot food and dirty plates. We laughed and joked about customers while we waited for Todd to produce our orders, and I felt like part of something again. I didn't realize how lonely I'd been since I walked out.

Gradually the crowd died down to a dozen or so, and I stopped to take a breather with my two best customers and a pot of Earl Grey.

"How's P.J.?" I asked, thinking of his Bobby Orr repetition.

"I don't know," Jaundice murmured.

"He's still at Whispering Pines?"

"Nah. We picked him up yesterday morning and took him home." He scratched the bridge of his nose with a spindly finger, leaving his glasses askew.

"Well, he must be okay if they let him out," I reasoned.

"Sure, he's okay." Jaundice nodded. "He's just *different.*"

"Newer players," Max said, adding sugar to his coffee.

"What do you mean?"

"He's listing younger guys, like Kariya and Courtnall," Jaundice explained.

"What's wrong with that?" I was genuinely baffled by their concern.

"Skipping decades like that." Jaundice shook his head slowly. "It's not *wrong,* just different."

"I wouldn't worry about it," I said, with what I hoped was reassurance.

"When he's not listing players, he hums," Max said. "That's new. His hands shake a little, too."

"Something went wrong in there," Jaundice said, staring at his empty plate.

When Dean finally appeared in the cook's window, I made my way to the kitchen.

"Jody, how are you doing?" he asked, when I reached him. His white T-shirt was smoke stained and he looked exhausted.

"Fine, I guess." I shrugged.

"Thanks a lot for helping out front." He paused. "Have you found a new job yet?"

I was tempted to lie, but there was no point. As Dean leaned against the fridge, eating a tomato sandwich, I told him how disastrous the past few days had been. He listened carefully, chewing, swallowing, and waiting for me to finish complaining.

"So I was hoping I could get my check."

"No problem." He led me into the office and pulled out a stool for me.

I wasn't inclined to stay, but apparently it wasn't my choice.

Dean sat facing me, our knees almost touching in the cramped space.

"Before I give you the money and you dash out of here, I want to ask what you plan to do with your life."

I tried to ignore the blob of mayonnaise clinging to his chin like a tiny yet tenacious mountain climber.

"I have no idea." What difference did it make?

"Are you thinking about anything in particular?"

"Not really." The mayo was distracting. "Dean, you've got some stuff right here." I pointed to the approximate spot on my own chin.

He wiped the back of his hand across his face and missed it entirely. "There isn't a field that grabs your attention?"

"It's still there. It's, uh . . ." I pointed.

He took another swipe and just missed it again. "Maybe talking to a career counselor would help."

"Just a little more to the left. Your left."

"Jody, I'm trying to *talk* to you."

"I know, and I'm listening, but that mayo's getting on my nerves."

He grabbed a napkin and violently scrubbed his face. "Can we move on, now?"

"Uh, sure." *Why is he so touchy?*

"What about school?"

"What about it?"

He sighed with exasperation. "Do you want to go?"

"I don't know."

"Look, I'm asking what you plan to do because you can't come back here."

"Come back?" I laughed. "I'm just here to pick up my—"

"I saw you working out there, Jody. I know you really enjoy it."

"Well, I've missed it, but—"

"What I'm trying to tell you is I'm selling the place."

My heart stopped. "What?"

"I'm not a young guy anymore, and I've got family stuff going on. I have my mother's medical bills to take care of—"

"Dean."

"I don't want your sympathy, Jody. I just needed to warn you that this place can't be your safety net anymore. The guy who plans to buy it wants to use the space for a duplex."

"He's tearing it down?" I gasped. True, I'd been afraid I'd return to the Galley and slip back into my old life without experiencing anything new, but knowing the restaurant was closing almost brought tears to my eyes.

"I know," he said, patting my shoulder.

"What are your customers going to do?"

"There are other restaurants."

"Not like *this,*" I told him. "I can't believe you're selling."

"Hey, it had to happen sometime. To be honest with you, the thought of early retirement doesn't turn my stomach."

"I'm happy for you in that sense, but . . . *shit,* I really care about this place."

"Me too, but the Galley's days are numbered." He reached for a stack of envelopes. "I haven't told anyone else about this, and I'd appreciate it if you'd let me break the news in my own time."

"Sure." I shrugged, my shoulders almost too heavy to lift.

"Now, let's see here," he said, flipping through the envelopes. "Your check wasn't very big, since you left midweek, so I put a little extra in there. Kind of a bonus."

"You didn't have to do that."

"I wanted to. And I wanted to share something with you before you go."

Despite his depressing news, I cracked a smile in anticipation. In the seven years I'd known him, he'd never told me any Makah stories. He was a very private guy, but I'd always hoped he'd enlighten me one day on some magical, spiritual level. I hoped for a piece of tribal wisdom, a story or myth handed down from one generation to the next to illuminate the larger life picture.

He leaned over and pulled open the bottom drawer of his filing cabinet. After a moment or two of digging around, he produced a battered photo album and handed it to me.

"What's this?"

"Open it up. It'll make you feel a hundred percent better."

I lifted the cover, expecting some childhood black-and-whites of my boss and his family. Instead, the first page was covered with yellowed newspaper clippings. It took me a moment to realize that the clippings were comic strips. All *Ziggy* comic strips. I flipped to the next page, then the next, and discovered the whole book was filled with the same goofy little boob and his moronic thoughts of rainbows and sunny days. I loathed Ziggy and all the idealistic crap he stood for.

"You, uh . . . *collect* these?"

"Read them, Jody."

"Are you serious?" One look in his eyes and I knew he was.

"It's like life affirmation," he said.

"It's like a lobotomy," I muttered.

"Say what you will, but let me ask you, which one of us is always down in the dumps?"

"Me, but—"

"Exactly. You know, you can't waste your life, Jody."

"I'm not wasting it."

"You have to do something, *aspire,* set goals."

"I don't have time for goals," I snapped.

"And stop pissing and moaning like that."

"Truly inspiring words, Dean. Pissing and moaning. Did you get that from *Family Circus*?"

"Just give Ziggy a chance," he said quietly.

I wanted to tell him that Ziggy could kiss my flat ass, but shoved the book under my arm instead.

"I need it back, when you're ready," he said. "It's a loan, not a gift."

"Much appreciated," I said grimly. So much for the legends of the Makah.

I said goodbye to Todd as I passed through the kitchen and waved at Katie on my way to the front door. If nothing else, I had money in my pocket and wouldn't have to pick the scab off my wounded savings account.

"See you around, kiddo," Jaundice called from the counter.

"Not if I see you first," I teased halfheartedly.

"So you're serious about this quitting nonsense," Max said. "You're going to leave us with crappy service and lukewarm coffee."

"Not for long," I mumbled, too low for him to hear, and waved goodbye.

Max returned the gesture with a twist; only the middle finger was used. Apparently he had enough room in his pockets to carry a grudge.

As I passed the corner booth, Marty McDade was leering at me. I hadn't seen him come in.

"I guess congratulations are in order." He rested his fat fingers on his belly.

"Congratulations?"

"The wedding."

"Oh, yeah." I smiled with relief. "Always the bridesmaid . . ."

"Best wishes to you." There was something odd in his tone.

"I think best wishes are supposed to go to the bride," I said, with false cheer.

"I know." He laughed. "Best wishes, Jody."

I wrinkled my nose. "I'm not the—"

"We don't have a lot of room, but Lucas says you two lovebirds will be just fine in the basement."

"What?"

"And welcome to the family, of course. I know we're gonna get real close." He snickered.

I dashed out of the restaurant and into the street, hoping to be struck by a bus, knowing full well that, with my luck, it wouldn't have finished me off.

fifteen

Instead of being struck down by traffic, I ran into Hannah Baxter, which was infinitely worse. She grinned at me and I noted, with great relief, that her children weren't with her.

"Jody! *Oh, my God.* I've been looking all over for you!"

"Where did you look?" How hard could it be to track me down in the booming metropolis of Bent Harbor?

"Erin's place. But you weren't there."

"Quite a thorough search," I murmured.

She didn't hear me, mainly because she wasn't listening. "I've found the most gorgeous invitations at Occasions and I want you to take a look."

"Oh, Hannah. I'd *really* like to." I lied through my teeth. "But I need to get to the bank before they close, and then I've got to get home."

"It's almost seven, Jody. The bank's closed."

As was my window of opportunity.

"I just can't do it tonight," I told her. If only my plans went beyond terminating my fictional engagement to Lucas McDade.

"But you're my maid of honor." Her grin melted into a quivering frown.

"*Maid of honor?* No, I'm . . . I thought I was just a bridesmaid."

Hannah shook her head and gazed at me with rapidly misting eyes. "Maid of honor."

"I'm sure you said I was only a . . ." The tears were looming. I tried another tack. "You don't want my input on the invitations, Hannah." I'd be too tempted to call it a re-re-remarriage.

"But—"

"What I mean is you did *such* a lovely job with all of your, uh . . . other invitations, that I really do consider you an expert."

"Oh, thank you!" she squeaked.

"I think my poor taste would only get in the way. I have no eye for color, and—"

"Say no more, Jody. I see what you're wearing, and you're right. I'm probably better off on my own."

"Great," I said, backing away from her.

She stopped me with a hand on my sleeve. "I haven't heard anything from you about the reunion," she accused.

"Oh, I don't think I'm going to go." Actually, I *knew* I wasn't.

"Oh, you've got to, Jody. Everyone will be there."

"That's the problem."

"It'll be *fun.* I mean, how often does an opportunity to see your graduating class come up?"

"Uh, every ten years, apparently."

"Jody." She rolled her eyes. "Why don't you want to go?"

"I'm just not in a good place right now."

"Oh, yeah." She frowned. "I forgot you're unemployed. How's the job hunt?"

"Well, I don't have one, if that's any indication."

Her eyes widened and she gasped, "Oh, oh, oh, I saw an ad in Wednesday's paper for something here in town. Now what was it?" She closed her eyes to think.

Typical. I'd spent Wednesday moping instead of scanning the paper. "Hannah?" I prompted, watching her eyelids flicker with the effort to remember.

"Got it!" she sang triumphantly. "It was a waitressing position at Dean's Ocean Galley."

Dear God.

"That was *my* job," I said, sighing.

"Oops. Well, I'll keep my ears open."

Hannah and I finally said our goodbyes, and I started to trudge back to Erin's, when an orange Dodge Dart pulled up next to me. It was Josh's girlfriend, Muffin Zone Amy, offering me a ride I gladly accepted. The footwell was filled with crumpled muffin bags and tiny margarine containers.

"Want a wheat germ special?" She pointed to a full bag on the back seat. "They're zucchini."

"I'm not so keen on vegetables masquerading as desserts."

"It's a breakfast food."

"Same difference." I shrugged. "No, thanks."

"Could you pass me one?"

I handed her a muffin and noticed her eyes were puffy from crying. She wasn't the most attractive girl to begin with; her hazel eyes always looked stunned and her limp, dirty-blond hair was in need of either a blow-dryer, a curling iron, or a hat.

My life was already a soap opera during sweeps week, and the last two things I needed were drama and tears, but I felt sorry for her. Against every instinct I possessed, I asked her if something was wrong.

She responded by shaking her head and ripping the top off her muffin, chewing listlessly.

I waited for her to swallow and asked her again.

"Yeah, I guess you could say there's something wrong. It's your brother."

"Great." More of Josh's problems. "What did he do?"

"I don't think I should say," she sniffed.

"I understand," I murmured, hoping she couldn't detect my relief. I'd done my duty by asking, and I wasn't about to pry, so I was off the hook. There was no need to get involved.

"I think he's selling dope again."

Shit.

Why did she have to open her stupid, muffin-packed mouth? I felt a sharp pain in my forehead and knew I was on my way to a migraine. Details meant getting involved, and I didn't want to be put in the position of deciding whether to tell my parents, confront my brother, or wait until the dumbass got busted. Once Mom and Dad found out Josh was screwing up again, it would ruin everything for both of us. It was a classic case of guilt by association.

"Is that right?" I asked disinterestedly, hoping she'd drop the subject.

"Yeah. I told him I'd leave if he ever started again."

"Good idea." I stared out the window. Too bad *I* couldn't leave him.

"I can't believe he'd risk everything we have for a few measly bucks." Her lip trembled as she spoke.

Everything they had appeared to be casual sex and a love of baked goods. *Is it really so much to lose?* "How long have you been together, anyway?"

"Tomorrow's our five-week anniversary!" she wailed, steering the car to the curb and cutting the engine.

The convenience of a ride wasn't worth the hassle.

"You know, Amy," I said, "after he was caught the last time, he swore he would never do it again. I know it doesn't sound like much, but I'm sure he has more sense than you think." I wanted it to be true. *Desperately.*

"But I saw him." The tears streamed down her face, and all I could find to give her was the greasy napkin from her muffin bag.

"Saw him what?" Why was I letting myself get sucked in?

"When he came over a couple of nights ago—" She choked on a sob, then shoved a chunk of wheat germ special into her mouth while I mentally reviewed the steps of the Heimlich maneuver.

"Yes?" I waited to hear about the bags and small bills.

"He was covered in—"

Dirt? Maybe he was growing the plants outside this time. That little bastard *was* doing it again!

"—bruises," she finished, and my thoughts ground to a halt.

"Bruises?"

"Yeah, all over his chest. Someone had beaten him up, Jody. And why would anyone do that?"

Because their father forced them and they were anxious for a pork roast dinner. I cringed, visualizing my own rapidly yellowing bruises. "What did he say about the bruises?"

"He wouldn't tell me anything."

"Hmmm. Was there any other evidence?"

"No." She paused to sniffle. "I just can't believe he's doing it again. I mean, I *love* him, Jody."

I was getting awfully sick of that word. "Listen, Amy, the bruises were my fault."

"Huh?"

"Josh and I were boxing at my parents' place the other night and I gave him those bruises."

There was a long moment of silence before she spoke, and when she did, her voice shook. "I would have expected more from you. You're his *sister.*"

"What?"

"Why are you covering for him?" Her red-rimmed eyes were filled with disgust.

I explained Dad's rules, the sandbox, the gloves, the audience, and the adrenaline rush, but when I'd finished, Amy started the car without a word.

"What's wrong?" I asked as we rocketed through town.

She didn't answer, so I directed her to Erin's place. When she pulled over and I reached to open my door, she said, "I can't believe you'd sit here and feed me a bunch of bullshit."

"It's *not* bullshit. Josh was probably embarrassed to tell you the truth. He's a guy, Amy. Guys don't like to admit their sisters can beat them up." It seemed like a fair assumption.

"Why are you lying?"

"Why would I make that up?"

"I have no idea, because it's one of the dumbest things I've ever heard. You must think I'm a total idiot, Jody. I mean, what kind of a fucked-up family settles arguments by boxing in the backyard?"

"Mine," I said, growing weary of trying to convince her.

I exited the car and closed the door. As I leaned over to thank her for the lift, she peeled down the street before I could open my mouth.

"Not my problem," I muttered, washing my hands of the whole mess. Josh could deal with her.

I climbed the front steps, exhausted by the day's events. I had enough crap on my plate; I didn't need a side order of everyone else's problems.

I trudged into the living room, prepared to curl up on the couch with my new best friend, the remote. It was time to drown my sorrows in catchy theme songs and dramatic, cliff-hanging episodes. TV was all I had left and, the way things were going, Erin's couch would be my final resting place.

"Jody?"

I spun around and saw a man sitting on the couch. I didn't recognize his face, but I knew exactly who he was. He wasn't as slight as he'd looked by moonlight, but clothing probably added mass. The inevitable moment had come; I was face-to-face with Batman.

"Uh, hi," I said, somewhat disarmed by his appearance. Erin normally chased blonds.

Batman had the kind of hair that always looked casually mussed and intensely appealing. It was short, dark, and cut close over the ears. His pale blue eyes had a comforting familiarity about them that bred confidence, but it was the lips that really caught my attention. They were pink, damp, and smiling.

It's not fair.

Erin had sampled every male from Bent Harbor to Fillington, and beyond. She'd had her fun and frolic, never giving a damn about their feelings, always certain there was another man around the next corner. The fact that her last turn had provided her with this perfect specimen was enough to make me sick. For those broad shoulders and the thick-fingered hands resting on his knees, even *I* would have tolerated the superhero fetish. *It's not fair.* He wore work boots, jeans, and a chamois shirt, softened with age and ragged at the collar. I *loved* chamois shirts. He smelled like pine. He had a cleft in his chin. His eyes *twinkled,* for Christ's sake.

It's not fair!

I didn't want to squeeze in next to him on the couch, and the rocking chair wasn't as sturdy as it had been in Gammy's day, which left the dreaded beanbag chair. I lowered myself into it as gracefully as I could, wincing as one of its many holes widened and a fresh stream of pellets poured onto the hardwood floor. I felt the heat of embarrassment flush my cheeks, then burn as I remembered the brown smear of dried gravy on my pants.

I had no idea how to address the topic of our previous encounter, so I decided to pretend it had never happened.

"Wow," he said, in a warm, husky voice. "You look better."

My head snapped up in shock. "Is that right?" I asked through gritted teeth.

"Yeah. A lot better." He smiled as though it weren't an insult, exposing slightly crooked but exceptionally white teeth.

Jackass.

I tried to smile. "Thank you. Where's Erin?"

"Getting changed." He paused. "Which is good, because it gives us a couple of minutes alone."

"What? Why do *we* need time alone?"

"I haven't been able to come by and see you."

"Why?" *Come by and see me?*

"I've been spending most of my time in Fillington."

"That wasn't what I—"

"I'm not getting enough action here, which is a shame."

"That's funny," I stammered, shocked by his bluntness. "There seems to be plenty of action here." *Whenever I'm trying to sleep.*

"Not enough to keep me busy."

"That's rich." What was he trying to prove, that he was some kind of industrial-strength Casanova?

"I'm serious. Some of the older women here in town won't give me a chance."

"What?"

He shook his head. "They don't understand that it's more than spreading seeds."

I squirmed in my chair, causing another dribble of pellets. Where the *hell* was Erin?

"I mean, it's a dirty job, but—"

"Somebody's got to do it?" I snapped. "Give me a break."

"What's wrong?" His eyes met mine and I damned the twinge of interest that fluttered in my stomach.

"Maybe we should get Erin in here," I snapped. "I'm pretty sure she'd like to hear this."

"Hey, Jody, slow down. Maybe we can include Erin later on, but right now, there are some things I want to keep between you and me."

"You son of a bitch!" It was bad enough I'd heard him suggesting a threesome on the night of kitchen sex, but to make a move while Erin was mere yards away was lower than I'd expect anyone to go.

"What?" His eyebrows furrowed with confusion.

"I can't believe this!" I struggled to get out of the beanbag chair, flailing around and eventually giving up. "I've been listening to her carry on about you for days, and now you want to treat her like shit?"

"Jody—"

"She's in *love* with you, asshole, and for the life of me, I can't figure out why. It sure as hell isn't that weak little number between your legs because I've seen it, and believe me, it's no great shakes!"

"But I—"

"Hold on there, crackerjack, I haven't even mentioned the lame-ass superhero thing." It was my big chance to address the real problem. I took a breath before continuing, but before I could say another word, I was interrupted.

"What are you doing?" Erin asked, and I turned to see her leaning in the doorway.

"I'm giving this reptile a piece of my mind." I was defending what little honor she had, as a matter of fact. She was lucky to have a friend like me. Some women would have looked at her hunk and a half of boyfriend, and jumped at his offer of "action."

"Do you know who this is?" she asked.

"Of course I do, it's—" I stopped when I saw her twisted smile.

"Who is it?" she asked, a sadistic gleam in her eye.

Suddenly, I wasn't so sure. And if I wasn't sure, and the gorgeous, blushing guy on the couch wasn't Michael . . . what if I'd . . . and if I'd never seen . . . had I just called a complete stranger an *asshole*?

He cleared his throat. "I'm Justin McDade." He paused. "Lucas's brother."

"Lucas's brother," I murmured, swallowing hard.

"Lucas's brother!" Erin could barely contain her glee at my blunder.

"*Oh, my God.*" The eyes. They were the exact shade of Lucas's.

"Who did you think he was?" Erin smirked.

"It doesn't matter. It was a simple misunderstanding." In the midst of my tirade, had I insulted his *genitalia*?

"Come on, Jode. Tell me," Erin sang.

"Can't we just let it go?" I asked.

"Nope." She crossed her arms.

"Fine. I thought he was . . . Batman."

"Batman?" Justin asked, starting to laugh.

"You already met him," Erin said.

"Well, that was a long time ago—" Justin began.

"Not you," Erin interrupted. "Batman."

"It was dark," I explained.

"You met *Batman* in the dark?" Justin asked, clearly confused.

"No. I mean . . . yes, I met *Michael,* but only briefly and, like I said, it was dark."

"Who's Michael?" Justin asked.

"Batman," Erin and I said in unison.

"I give up." He shrugged and leaned back against the couch pillows.

"Why would you think *he* was Michael?" Erin asked, jerking her thumb in his direction.

"Because he was talking about his sexcapades—"

"*I was not!*" Justin interjected. "You two are nuts."

"You know." I turned toward him, feeling the blush creeping toward my hairline. "Getting action, spreading seeds, dirty job . . ."

His beautiful lips curled into a smile. "I just started a landscaping business."

"Oh." I gulped. My big mouth was taking no prisoners.

sixteen

Justin was gracious enough to look past both my false accusations and stupidity, but that didn't stop my apology marathon. Erin parked herself next to him on the couch, clearly prepared for a show.

"Could we maybe talk privately?" Justin asked.

While Erin's eyebrows rose to her hairline, I led him outside for a walk around the neighborhood.

"So," he asked, hands thrust deep in his pockets, "I *have* to ask what the Batman thing's about."

"I'm probably not supposed to mention it," I said, wincing.

"I think you've already crossed that line. Consider it mentioned."

"It's Erin's boyfriend, Michael," I told him. "Let's just say the guy's got a fetish."

"Enough said." He laughed. "You know, when I found out you and Erin were living together, I wasn't sure . . ."

"It's a temporary arrangement," I assured him. "We aren't a *duo.* For crying out loud, aren't women allowed to be roommates anymore?"

"What? I never thought . . . I was going to say, I wasn't sure of where to find you."

"Oh." I could almost taste the rubber soles of my Nikes as I warmed up for yet another apology.

"So," he said, "why are *you* so mad at *her* superhero?"

I haltingly explained that Michael and I'd met under nude circumstances. "When I thought you were him, and you said I looked better—"

"I meant better than in elementary school. You used to have that frizzy hair."

"I still do." I grimaced in the darkness.

"And you always wore those half-pants/half-shorts things."

"They're called *culottes,* Justin, and they happened to be *very* fashionable at the time."

"Aside from the fact that you were the only kid wearing them, of course."

"I'm surprised you remember something like that."

"I remember." He looked at me, then away again. "You were a grade younger, but the only girl who gave me Valentines."

I didn't mention that I gave them to *everyone,* suddenly feeling like a Valentine whore.

"It feels strange to be back here," he murmured.

"I guess it would. I bet the town looks a lot different."

Despite the economic downswing Bent Harbor couldn't seem to shake, the town was far from stagnant. I supposed either the rich stayed rich or got richer, and their architectural fantasies had come to life on the plateaus above the harbor. Beautiful homes already speckled the beaches and new construction moved closer to the sea every year.

There may not have been jobs, but there was certainly development. We had a new aquatic center with two high diving boards and a wave pool. City Council had built an elaborate salmon fountain in front of the courthouse, funded in part by Marty McDade, who hoped the attention would increase car sales. The population was growing, thanks to the Hannah Baxters of the town, who seemed to produce children as often as they did their taxes, and there was talk of building another elementary school. I was sure Justin couldn't help but be impressed by the changes.

"Nah, it all looks pretty much the same," he said. "The trees at Dad's place are taller, of course."

I tried not to take the lackluster response personally. He was only a kid when he left, and probably didn't remember much to begin with.

"Where did you and your mom go, anyway?" I asked, intrigued by the McDade mystique.

"All over the place. We started in Boston because she has a sister there and it was about as far from Dad as she could get."

I nodded emphatically. "One time zone wouldn't have been enough for me, either."

"What?"

"Oh, your dad and I don't really . . ."

"Same as everyone else"—he sighed—"myself included. Anyway, we gradually started moving west. Spent a couple of years just outside of Chicago, lived in Boulder for a while, then we hit the coast. We spent some time in San Francisco, and now I'm here."

"Wow, I've spent my whole life anchored to the harbor."

"Why didn't you leave?"

"I never wanted to," I answered. "So, what brought you back?"

"Family stuff. That's part of why I wanted to talk to you. I needed to thank you for being so good to Lucas."

I felt a blast of guilt. I wouldn't describe my treatment of his brother as *good.* "Uh, no problem."

Was Justin also under the impression that I was *marrying* Lucas? Did he know about the cement mixer? The love proclamations? How could I explain that our "relationship" was a one-sided obsession without sounding conceited?

"Mom and I were kind of worried about how he'd adapt to life without a solid schedule and rules, you know?"

"Yeah, I guess army life is pretty rigid. From what I've seen in movies, anyway."

Justin stopped under the streetlight and turned to stare at me. "He wasn't in the army, Jody."

"Navy, air force, it's all the same to me," I said, laughing.

"No, I mean, he never enlisted."

"But he told me he just got out."

"No, he just left an intense counseling program in Denver."

"What?"

He looked puzzled. "You haven't noticed his erratic behavior?"

"Uh, it's kind of hard to miss, Justin."

"Yeah, he gets pretty wired from time to time."

"Excited, you mean?"

"More manic, actually. He doesn't like the meds, so he doesn't take them, and the next thing you know, he's off and running with these crazy ideas."

I sifted through what he'd said, feeling a bit unsettled. "So, Lucas's obsession with me is actually—"

"A chemical imbalance," Justin finished.

"How flattering."

"You're disappointed," he said, frowning.

"No," I assured him. "Not disappointed, but I guess my ego's a little deflated."

"It shouldn't be," he said quickly, and in the glow of the streetlight, I could see he was blushing.

I felt the tickle of excitement in my stomach. "Oh."

"So." He cleared his throat. "My dad refuses to believe anything's wrong with him."

"With who?" I asked, mesmerized by the cleft in his chin.

"Lucas."

"Right, I'm sorry."

"So, Dad's seen all the records, but he had custody of Lucas when Mom and I left, and he doesn't want to think it's his fault."

"He must know it isn't." Even Marty wasn't that stupid.

"Like I said, as far as Dad's concerned, nothing's even wrong. He's hired Lucas to work at the dealership."

"Maybe being close to family will be good for him."

"Nope. Dad won't medicate him. He's supposed to be taking lithium, and I'm here because someone needs to take care of him."

"What about your mom?"

"She won't come back here." He didn't add anything further, and I didn't ask.

"If there's anything I can do to help . . ." I wasn't sure what I was volunteering to do.

"Thanks for the offer."

We walked in silence for a few minutes while the information sank in.

"So," Justin eventually said, "now that I've darkened your evening . . ."

"You haven't. I'm glad you told me."

"Well, I think that's enough of the McDade saga for one night." He smiled, and my breath caught in my throat. "Why don't you tell me what you've been doing for the past twenty years?"

We continued to walk, and I don't know whether it was his openness about Lucas, my own loneliness, or the dark of the night that made me do it, but I told Justin McDade about *everything.* I talked about things I'd never mentioned to Chris, or to Erin, while he listened attentively, never interrupting. He was easy to talk to, like a familiar stranger, and I shared the frustrations and heartache of the past week as though he were a fellow passenger on an airline, someone I'd never see again once the plane landed.

When I spoke at length about my unemployment and the cursed dip into my savings account, he was kind enough to suggest I work with him on landscaping.

"I thought you were the guy who isn't *getting enough* in Bent Harbor," I reminded him.

"That's right." He laughed.

"Thanks anyway, though."

"You don't want to go back to the Galley?"

"Dean's selling it." I almost teared up.

"No way! I love that place."

"Me, too," I said.

"So, the taffy place is a definite no, but did Wallace Enterprises ever call you back?"

"Nope. They hung me out to dry."

"Why don't you call them?"

"Because I never want to see that woman again. The jump-start kind of woke me from the dream."

"Maybe something came up and she couldn't call you."

"I doubt it. You didn't see the look on her face."

"You have to at least try," he said.

"No I don't."

"The squeaky wheel gets the grease."

"Good things come to those who wait," I countered.

"That might be true, but how long can you wait? How many bank withdrawals will it take?"

It was a hard hit, mainly because we'd arrived at Sitka Point, my fantasy neighborhood of the future. I didn't answer the question, but showed Justin the houses I'd spent years admiring. They were out of my price range, but that could all change if I didn't annihilate my savings and found a new job.

"I just want something that's my own, you know?" I murmured. "Relationships end, jobs end. A house is something I'll have control over, something that's *mine*."

"I know what you mean."

"I love that one, up in the trees," I said, pointing at my favorite house. It was two stories of gray shakes and white trim, surrounded by a garden I knew from years of spying would bloom into a Technicolor crowd of roses, irises, and patches of wildflowers.

"Nice landscaping." Justin said, eyeing the stone retaining wall and lattice fences shadowed by roving clematis.

"Big bucks." I sighed. "And they'll never sell anyway."

"You don't know that."

Despite his dysfunctional family, Justin talked as if there were no doubt everything would work out in the end. I wished I could feel the same way, and it made me realize how much time I'd spent bracing myself for life to kick me in the teeth. He was right about Wallace Enterprises. If I wanted a job, I needed to pursue it.

When we turned back toward Erin's house, I was equipped with a lovely new sense of calm.

We strolled and talked, and I took the opportunity to check him out a little more thoroughly. He didn't have his brother's frail build, or his dad's pear format, but a lean body a couple of inches taller than my own five foot eight. A perfect height differential for kissing.

"Lucas says your reunion is coming up. Are you going?"

"No way."

"Why not?"

"Because . . . I don't know. Because I don't have anything to show for the past ten years. I'm like a time capsule."

"Come on. Think positively."

"Well, I *do* have my health, which would be a real coup if this were our sixty-year reunion. Unfortunately, I don't think it will compare to the success of my classmates this year."

"They might be a bunch of heroin addicts," he said hopefully.

"In which case, I wouldn't want to spend an evening with them."

"What are you so worried about? Your problems seem pretty normal. I'm sure other people are feeling the same way."

"I doubt anyone else has lost everything in the past seven days. Maybe some of them have crappy jobs, but at least they're employed. And surely some will be single, but a bunch will be married."

"Do you want to be married?"

"Not right now."

He cleared his throat. "Would you be more comfortable if someone went with you?"

"I'm not going."

"Would you, if you had someone to go along?"

"Erin might go, but it just isn't the same."

"Jody." He sighed. "I'm asking if I could take you."

"Oh." *Could I be a little more obtuse?*

"Well?"

"I guess we could go together. As long as you don't mind." Arriving on the arm of Justin McDade might make the whole ordeal tolerable.

We reached Erin's and he walked me to the front door.

"Are you doing anything tomorrow night?" he asked.

"No." My heart pounded.

"Do you want to go for dinner and see a movie or something?"

"Do you mean, like a *date*?" I asked, feeling like a fool. *Date?* No one had used the word for at least decade. People *went out,* or *hooked up.*

"Yes, like a date," he said, chuckling softly.

"That sounds great." Better than great. Fantastic. Incredible. Unprecedented. *Terrifying.*

We agreed he'd pick me up at seven and I stood at the doorway for a moment, hoping for a kiss that didn't materialize, before we said good night. I nearly floated into the house.

A date.

I'd never really been on one before. Any relationships I'd had began with a group of friends going out together, which eventually morphed into a pairing off of sorts. Chris had never technically asked me out, but appeared at my house with a video rental and stayed for the evening. Our friendship blurred into coupledom after some drunken encounters and several nearly chaste sleepovers, and the next thing we knew, we were living together.

A date was a whole new ballgame.

"Well, well, well. She returns with a big smile," Erin said, when I entered the kitchen.

"It was a nice walk." I shrugged, wanting to keep the rest to myself.

"I guess so. You've been gone for two hours. Do I sense romance?"

"Maybe."

"You'll have to do better than that." She took a drag on her cigarette.

"We're going out tomorrow night."

"Aha! I *knew* it! You're a fast mover, Jody Rogers. Should I stay at Michael's so you have the place to yourself?"

"No!"

"Uh, that's right. You're not that kind of girl. *I am.*" She giggled. "So, what was the big secret?"

Justin hadn't sworn me to secrecy, but I told Erin about Lucas under the condition she not spread the information all over town.

"No shit?" she asked, when I was finished. "He's a nutjob?"

"No, he's just—"

"Clinically off?"

"Erin, come on. He's got some problems beyond his control."

"Is it hereditary?"

"I don't know. Why?"

"Well"—she took another drag—"if you and Justin are—"

"Going out for *dinner*? Talk about jumping the gun, or, in your case, the bones."

"If you two get serious, you might want to do some research."

"It isn't going to get serious," I assured her, hoping it wasn't true. "It's a one-time thing. Well, two actually."

"He's booking in advance?"

"He's taking me to the reunion."

"Interesting." She smiled.

"You're going, aren't you? You have to."

"Yeah, I'll be there. I wouldn't pass up the opportunity to see those losers try to outdo one another."

We stayed up for another hour, and when I finally went to bed, I had the best sleep of my week, thanks to Justin McDade.

In the morning, I took Justin's advice and called Wallace Enterprises. I asked to speak to Mrs. Wallace and was connected without hesitation, which seemed to be a good sign.

"This is Jody Rogers," I said, when I had her on the line. "You interviewed me the other day?"

"Oh, yes. That's right." The tone was hard to read, but at least she remembered me. Then again, the jump-start wasn't the sort of event one would forget.

"I hadn't heard from you, and you'd mentioned calling me back."

"I said we'd call if we were interested in a second interview."

"Right," I said eagerly.

"We didn't call you back."

Was it a question? "No, you didn't."

"Which means we aren't."

"Aren't?" If the conversation were any more cryptic, I'd need a decoder ring.

"We aren't interested in a second interview, Miss Rogers."

Ouch! "May I ask why not?" *As if I didn't know.*

"The fact that you broke my second toe when you lunged onto me isn't enough?"

"*Lunged?* Well, I kind of hoped you'd see that as the accident it was."

"And what about your doctored résumé?"

She had me there. "Oh, I uh—"

"I don't look kindly on liars, Miss Rogers. I called Dean's Ocean Galley to verify your employment history. You were a waitress, not an assistant manager. When I mentioned the discrepancy to your former employer, he actually had the nerve to try to lie for you."

"It wasn't a lie, but an embellishment."

"Please don't embarrass yourself any further. Good day, Miss Rogers."

seventeen

I was too excited about my evening with Justin to let the Wallace Enterprises disappointment bother me; too nervous about what to wear to worry about anything as insignificant as a job rejection. Erin had the day off and offered to help with an outfit.

"I should be paying you a consulting fee, or something," I told her.

"Try this on." She handed me a vinyl mini.

"Maybe I spoke too soon. He's taking me to *dinner,* not pimping me out."

"Then what about this?" She held up a flowing, flowery, ankle-length skirt.

"Is there a peasant blouse to go with that? Or maybe a Phish T-shirt?"

"Okay, I guess you aren't nouveau hippie."

"I'm not nouveau *anything.* I just want to look, you know, nice."

"So, this is a date?" she asked, watching me from behind the smoke of her umpteenth morning cigarette.

I nodded, dressing in a pair of khaki pants and a periwinkle blouse. "What do you think?"

"If the Gap was a restaurant, you'd be maître d'."

"If smoking was sexy, you'd be a porn star."

"You know I'm trying to quit," she growled, extinguishing it in an overflowing ashtray.

"Since when?"

"Since Michael." She blushed.

"So, what do you really think I should wear?" I asked.

"Something low cut. And you've got to step heavy, so your boobs jiggle."

"I'm serious," I whined.

"Too serious. Try that navy wrap skirt and cardigan."

When I added sandals and a silver pendant, it was perfect, which meant I was ready for my date a mere *eight hours* before it was due to begin.

She brewed a pot of Raspberry Raindrop tea and I flipped through the latest edition of the *Bent Harbor Times.* The Avon ad was still in there, along with the paper route, and there was a listing for a movie usher at the Starscope Theater. The Wallace Enterprise position I'd failed to get was also listed—in bold print.

"Maybe I should start my own business," I mumbled.

"Doing what?"

"I said *maybe.* I don't have an actual idea."

"In that case, maybe I should be an astronaut."

"Very funny."

"Justin has a business. Maybe he needs help."

"He offered me a job, but he was just being nice."

"You've got to hate that, right, Jode?" She rolled her eyes. "A guy that goes out of his way to be nice. I think he's a keeper."

"Let's not place any bets, just yet."

"It didn't take long for Michael and I to realize we had something," she said wistfully.

"Speaking of which, have you told him how you feel?"

"Not exactly."

As it turned out, she'd told him she loved his *shirt,* his *hair,* and his *hands,* thinking he'd be able to piece the clues together and figure out that she loved *him.* She sighed and told me her boyfriend was no Sherlock Holmes. Before I could attack her logic, the phone rang. Erin answered and passed the receiver to me, mouthing something a champion lip reader couldn't have deciphered. I took the call anyway.

It was Dean. "Your mom gave me your number. I'm sorry to bother you, but I've got a favor to ask."

"What's up?"

"Someone called, wanting a referral for you, and I think I screwed it up."

"You didn't," I assured him. "I'd already taken care of it by then."

"Oh, you got the job?" He sounded disappointed.

"Hell, no."

"If you'd warned me about the assistant manager thing, I might have been a bit smoother on the phone."

"Sorry I put you on the spot, Dean." I paused. "So, what's the favor?"

"I wouldn't ask if I wasn't desperate."

"What's wrong?"

"My niece was arrested in Tacoma last night, and I need to go take care of things."

I didn't ask what the charges were, considering how much I hated people nosing around in Josh's legal affairs. "I'm sorry."

"Can you watch over the Galley for the next few days?"

"Geez, Dean, I'm kind of in the middle of a job hunt." My exaggeration skills were getting stronger every day.

"You wouldn't have to wait tables, or anything. I just need you to check in on the place a couple of times a day to make sure everything is running smoothly. I'll pay you full wages, regardless of how much time you actually spend there."

"What happened to selling the place?"

"It's taking longer than expected. I *really* need your help."

I heard the desperation in his voice and felt the desperation in my wallet. "I'll do it."

"Thanks a million, Jody. You're a lifesaver. I'm leaving tomorrow morning and I'll be back in a couple of days. Three, tops."

"Don't worry about anything," I told him.

"By the way, have you looked over the Ziggy book yet?"

"I haven't had a chance."

"Just give it a shot, okay?"

I agreed, mainly to get him off my back, and when I hung up the phone, I told Erin what I'd agreed to do.

"Well, it's money, isn't it?"

"I suppose, but it'll slow down the job hunt a bit."

"I don't think that's possible, Jode."

We made egg salad sandwiches for lunch and flipped through Erin's stash of fashion magazines to kill time. We wasted part of the afternoon driving to the Fillington Safeway, where Erin could actually do her own shopping, and we stopped at the bank on the way home, where I cashed my check and made a mortgage contribution to my best friend. After a couple of errands she'd been putting off, we headed back.

We arrived at the house at six-thirty and sat at the table to wait. I couldn't stop tapping the tip of one sandal against the table leg and Erin showed remarkable restraint, although it must have driven her nuts.

Just before seven, we heard someone on the front steps.

"That's him." I choked, rising to smooth my skirt. "How do I look?"

"Same as you have all day. Nice."

"Are you sure? I can still change—"

"Just answer it, Jody." She grinned.

I walked toward the door, adjusting my hair and taking a deep breath before opening it. Instead of Justin McDade, Hannah Baxter stood on the doorstep with one of her children. Luckily, Erin hadn't been devastated by the demise of Gammy's vase, but I doubted she'd be pleased to see the Baxters back on site. I wasn't thrilled, myself.

"Hannah, hi," I said, peering over her shoulder to look for Justin.

"Jody, I'm so glad you're here. I've been running all over town trying to find fabric for the bridesmaids' dresses with no luck."

"I'm sorry, but I'm just on my way—"

"So I thought you could go to Fillington with me tonight."

"Tonight?"

"There's a shop in the SeaMist Mall that's open until eight."

"Actually, I have a—"

"You'll have to drive, of course. David has the car."

"How did you get here?"

"He dropped us off. Oh, and we've got to stop for some new underpants on the way. Someone's had an accident." She tickled the kid's chin and I suddenly caught a whiff of urine.

"I don't have a car," I said, delighted by the fact, for once.

"I'm sure Erin can loan us that little Honda. We've just got to get there tonight, because the woman I spoke to has barely enough silver lamé in stock for my order."

"She can't hold it for you?"

"She *won't*." Hannah's lower lip trembled and I knew I was in for another batch of waterworks.

"I'd really like to help, but I'm going out tonight."

"Jody, you're my maid of honor," she whimpered.

"If you'd given me some advance notice, I might have been able to work something out, but—"

"Where are you going? Can't you cancel?"

"No," I said firmly.

"But this is *important.*" Tears rested in the corners of her eyes, waiting to trickle at just the right moment.

"She has a date," Erin said, from behind me.

"A date?" The tears were sucked back in, forgotten in the face of hot gossip. "With who?"

I didn't want to tell her. Once she knew, it was only a matter of time until the whole town found out. "Just a guy."

"It's not Chris, is it? I was so mad when I saw him and your cousin on Valentine's Day, I could have screamed."

"Valentine's Day was *three months ago*!" I gasped. "Why didn't you tell me?"

"I thought you knew," Hannah said, looking confused.

"What?"

"Well"—she covered the kid's ears—"when David had that fling with Beth a couple of years ago, I knew all about it."

"Your husband and my cousin?"

"What a *slut,*" Erin said. "And coming from me, that's quite a statement."

"I'll say," Hannah agreed. "Anyway, I figured I might as well let him sow his wild oats, but it bothered me that everyone in town was talking about them. Just like Beth and Chris."

"People knew about them?" I asked, barely breathing.

"Not just people, Jody." She lifted her hands from the ears below her. *"Everyone."*

"I'm going to be sick."

"I didn't know," Erin murmured, as consolation. "If I had, I wouldn't have let you wander around town like some starry-eyed Pollyanna."

"Thanks."

"Playing the fool."

"Okay," I said.

"Totally oblivious to the fact that you were being cuckheld." She frowned. "Is that the right word?"

"It doesn't matter," I snapped. "The point is made."

"Don't feel too bad, Jody." Hannah rubbed her pregnant belly. "No one thought you were stupid. Just blind."

"That's very reassuring. Now, if you'll excuse me, I'll call you a cab home."

"I don't have any money."

"How were you planning to buy the dress fabric?"

"Layaway, I guess."

"I'll drive you home." Erin sighed.

At that moment, Justin pulled a red pickup into the driveway and I hurried down the steps to meet him. There was no reason to introduce the bride-to-be-again.

He looked even better than the night before. Granted, he probably hadn't been tarted up and twiddling his thumbs for eight hours like me, but his dark green shirt was tucked into his perfectly creased khakis. His belt matched his shoes and I was pretty sure he'd added some salon products to his carefully tousled hair.

"You look nice," he said.

"Thanks. So do you." I smiled as he opened the truck door for me. Definitely a first.

I heard Hannah's squawk of approval and cursed her under my breath.

"Sorry it's not the cleanest vehicle around," Justin said, as I waved out the window and we headed toward Fillington.

"It's fine," I told him, enjoying the sensation of towering above the rest of the traffic.

"I wasn't sure what kind of food you liked, but there's a place right on Simpson Bay that's supposed to be really good."

Actually there were *two* places right on the bay, and one was the Salty Beaver, a steakhouse commonly mistaken for a strip club. If I had to tell Erin I'd spent the evening at the Salty Beaver, she'd die laughing.

I held my breath as we pulled off Old Marine Highway, into the bay, and didn't release it until he parked in front of the Blue Heron. I'd never been there, but everyone raved about the menu.

Once we were seated in a cozy, candlelit booth, surrounded by cranberry-colored walls, a feeling of well-being swept over me. Not even a week had passed since the Chris fiasco, and I was already moving on to greener pastures. I glanced across the table. *Much greener.*

We started with salads, followed by grilled salmon, roasted potatoes, and asparagus. I barely noticed the other patrons, whose hushed tones and clinking silverware sounded faint and distant. I listened to the rise and fall of Justin's voice, watching his expressions change as he told stories from his post-Harbor childhood and beyond. It felt good to be with him, and I wanted the meal to last forever.

"So, did you call Wallace Enterprises?" he asked, as we waited for dessert to arrive.

"This afternoon." I nodded. "I didn't get the job."

"I'm sorry."

"So am I, but what can I do? I'll just keep looking."

"I guess you've been pounding the pavement."

"Not as much as I should have," I admitted. "Sometimes it seems hopeless."

"Don't worry. Something will come up."

If the words had come from Erin, Hannah Baxter, or any member of my family, I would have told them to shove it, but in the soft glow of that candlelight, I smiled and thanked Justin for his support.

After chocolate mousse rich enough to twist my tongue, we left the restaurant and climbed into the truck.

"What do you want to do now?" he asked.

Kiss you, I almost blurted.

The only show playing at the Starscope was a horror movie neither of us wanted to see, so we took the very long way home, enjoying the clear night skies. The back of his hand bumped my knee when he shifted gears, leaving the discovery of a new erogenous zone in its wake. The engine was too loud for us to talk, but the silence between us was satisfying.

When we pulled into Erin's driveway at the end of the night, her car was gone, which meant I had the house to myself. I wasn't prepared to say good night, but wasn't ready for the big invite, either.

I'd never made a first move in my life, so if there was going to be a kiss, he'd have to initiate it. He turned off the engine and we sat quietly, just like the night Lucas dropped me off, not that I wanted to think about the similarity.

"Thanks for the dinner," I said, in an unnaturally high voice I must have been saving for the moment. "It was really good." *Really good.* I was a regular wizard of words.

"I'm glad you liked it."

I waited for him to say more, but he didn't. Was he waiting for me to get out of the car? "That salmon was delicious. I'll have to take my parents there sometime." Why was I dragging my parents into it? It seemed he'd lost interest in me somewhere between the restaurant and home. Was it something I'd said?

"We'll have to go again," he murmured, and I breathed a sigh of relief.

"That would be nice."

"Yeah, it would."

The silence filled every inch of the truck, until Justin cleared his throat. "This is really awkward."

"Yes." I nodded. "Yes, it is."

"I wanted to kiss you good night, but—"

"But what?" I bleated.

"I wasn't sure if the timing was right."

"Well, this *is* the end of the night . . ."

In one deft movement, he unfastened his seat belt and leaned over to my side of the car. I took a quick breath before his lips were against mine, warm, firm, and inviting. His tongue stroked first the outside of my lip, then inside as I opened up to him. His damp breath mixed with my own as we tasted each other. He tenderly bit my lower lip and I did the same. He was an even better kisser than his brother, but I tried to forget the comparison as soon as I'd made it. The flesh of our mouths chased, caught, and caressed each other slowly, then with increasing urgency. Heat pulsed through my body and I was absolutely caught in the moment, thinking of nothing else. That is, until two words popped into my head and I choked on my own laughter.

"What?" Justin asked, pulling away from me.

"No! Nothing, it's nothing." I chuckled again, but leaned toward him, hoping to get lost in the kiss again.

"What's so funny?" He frowned. "Am I doing something wrong?"

"God, no! This is . . . wonderful."

"Then why are you laughing?"

"It's stupid." I leaned toward him, but his interest was piqued. *What on earth had made me think of it?* I giggled again.

"Tell me."

I didn't want to say the words aloud, but he looked rather wounded.

"Tongue hockey." I couldn't help laughing as I spoke.

"What?"

"You know, what we all used to call this before we actually did it. *Tongue hockey.*"

"*Very* romantic," Justin said dryly.

"Well, what were you thinking about?"

"How good you smell, and how soft your skin is."

"Oh." *What kind of an idiot am I?* "Sorry," I said, reaching for the door handle.

Justin touched my arm, shook his head and smiled. "What position am I?"

"What?"

"Tongue hockey. Am I a forward, defenseman, or what?"

By the time he walked me to the door and said a final good night, we'd played one hell of a game. It was a close but fully clothed match that included several hat tricks, instant replays, and one long, languid stretch of overtime.

I crawled into bed, grinning at the thought of a rematch.

eighteen

I awoke the next morning to the sound of the doorbell and rolled onto my stomach, waiting for Erin to answer it. I closed my eyes and tried to recapture a fading dream, starring a certain Justin McDade. Five minutes of uninterrupted sleep was all I needed, but it just wasn't meant to be.

The bell rang three more times and I reluctantly threw off my blankets and stumbled down the hallway, wishing for a peephole so I'd know what I was up against at such an ungodly hour. At the final chime, I swung the door open and found none other than Hannah Baxter on the front step. *Again.* I was beginning to think Erin should charge *her* rent for the amount of time she spent parked on the welcome mat.

"Jody! I'm glad I caught you. I thought we could check out that fabric this morning." She spoke through a distracting layer of glossy pink lipstick.

"What time is it?" I asked, rubbing the sleep from my eyes.

"Eight-thirty," she said matter-of-factly, as though it were a perfectly acceptable time to drop by, unannounced.

"Nothing's open." I wanted to crawl back into bed even more than I wanted to shove her down the stairs. And that was saying something.

Hannah rolled her eyes. "The shop is in *Fillington,* remember?

By the time you're dressed and we take off, they'll already be open."

Doesn't she have children to raise, or laundry to fold? "Erin's at work and I don't have a car."

"I do, though. I drove David to work this morning."

I couldn't decide whether she was insanely persistent, or frighteningly obtuse. Either way, the lines of communication were disconnected and swinging in the breeze.

"Listen, why don't you come back in an hour or so and I'll be ready?"

"Waiting doesn't bother me." She pushed past me and into the living room, where she flopped on the couch and pulled a magazine from a stack on the coffee table. "Don't mind me."

"Now *that* is a tall order," I muttered, heading for the bathroom.

After a quick shower, I scrambled into jeans and a T-shirt, hoping there was no bridesmaid dress code in effect. I ran my fingers through the curly masses of my hair and met Hannah in ten minutes flat.

"I forgot to ask how your date was last night," she said, glancing up from her magazine.

"It was good." I was determined to keep the details between Justin and myself. And probably Erin.

"Who was that guy?"

"Hmm?" I gazed out the window in an effort to avoid the question.

"Jody."

"It was Justin McDade," I said, sighing.

"You've got to be kidding!" She dropped her magazine onto the table and licked her lips. "He sure got the looks in that family. I wouldn't mind having a piece of his action."

"Spoken like a woman in love with her reintended," I said, just as the phone rang.

It was my mother, asking to meet for coffee. *Finally,* a break in the silent treatment. I didn't know what had prompted her to call, but it didn't matter. I was just happy to hear her voice. I told her about my plans with Hannah and offered to meet her in the afternoon.

"Tell her to come along," Hannah suggested, from the doorway.

"Is she sure?" Mom asked.

"The more, the merrier," I said, grateful to have support on the fabric hunt. If I couldn't talk Hannah out of at least some of her stupid ideas, perhaps my mother could.

Mom picked us up in her minivan and gushed over wedding plans as though it were Hannah's first time down the aisle. Their chatter about flowers, music, food, and gowns was engrossing enough that they never tried to include me. I was able to slip into my own thoughts as I watched the scenery stream past the window. Naturally, those thoughts drifted to Justin.

After my hellish week, it was invigorating to have something positive to focus on. I'd wanted to talk to him that morning, which added to my reluctance to partake in a fabric mission, but he was probably hustling from one lawn job to the next. I could call him when I returned from Fillington, or hope that he'd leave a message while I was gone. Either way, it was nice to have something to look forward to.

When we reached Fabric World, Hannah made a beeline for the far wall, where I could see the glitter of sequins beckoning us. Mom and I followed her trail and found her rifling through bolts of gold, silver, and bronze lamé with an expression of sheer bliss. I noticed with a smirk that whoever had painted Fabric World's signs had left off the accent, which meant we were shopping in the Lame Department. Somehow, it was fitting.

"Mrs. Rogers, I don't know if Jody told you about my plan for the dresses," Hannah said, rubbing material between her fingers.

"No. In fact, I didn't realize she was in the wedding party until this morning." She shot me a piercing look.

"I forgot to mention it," I muttered. Little did she know, I wasn't going to do it.

"I want the girls to wear replicas of my prom dress," Hannah said.

Mom actually nodded her approval.

"I want the three other girls in silver and my maid of honor, Jody, in gold. The dresses will be form-fitting and floor length, with mesh trains."

"That sounds lovely, dear." Mom patted some plush blue fabric with her fingertips. "I don't know when I've seen mesh used in a wedding before."

She said "mesh" in a way that made it sound not only acceptable, but *good,* like satin or silk. Apparently she'd be little help during the negotiations.

"Hannah," I said. "I'm worried that all of our, uh, *glitter* is going to take attention away from you. It's your big day, so you should be the shiny, I mean, shining one."

"Don't worry about me." She offered a gorgeous smile. "I found a dressmaker to design my dream gown. It'll be white, with alternating layers of silver and gold lamé, with a silver gauze veil and train. It's going to be perfect."

I was beginning to think Hannah could use a few days of rest at Whispering Pines, along with P.J. Hardison. Fourth attempt or otherwise, no bride should spend their wedding day looking like the Tin Man in drag.

Hannah had the pattern and all of the other girls' measurements, so Mom set to work on me with a tape measure while the bride collected the unnecessary materials and carried them to the cutting counter.

"Can you imagine how hideous we're going to look?" I whispered to Mom.

Hannah hadn't mentioned the names of my bridesmaid underlings, so I could only guess at the identities of the losers I'd be saddled with. I didn't know who the groomsmen were, either, but suspected I'd be spending time with the old varsity football team in the weeks to come. I had to find a way out of the mess, and *fast.*

"Well, it isn't my cup of tea, but maybe it won't be as bad as it sounds. At least it's a wedding." She sighed.

"Meaning what?"

"Oh, nothing, really." She bit her lower lip and measured my waist, marking the digits on a small notepad provided by the clerk.

"Just tell me."

She stopped what she was doing and gave me a hesitant look. "Do you *ever* think about getting married?"

"Mom."

"I wouldn't say anything to you normally, but it's a bit awkward for me at bridge night sometimes. Most of the women there have already married their daughters off and—"

"I'm not getting married for the sake of your bridge club!"

"That's not what I meant."

"A wedding requires a groom, anyway." I was already feeling secretive about Justin and Mom's interest in running me down the aisle worked as lip sealant.

"Well, let's not talk about Chris. I tried to set you up with a very nice man the other night, and you refused to make the effort." She reached behind me, set the tape measure below my shoulder blades, and pulled the ends together under my breasts.

"*Dad* didn't even like him."

"Your father could grow to like anyone." She marked down the measurement and ran the tape from my hip to heel.

"How's he doing?" I asked quietly.

"He's hurt, Jody."

"I hate this situation. I never meant to upset him."

"I know. Why don't you come for dinner tomorrow night so you two can patch things up."

I was anxious to make amends with Dad and promptly accepted the invitation to a paternal ambush.

"I'm sorry about Arocknids, too, Mom. I should have defended your idea."

"It's okay, honey." She stood with a smile and squeezed my shoulders.

We gave Hannah the notepad and waited as a clerk cut the fabric. I hoped my replacement would be close to my size.

"I figure it'll be a little over a hundred each for the material," Hannah announced. "And the dressmaker said she'd only charge seventy-five apiece to make them."

A hundred and seventy-five dollars! Paying for the dress hadn't crossed my mind. Hell, wedding number three didn't cost me a dime, but apparently the Baxters had to start cutting corners somewhere.

"One seventy-five, huh?" My voice shook.

"I know it's a bit pricey, but at least you girls can wear them again."

Was she kidding?

"I just need to zip to the bank," I said, throat suddenly dry. My stomach knotted at the thought of my damaged savings account. At least watching over the Galley meant money was on the way.

"I'll come with you," Mom said.

Once we were outside the shop, she offered to pay for half of the dress. "I thought you were going to pass out right there in the store. Your face lost all color in a matter of seconds."

"I just didn't realize I was paying for it. I don't even want to be in the wedding."

"Are you okay?"

"Yeah, just shocked."

"I meant financially. You've been working so long, your father and I assumed you had money to live on while you're between jobs."

"I do." I shrugged. "I mean, I have my savings account. I've been dipping into that."

"I'm glad to hear it. That's what a savings account is for. It's a safety net."

"Actually, I'd planned not to touch it until I buy a house."

"Well, that's a long way off, isn't it?"

"I've got quite a bit stashed away."

"I thought you wanted to live on Sitka Point."

I nodded.

"It's an expensive area." Her lips were pursed.

"Some of the smaller cottages are more affordable." I'd pored over the real estate listings in the Sunday paper for years.

"I think you'd better have a realtor take you out to see some of those cottages, Jody. You might be surprised at how little you get for your money."

"I'm sure I can find something."

"Whatever you say, dear. But take a good look."

The last thing I needed was someone dumping on my dream. "Okay, Mother."

"How's the job hunt going, anyway?"

"Fine."

"Have you had any interviews?"

"Three."

"Only three? You've been off work for over a week!"

"I know that."

"So, how did they go?"

"Well, I'm still unemployed."

"Are you *really* trying to find work?"

"Of course I am," I snapped.

"It's not a good time to be picky."

"As if I can afford to be picky! There are *no* jobs."

"Dean was a wonderful boss—"

"He's selling the Galley."

"Well, maybe you could—"

"Live there? It's going to be torn down and replaced with a duplex."

That stopped her cold.

By the time we reached the bank, I'd decided to pay for the dress myself. It was a matter of pride, and of principle. I wasn't some deadbeat loser, and I'd be damned if I'd let Mom pay for anything she could hold against me later.

When I handed over my cash, Hannah was keen to do more shopping, and we humored her for a couple of hours. By noon, I'd had quite enough of her company, so we dropped her at Erin's to pick up her car and Mom and I carried on to Pasta Haven for lunch.

We were seated in a back corner, perusing the menu, when Chloe Patterson and Sara Temple walked in. I hadn't seen them since graduation, and I'd liked it that way. They were senior cheerleaders and professional snobs. I hid behind my menu, praying they wouldn't see us.

"Isn't that Chloe?" Mom asked, peering at the women as they were led to their table.

"Affirmative." I slouched down as low as I could.

"I haven't seen her in *ages.* I wonder what brought her back to town."

"There's a ten-year reunion coming up." I rolled my eyes.

"Oh, how wonderful! Your father and I had such a great time at ours." She paused and squinted at me. "You *are* going, aren't you?"

"I guess so." Only because I would walk in on the arm of Justin McDade.

"Why don't you go over and say hello to those girls?"

"I'd rather eat larva."

"You can't say a simple hello?"

"We weren't friends."

"It doesn't matter anymore. It's been *ten years,* honey. Everything will have changed."

Before I had a chance to debate the point, Chloe spotted me and nudged Sara. I smiled tightly as they approached our table, looking as if they spent the majority of their time in tanning booths. The golden skin contrasted perfectly with their outfits; Chloe's off-white sweater set, and Sara's mauve silk blouse.

"Jody Rogers? I *thought* that was you," Chloe cooed artificially, looking me over with bright blue eyes. Her hair was still bleached blond, and she somehow managed to make dark roots look not only deliberate, but *stylish.* I could feel her gaze hovering on my T-shirt and jeans before roaming to my mop of hair and unmade face.

"You look the same as ever," Sara said. Her similarly bleached hair bounced with every syllable that slipped through her newly capped teeth. She was "Snaggletooth" in elementary school, but a ninth-grade growth spurt that propelled her breasts to a double D made all the boys forget her chops.

"So do you two." I strained to continue smiling.

"It's nice to see you, too, Mrs. Rogers," Sara said, while Chloe nodded an affirmation.

"We're in town for the reunion," Chloe explained.

"That's what I figured," I told them.

"I wasn't sure if I'd make it. The firm's been so busy, it was difficult to get away."

Aware of the bait, I didn't bite, but Mom didn't seem to understand the dynamic at all. "What type of firm?" she asked.

"Architectural," Chloe bragged. "I'm working on a new bank tower in the city."

"That sounds fabulous!" Mom said, and it took all the restraint I had not to kick her under the table.

"I'm the co-owner of an interior design business," Sara piped in. "Sometimes Chloe and I work on the same projects."

"Interior design. I could use a bit of that myself," Mom said, and Sara handed her a business card. I didn't ask for one, but received it anyway, as well as a card from Chloe. I had nothing to hand them but an old movie stub and a grocery receipt, so I sat with my eyes downcast, waiting for the inevitable interrogation. It didn't take long.

"So, where are you living these days, Jody?" Chloe asked.

"Here in Bent Harbor," I said.

"Oh, you came back after college?" Sara asked.

"I never left."

"But there's no coll . . . oh," Sara said, as the light went on over her struggling brain.

"So, what kind of work are you doing?"

"I'm between jobs at the moment."

"That sounds interesting," Chloe murmured.

Did she hear what I said? It didn't matter, because the questions suddenly hit a rapid-fire pace.

"Are you married?"

"No."

"Divorced?"

"No."

"Boyfriend?"

"Well . . ."

"Kids?"

"No."

"Have you bought a place here?"

"No."

"Are you renting?"

"Not exactly."

"Meaning?"

"I live with Erin Milne."

"Oh, so you're a . . ."

"No." *Boy, am I sick of that one.*

"Well, it was terrific seeing you," Chloe lied as they backed away from our table, confident that I would pose no threat to their reunion domination.

"Yes, you too," Mom said, offering a little wave. When they were out of earshot, she reached over and patted my hand. "Now, that was easy as pie, wasn't it?"

There was no way in hell I'd be attending that reunion.

nineteen

As soon as Mom dropped me at Erin's place, I raced inside to check the answering machine. To my delight, relief, and joy, there was a message from Justin, offering dinner at his place that very night. I dialed the cell phone number he'd left to accept the invitation.

The conversation was brief, but rewarding. He was working on a couple of jobs in Fillington and would be there for most of the afternoon, but home in time to serve me dins. When we talked about the previous night, we spoke the same language. He'd been thinking about me as he shoveled dirt, I'd been thinking of him as I shoveled Hannah's shit to the tune of one hundred and seventy-five dollars. We were both looking forward to seeing each other at six-thirty. All in all, a lovely call.

It was still early in the day, so my next move was to find a realtor. Mom spooked me when she'd spoken of how far money wouldn't go on Sitka Point, and I was in need of some hard-and-fast reassurance that my dream could indeed be a reality. I made an appointment to meet with a Sunny Dandridge two days later and smiled with satisfaction.

After a quick stop at the Galley, which was running like clockwork, I should have searched for jobs on the Internet, but instead I searched my closet for a suitable outfit for dinner. I waded through the sea of blouses, jackets, and sweaters, trying and discarding one item after another, finally settling on exactly what I'd started with; a blue silk blouse and cotton pants. I indulged in a cucumber-melon bubble bath for well over an hour and was in the middle of dressing in my room when Erin and Michael entered the house with a slam of the door.

"I can't *believe* you'd try to pull something like that!" Erin shouted as she stormed through the hallway.

"I didn't *try* anything!" Michael yelled after her.

"Bullshit!"

"What was I supposed to do? Tell her to leave the restaurant?"

"What do you think, *asshole*?"

Tension amid the tenderness. I elected to weather the storm in my room.

"Be reasonable!" he shouted after her.

"Reasonable?" She stomped through the hallway again. "She's your girlfriend."

"Ex-girlfriend! Why can't you get that through your thick head?"

"Excuse me?" she roared.

"I keep telling you she doesn't mean anything to me!"

"Then why did you visit her table?"

I'd never known her to act jealous before, and couldn't help giggling. What was she going to say when Michael found out she'd bedded every eligible bachelor (and some who weren't so available) in the region?

"I already told you, Erin. I wanted to congratulate her on her new job."

"It took you long enough."

"I introduced *you* as my girlfriend. What more could I do?"

"Ask her to leave!"

"She was midway through her meal!"

"And what was she eating?"

"Steak."

"Exactly!"

"What are you talking about?"

"This is about me being a vegetarian, isn't it?"

"Erin—"

"You want her back, don't you?"

"Admit it!"

"Erin."

"Will you just admit it? I saw the way you looked at her!"

"Erin, for Christ's sake. I'm in love with you."

There was a lengthy pause, and all I could hear was Erin's ragged breathing.

"You're what?" she finally gasped.

"I'm in love with you."

"Oh, Michael," she whimpered. "I love you, too."

Her voice was muffled and I imagined a tangled lover's embrace. It sounded so *easy* for them to say those words, I couldn't believe I'd never done it.

I sat on the bed and waited for them to relocate. If I could exit quickly and quietly enough, they'd never know I'd been there.

"So, are we okay?" Michael asked.

"Yes." She sniffled. "I'm sorry I blew up at you. I was so jealous, I didn't know what to do. Of *course,* we're okay."

I was glad they'd patched things up and felt ready to rendezvous with my own taste of romance. That is, until Michael said four small but terrifying words.

"I'll get my cape."

Shit.

The sex seemed to move from room to room with alarming speed. They bumped into walls, groaning with pleasure, while I gazed at my watch, hoping they'd make it snappy. But they took their time, hoarsely whispering sweet nothings as they got frisky on the kitchen counter, the dining room table, and, to my chagrin, even the beanbag chair.

Finally, when I'd almost given up hope of leaving the room that night, Michael mentioned he was going to be late for work, so they had one last go of it, ending with a joint cry of "to the Batcave!"

After history's longest goodbye, a suckling, smooching affair, Michael clomped down the front steps and Erin turned on the shower. When I was sure the coast was clear, I made my break for the front door.

Justin's house was only a few blocks away, and I walked briskly with anticipation. Most people in town owned their homes, but there were a few perennial rentals around, and I knew his little yellow cottage on Rose Run was one of them.

The walk only took about ten minutes, thanks to the speed of my footsteps, and when I arrived at the front door I rapped my knuckles against it. When no one answered, I peered through the window next to it, into a darkened hallway.

Justin stood in a well-lit kitchen, waving a hair dryer at a large cloud of smoke, apparently urging it away from a fire alarm. Rather than waiting for him to notice me, I opened the door, plugged my nose, and greeted him in the kitchen.

"Is everything okay?" I asked.

He spun around to face me and fumbled for the power switch on the dryer. "Jody, you're here."

"Justin, I am."

I glanced from one corner to the next, taking in the scorched saucepans and piles of dirty bowls. Spoons and forks, dripping sauces and syrups, were all over the countertops, as though a utensil bomb had exploded. A yellow substance was boiling over on the stove and the burner was sizzling with defiance. A small carcass sat on the island in the middle of the room, every inch of it charred black. "It's a good thing I like it crispy," I said, trying to bite back a laugh.

"I can't believe this mess." He surveyed the scene, one hand on his hip, the other still clutching the dryer.

"What happened?"

"A lot of things, actually." He bit his lip. "I couldn't remember whether I'd told you six or six-thirty, so I was rushing to get the chicken done."

"I'm sorry, the what?"

"The chicken." He pointed to the carcass.

"Oh, is that what it is?"

"Very funny." He rolled his eyes. "Anyway, I turned the oven up to broil and forgot about it."

"What do I smell cooking right now, then?"

"When I saw what I'd done, I brought in the infantry."

"What?"

"You know, the Colonel." He smiled sheepishly, endearingly, *gorgeously.* "We're still having chicken, just not the original bird. I was trying to finish the rest of the meal myself, though, making mashed potatoes, corn on the cob, and gravy. Apparently, they don't all require the same cooking time."

"No, they don't. And might I mention, the Colonel makes all of those items, as well?"

"I know, but I wanted to try doing it myself."

I glanced at the mess on the stove. "What's the yellow stuff?"

"Lemon filling for a meringue pie."

"You were making me a meringue pie?"

"Yeah." He put the hair dryer on the counter and wiped his hands on his jeans, adding a smear of yellow to the shades already there.

"I can't believe you'd go to all this trouble for me." I shook my head. A *lemon meringue pie,* for crying out loud.

"Why not?"

"Well, for starters, you obviously can't cook."

"I should have taken you out," he said, groaning.

"I disagree," I said, stepping closer to him. "If you'd taken me out, I'd have been too self-conscious to do this." I reached for his face, held his cheeks in my hands for a split second, and pulled him down to kiss me.

Prompted by the pornographic decathlon I'd listened to at home, and the overwhelming thrill I felt, knowing he'd tried so hard to cook for me, I didn't wait for a slow escalation of the kiss. It was ardent from the second our lips met and my hands slid to the back of his neck.

Justin wrapped his arms around my lower back and pulled my body closer to his. I could feel his hips pressed against mine as we swayed, a little unsteady on our feet. His tongue curled around mine and goose bumps rose all over my body.

After what seemed like forever, we broke apart and stared into each other's eyes at close range.

"This is moving very quickly," he said quietly.

"I know."

"I'm glad."

"I'm glad, too." In his arms, I felt safe, comfortable, and extremely aroused.

"So, what do you think about . . ." He tilted his head toward the back of the house and, I assumed, the bedroom.

I nodded. "Considering I'm about to prove myself wrong, it may be pointless to say this . . . but I'm not normally that kind of girl."

"You're not?" He gave me a look of mock horror.

"Well, I haven't been, until now."

"Same goes for me." He smiled, and the oven timer started buzzing. "Should we eat first?"

"Forget dinner," I said, slipping out of my shoes.

On the way to the bedroom, we left articles of clothing dangling from the arms of chairs, pooled on the floor, and even caught in the leaves of a large tropical plant.

"Is this your stuff?" I asked, between moist kisses.

"Came with the house," he murmured, opening the bedroom door.

We fell onto the duvet together, naked, curious, and playful. For the first time ever, I was uninhibited. Our pace gradually slowed, our movements reduced to tender strokes. He massaged my back and arms, whispering to me as he worked, and I did the same for him. We ran our hands over each other's skin, trying to delay what we most looked forward to. It was like the final month before Christmas, each moment a new window on the Advent calendar and more gifts under the tree. That May night, Christmas was in the air, and I got everything on my wish list.

When I awoke to the shrill beep of an alarm clock, Justin's warm body was spooning mine.

"I guess I better get up," he moaned, rolling away from me.

I felt an immediate draft of cold air down my backside, and wanted him back in bed.

"Did you sleep okay?" he asked, kissing my shoulder.

"You know perfectly well that I didn't." I smiled, recalling our escapades through the night. "And neither did you."

"And yet, I feel strangely energized." He grinned as he left the room.

While he showered, I cooked scrambled eggs and toast. I even made a halfhearted attempt to clean the dishes, amazed at my sudden swing toward domesticity.

When he appeared in the kitchen, dressed and shaved, we smooched for a couple of minutes before sitting down to eat, but we were soon interrupted by the phone. At his insistence, I dug into my breakfast while he took the call. He was silent for several minutes, nodding as though whoever was at the other end could see him. When he hung up, he looked worried.

"Is everything okay?" I asked.

"It's as good as can be expected," he said, sighing. "Lucas admitted himself to Whispering Pines yesterday afternoon."

"He did? I mean, I had no idea . . . you never said anything."

"I wanted to have a normal evening." He paused and smiled shyly at me. "Well, much better than normal, actually."

I blushed in response. "Is he all right?"

"I think so. The nurse just said they had to sedate him late last night, but he seems better this morning."

I didn't know what to say, and he didn't look like he wanted to talk about it. We finished eating and he complimented me on my prowess, culinary and otherwise, before asking me to lock up when I left the house. We kissed goodbye on the doorstep, like some kind of Rockwell print, aside from the fact that I was wearing nothing more than one of Justin's T-shirts, which barely covered the flat ass that hadn't even fazed him.

On my way back to Erin's, I ran into none other than Marty, the only McDade I hadn't kissed and never would. I was surprised to see him on foot, considering he usually drove his merchandise everywhere he went, including the two-block jaunt from his dealership to the Galley. He looked odd, trudging down the sidewalk, and when I got closer I saw that he had huge bags under his eyes, and his usual sneer was reduced to a slack-jawed numbness.

I offered a tight-lipped smile as I walked toward him, braced for whatever insult he'd throw my way.

"Hi, Jody," he said, when we were just a few feet apart.

"Marty." I nodded briskly. "How are you?"

"I haven't seen you at the Galley in a while." He almost looked through me.

"I don't work there anymore."

"Oh, yeah. That's right," he mumbled, walking past me without another word. No insult, no pickup line, not even an attempt to touch me, as if he were somewhere else entirely. I could only assume he was worried about Lucas.

I decided to detour past Whispering Pines, after what Max and Jaundice had said about P.J.'s odd behavior. I peered through the bars at a huge Tudor home which had been transformed into one of the most expensive facilities in the state. I noted the carefully mowed lawns and thriving gardens, certain that Whispering Pines was no Bedlam.

I followed a brick pathway leading to the main entrance and stepped inside. The walls were painted lemon yellow, with white-trimmed windows, and while the wire on the outside of the glass was barely visible, it was a reminder that most of the guests were not staying voluntarily. The reception area smelled like any hospital, a mixture of cleaning supplies and human emissions. The floor was freshly polished and the lounge, with its stacks of magazines and cheerful artwork, gave the impression of a clean and pleasant environment.

I approached the front desk and was greeted by a young nurse wearing a pink cardigan over her whites. "May I help you?"

"Yes, I'm looking for a new patient. Lucas McDade?"

"Let me check the computer," she said, disappearing behind a frosted-glass partition.

"He arrived yesterday afternoon," I called after her.

After a moment she reappeared, shaking her head. "I'm sorry, Mr. McDade can't be seen today."

"I didn't need to see him, I was just . . . *why* can't he be seen?"

"He's being evaluated right now."

"So, can I see him later?"

"I don't think so."

"I don't understand. This is a hospital, right? Not a prison. He checked himself in."

"Are you a family member?"

"No, I'm—"

"I'm afraid I can't give you any further information."

"All I want to know is whether he's *okay*."

"He's fine. The doctors are assessing his condition and determining the best way to treat him."

"He's supposed to be taking lith—"

"Perhaps you could come back another time."

"Perhaps I will," I snapped.

As I left the grounds, I saw a nurse on the lawn with a couple of patients. One was babbling while the other walked in dead silence. The sight reminded me again of P.J. Hardison, and I wondered just what kind of peace of mind Whispering Pines provided.

twenty

After stopping by the Galley to place a fish order and check on things, I returned to Erin's. She wasn't home by late afternoon, so I left her a note when I headed over to Mom and Dad's for dinner and a reconciliation. As I walked, I considered the different ways I could approach my father. He wasn't one for sentimentality, and was more inclined to act like a bear awakened in mid-hibernation than welcome an emotional scene. I figured my best bet was to be straightforward and explain that I never meant to hurt his feelings and ours was a simple misunderstanding that had gone too far.

When I arrived at the house, I entered without knocking to avoid setting off the Ruby alarm. I found Mom in the kitchen, layering a lasagna. She wore the paisley apron I made for her in home ec, the one she had to entirely restitch due to my poor sewing skills.

"Mmm, smells good," I said.

"Oh, you're here." She smiled and licked some tomato sauce from her thumb. "We could have picked you up, you know."

"I had a nice walk over." I peered into the living room and saw no sign of Dad, aside from the imprint of his buttocks on the recliner. "Where is he?" I whispered.

"In the den, watching TV. Dinner won't be ready for a while, love, so maybe now's the time to talk to him."

I found him channel-surfing on the beige recliner that had been bumped from the living room by the new La-Z-Boy. I felt like a kid again, seeing him in that familiar, ratty old chair. Ruby sat next to him, giving me a dirty and proprietorial look. Her asinine pink bow was coming undone, but I knew someone would fix her up in no time. After all, she was their furry little child now.

Dad glanced at me, then back at the TV, pausing on a figure-skating competition.

"What are you watching?" I asked, perching awkwardly on the arm of the old Hide-A-Bed.

"Skating." He didn't even look at me.

"Can I talk to you?"

"I'm in the middle of a program."

"You don't even *like* skating," I reminded him.

He reached into a plastic container and pulled out several bone-shaped dog treats. "My little girl likes it," he simpered as the bitch lathered his fingers with saliva. "Don't you, Ruby?" She wagged her wilted tail and panted as if she were crossing the Sahara. "Who's my girl? Who's my girl?"

"I am," I said quietly.

He handed the dog another treat and looked at me. Rather than turning the TV off, he hit the mute button. I was making headway.

"What do you want?" he asked gruffly, reaching for some mixed nuts.

"To apologize for the other night. I upset you, and I honestly didn't mean to."

"I don't know what you want me to say, Jody." He picked out a couple of cashews and popped them into his mouth.

"Well, I'd like you to accept my apology."

"Do you know *why* it upset me?"

"Yes," I answered, but apparently it was a rhetorical question.

"Because I thought I raised you to respect any job a person had. If someone is hardworking and honest, they should earn that respect."

"They do, Dad. It's just that—"

"I'm sorry it *embarrasses* you that the old man made a living at the pulp mill instead of some white-collar job."

"It doesn't embarrass me." When had I ever said, felt, or thought that?

"I was proud of your job at the Galley. You worked hard for a good, long time, but then you dropped it like it meant nothing. Like Dean meant nothing."

"It just didn't seem to be going anywhere," I mumbled.

Dad continued, as though I hadn't spoken. "Maybe if you'd had a plan, like going back to school, I'd have understood. But to quit a perfectly good job during a recession was an act of stupidity I'd never expected from you. Your brother, maybe, but not you."

Talk about a low blow!

"I was being sexually harassed at work. I told you about it before."

"I didn't raise my kids to back down from a fight. You just gave up too damn easily."

The dog whined for another treat, and Dad ignored her, for once. Ruby rested her head on his lap in defeat.

"Sometimes you have to quit," I said. "Like my relationship with Chris. He *cheated* on me, Dad. I couldn't stay with him."

"I'm not talking about Chris. You did the right thing by leaving him, although you should have kicked his sorry ass first." He chuckled before getting serious again. "But you *liked* that job, Jody."

"Parts of it," I had to agree.

"You liked your boss, your co-workers, even most of the customers." He counted each point off on his fingers and Ruby lifted her head to lick the salt from the tips. "That's more than a lot of people find at work."

"Dean asked me to cover the restaurant while he's out of town."

"See? That's what I'm talking about. You had a boss who trusted and respected you. I hope you're going to do it."

I nodded.

"You're a great kid, Jody. You just need to learn how to appreciate the good things in life. Sometimes they're simple, like an honest day's work, but isn't simple a hell of a lot better than complicated?"

"I guess so."

"I know you can do anything you want with your life, Peanut. Just make sure you do *something,* okay?" He pressed the mute button again and skating scores filled the room. Evidently, our heart-to-heart was over.

"Thanks, Dad," I said, and walked back to the kitchen, where the lasagna was in the oven and Mom was loading the dishwasher.

"Is everything settled?" she asked.

"I think so."

"Good. Would you mind setting the table for me?"

I dug three sets of cutlery from the drawer next to the fridge and started toward the kitchen table.

"Why don't we eat in the dining room, honey?" Mom asked.

I pulled a tablecloth from the linen cupboard, knowing how protective she was of the cherrywood tabletop.

"And set it for four," she said, as the door swung closed behind me.

I turned to push it open again.

"Is this another setup?" I demanded, dreading the answer. "Because if you think I'm going to sit through another blind date, you'd better guess again."

"Don't you take that tone with me." She pointed a fork at me.

"It *is* a blind date! Mom! How could you set me up like this again?"

"Will you calm down? The way you look at the negative side of everything, I'm amazed you can get out of bed every morning." She shook her head. "Your *brother* is joining us for dinner."

"Oh." I breathed a sigh of relief.

"We never seem to get together as a family these days, so I thought it would be nice to eat in the dining room. *Is that okay with you?*"

I nodded and slunk out of the kitchen, four sets of cutlery in hand.

Josh arrived on time and informed us he'd been promoted to assistant manager at Video Nook. Naturally, Mom and Dad acted like he'd found a cure for cancer, or saved the world from plague and famine, patting his head and spouting congratulatory remarks. I had to admit, even *I* was pleased for him. After three years on the job, he'd certainly earned full-time hours and a pay raise.

"Any luck with your job hunt, Jode?" he asked, cracking open a beer.

"Not yet."

"Did you get my message about the pizza place?"

"Yes, I did, Josh. But doesn't a delivery driver need, oh, I don't know . . . *a car*?"

"Oh, yeah. I guess they would. I'll keep my eyes peeled for something else."

Obviously Video Nook didn't base their promotions on cognitive powers.

"Your girlfriend gave me a ride the other day."

"Caroline?"

"*Amy*. The Muffin Zone girl."

"Oh. We broke up."

"I thought you might. I'm sorry, Josh."

"I was, too. I really liked those wheat germ muffins."

Even after losing the mysterious "all" that he and Amy had had together, he was still willing to soldier on. My brother, the trouper.

The family ended up sharing a very enjoyable dinner together. As always, Mom's lasagna was fabulous, and we teased each other the way we had in the past. Josh actually made me laugh hard enough for milk to come out of my nose, which might not be considered a highlight at most tables, but it was a golden moment at ours.

I felt lucky to have a decent family, especially considering Justin's dysfunctional nightmare. I was even grateful for Ruby, who sat on the floor next to Dad's chair, wolfing down the clumps of ground beef he fed her until she could barely stand.

Josh eventually had to leave for yet another Fillington party, and I declined his offer of a ride home, opting to hang out with my parents a little longer.

"Honey, I'm doing some painting tonight, if you'd like to help," Mom said, so I followed her into my old bedroom.

The number of completed ladybugs had doubled since my last visit, a case study in overstocking, but there was no sign of other creatures. She handed over one of Dad's old work shirts to wear as a smock, and assigned me to the task of painting red bodies.

When I had finished a dozen of them, I reached for the black paint.

"I'd rather you didn't do that, Jody." She pulled the paint toward her side of the table.

"I was just going to paint the dots," I explained.

"It's not that easy."

"Sure it is. They're *dots.* I can copy the ones you've already done."

"It takes a very steady hand."

"I think I can handle—"

"I said no."

"Mom, I'm not trying to take over, or anything."

"Your dad and I have managed to survive the last fifty-some years doing things our way. We both know what works for us."

"Okay, Mom."

"You don't have to try to change everything."

"Okay, already. I'm sorry."

"It's all right, dear. Now, let's get moving. I want to finish at least three dozen tonight."

I couldn't imagine why.

I painted with Mom for another hour, refraining from making suggestions about the new business. Dad and I shared a tight hug before Mom drove me home, and it seemed everything was just fine between us.

When I returned to Erin's, I found the house empty, no note on the fridge, and the answering machine was devoid of messages. I was disappointed not to have heard from Justin, but stayed up for a couple of hours, watching TV, and hoping either he would call or Erin would appear. When neither had happened by eleven o'clock, I went to bed.

The following morning I met Sunny Dandridge at West Coast Realty for my home tour. She was exactly what I expected; blond, bubbly, and almost frighteningly cheerful. Luckily, I was in the mood for cheerful.

"So, you're interested in Sitka Point," she said, handing me a Styrofoam cup of coffee.

"Yes. I know a lot of the homes up there aren't in my price range, but I've seen a few advertised in the paper that seem to match my budget."

She asked me where I worked, so I lied and told her I was still at the Galley. I also bumped my annual salary upward by a few thousand dollars, figuring a few white lies wouldn't hurt. I wasn't *buying* that very day, just getting an idea for the future.

After our brief interview, Sunny loaded me into her silver BMW and drove along Old Marine Highway until we reached the turnoff for Sitka Point. As always, I was impressed by the most glamorous houses I saw, but knew they were way out of my league.

"This one's a bit higher than the price range we discussed," Sunny said, pulling up in front of a two-story shake house with a wraparound porch. I'd passed it a thousand times, but never considered it a possibility. "But it's a lovely home."

"How much is a bit?"

"About sixty thousand more than you want to spend."

I gasped. Sixty thousand was no small potatoes.

"Shall we take a look inside? I have a key."

"Sure," I said, smiling weakly. It wouldn't hurt to know what was behind the shuttered windows.

When I stepped inside, it was as close to my dream home as anything I'd imagined. It had three bedrooms, perfect for the family I didn't have, two bathrooms, beautifully tiled, and a kitchen that could have inspired me to culinary greatness. Along with the infinite counter space were brand-new appliances, an island, and a skylight. Granted, I would gladly ditch the busy floral wallpaper, which would mean stripping the walls of every single room, but it would be a labor of love. The floors were all hardwood, and the unfinished basement was big enough for just about anything.

Suddenly, sixty thousand dollars *was* small potatoes. Hash browns, even.

"So?" Sunny asked, as I marveled at the back deck, already planning summer barbecues and parties.

"It's beautiful." The word didn't begin to encompass my feelings about the house.

"I'll take you to see something closer to your price range," she said, knowing full well a cheaper house would pale in comparison.

As we left, I paused on the front lawn for a final look, my heart aching with the knowledge that I couldn't afford it.

We drove down a couple of side streets, where Sunny pointed out some extravagant homes, listing their attributes and prices for me. I had the sinking feeling my life on Sitka Point was farther in the future than I'd thought, and I hated to admit that Mom was right.

Sunny stopped the car in front of a sad little bungalow with peeling paint and a sagging roof.

"This is what you'd be looking at," she said, her voice rich with apology.

"Sixty thousand makes quite a difference," I murmured.

"I'm afraid it does."

I tried to look past the overgrown garden, ignoring the rusty gutter pipes and the three-legged couch on the front porch, and *almost* seeing potential. However, the idea of blowing my entire savings and much more for the opportunity to use up a life supply of elbow grease was less than thrilling.

"Would you like to look inside?"

"I guess so," I told her. Better to know what I'd be in for ahead of time.

Sunny led me up a gravel path to the front door and told me the owner had promised his tenant would be home for the day.

"We're a touch earlier than I told him, but that shouldn't be a problem. By the way, the owner is very eager to sell."

Eager to sell? I had no doubt about that.

Sunny lifted the door knocker and the unit broke off its hinges and fell onto the doorstep.

"Easy to fix," she whispered. "All you'd need is a screwdriver."

She knocked on the door itself and received no response. Smiling at me with reassurance, she rang the doorbell, which sounded like an ancient gong.

"You could always replace that with something more contemporary," Sunny whispered, just as the door swung open.

To my absolute astonishment, standing in front of us, wearing nothing but a bedsheet and a scowl, was my cousin Beth.

"What are you doing here?" she barked, like the bitch she was.

Before I could answer, Sunny stepped in. "Hello, dear. I'm Sunny Dandridge, and I'm looking for Mr. McAllister."

McAllister. The name was familiar, but why?

"What do you need him for?" Beth asked, glaring at me.

"Well, I'm a Realtor and—"

"I'll take care of it, Beth," a male voice said.

The next thing I knew, Russell the blind date was standing in the doorway, wearing a bathrobe. He looked shocked to see me, but managed to regain his composure and smile at Sunny.

Beth clutched his arm and shot threatening looks in my direction, warning me not to tell Chris, I was sure.

"Oh, my," I said, shaking my head and barely containing a smile.

"It appears we've come at a bad time," Sunny stammered. "Perhaps we can make an appointment for a later date."

"I think that would be for the best," Russell agreed.

On the way to the car, Sunny apologized for wasting my time and promised to reschedule a viewing for me.

"No problem at all," I assured her, my grin so wide I thought my lips might split. "That's just what I needed."

twenty-one

When I got home, I found a note from Erin taped to the TV. She and Michael were off to Portland for a few days to visit friends of his. There was no flashing light on the answering machine, and I did my best not to take it personally. Considering Justin and I had shared the most intimate of human experiences, I was more than a little rattled he hadn't called me for two days following the main event. Of course, I knew he had a lot on his plate, dealing with Lucas. Hell, Lucas was a full plate plus a couple of Tupperware containers of leftovers in the fridge, but surely Justin had time for *one measly phone call.* Maybe our night together meant more to me than it did to him, and when I looked at it that way, I had no intention of calling him first.

I phoned to check in on the Galley, and Katie said everything was running smoothly, which meant I had nothing to do.

I wandered around the house, straightening magazine stacks that didn't need it and absently wiping Erin's counters and tabletops, despite the lack of dust, dirt, or interest. I even scoured the bathtub, all the while waiting for the phone to ring. Just as I was about to arrange the contents of her cupboard in alphabetical order, it did.

I was saved from countless hours of unspent self-pity by none other than Hannah Baxter. "Jody? Is this a good time?" she whispered.

"It's fine." What did she *think* I was doing at two in the afternoon?

"You don't have . . . *company,* do you?"

"Not at the moment." Although I was greatly looking forward to having company again, as soon as possible.

"Good, because I didn't want to interrupt, well . . . you know."

"Yes, Hannah. I get it. You're about as subtle as a pipe bomb."

"I was hoping we could get together this afternoon to look at churches."

"*Churches?* As in more than one?"

"Well, I need the perfect setting."

"Do you have a particular faith in mind?" Other than blind, ideally.

"It doesn't really matter. Baptist, maybe?"

"Your last one was Lutheran," I said, puzzled.

"I'm aware of that, Jody. I think it's time for a change of pace."

"You know, some churches might not book a wedding if the couple is of a different faith."

"That's what my mom said, too. Don't you think that's prejudiced?"

"No, but some churches won't allow a fourth wedding, either."

"That's why we need to shop around."

Did Hannah Baxter's very existence make God feel like a mad scientist?

Within the hour, I climbed into her Pinto, relieved to learn she'd left the kids at her mother's house. As we drove, she asked how things were going with Justin and I tried to be noncommittal. It wouldn't do me any good to swoon and blather on if he was planning to ditch me, or had already done so. How had I misread the situation the morning we parted, after the best sex I'd ever had? Why had I jumped into bed so fast? *Because I wanted to.*

I sparked a subject change by asking what was new on the wedding front.

"I chose the invitations and they'll go out next week. I'm too busy with the reunion right now to do much else. Have you changed your mind about going?"

"To the *reunion*?" I thought about my Pasta Haven brush with the cheerleaders of yesteryear. "I don't think so." I'd forgotten to tell Justin his services were no longer required. Of course, he may have changed his mind about taking me anyway.

"It'll be so much fun, Jody. People are starting to pop up all over town."

"Yeah, I noticed."

She drove past Simpson Bay and several miles beyond, eventually pulling into the parking lot of a little church I'd never seen before, on Walter Way. The building was white, with dark blue trim and stained-glass windows every few feet, overlooking a small cove.

"What kind of church is this?" I asked.

"Uh, there's a sign over here," Hannah said, walking toward it. "Anglican?"

"As in Church of England? What's it doing in our neck of the woods?"

"I don't know." She shrugged. "But this is the place I want."

"Well, let's go inside and see whoever's in charge."

We entered an arched doorway. To our right was a stairway leading up, and to the left, what looked like an office. I pointed Hannah toward the latter, but she was already climbing the stairs. I followed her, feeling like an unwanted intruder.

"I don't think we should be going up here," I whispered.

"It's a *church,* Jody. It's, like, open to the public."

She disappeared around a corner, and when I caught up with her, we were at the heart of the most beautiful room I'd ever seen. The stained-glass windows included every color imaginable, and tinted sunlight shone onto the deep red carpet leading to the altar. The pews were made of dark, rich wood, gleaming with varnish and lined with red leather cushions. I felt a wonderful sense of calm and wished my family had made it to church more often, if not for the sermon, then the serenity.

Blue and red bound hymnals were carefully stowed in the back of each pew, awaiting pious or distracted fingertips to follow each line.

"This is *perfect,*" I murmured, admiring the dark beams fitting the ceiling like a ship's hull.

"Let's book it," Hannah said, retreating in the direction of the office.

We were welcomed by an elderly minister who, like the church itself, fit the role perfectly.

He was white-haired, with rosy cheeks and a hooked nose, like the beak on a bird of prey. His ears were large and rubbery, his posture stooped, as though God were using him as a personal footstool.

We introduced ourselves, and his gaze lingered on Hannah, who, aside from the jean jacket and chewed fingernails, looked like an angel. His smile was beatific, as though he were waiting for heaven-sent words to spill from her lips. When she told him she wanted to be married in the church, his eyes sparkled.

"I assume you're Anglican," he said, in a wavering voice that carried the faintest trace of a British accent. He pulled some forms from a folder behind him.

"No."

"No?" he asked, laying the papers on his desk.

"No."

"Is your fiancé?"

"Not exactly."

His confusion was made apparent by the lifting of one eyebrow and the slight droop of a frown. "May I ask what church you *do* belong to?"

"Well, I've gone to Christmas Mass a couple of times at St. Peter's. You know, the Catholic one in Bent Harbor?"

"Yes?" He looked absolutely baffled.

"My first wedding was Episcopalian," she said, "and the third was, uh . . ."

"Lutheran," I reminded her.

"I see." He grimaced. "And the . . . er . . . second?"

"City Hall," she said. "Just the two of us and a couple of witnesses."

The minister glanced from Hannah to me, and back again, jaw dropping momentarily. "You don't mean . . . ?" A bent index finger danced between us.

"We're not a couple," I explained.

"No!" Hannah gasped. "I meant my ex-husband and fiancé."

"Both will attend this service?" the minister asked.

"They're the same person," I said, cringing.

"All right, then. Your *former* husband is also your *future* husband."

"Yes." Hannah smiled.

"If I may ask, how many other grooms have there been?"

"Just David. I've married him three times, and this will be our fourth."

"Are you planning to try different denominations until one of the marriages, er . . . *sticks*?"

"No. I mean, we're just . . . ," Hannah began.

"What is your reason for choosing our church?"

"It's a gorgeous spot," Hannah said timidly.

"That I am aware of." He rested his glasses on the bridge of his nose. "But what about the service?"

"What about it?"

"Our marriage vows do include the words 'till death do you part.' "

"I know," Hannah said, too quickly. "All of our vows included that. It's like, the *standard.*"

"That may very well be, my dear. But in this case, we mean it."

I could almost hear the creaky wheels of Hannah's brain. "So, what would it take for me to be married here?"

"Were you or the groom christened?"

"I'm not sure." She bit her bottom lip. "Could we do it just before the wedding?"

"Dear Lord," he muttered.

"What else?"

"Premarriage counseling is a mandatory course offered through the church, for a nominal fee."

"Premarriage counseling? I've never heard of it."

"I don't doubt that at all," the minister said, offering me a pained smile.

"A mandatory course?" she continued. "That's ridiculous. David and I don't need counseling."

"Hannah," I murmured. "Three of your marriages have ended in divorce."

"I know, but *counseling*?"

"And, of course, there's the fee for the service," the minister said quietly.

"How much?"

"Seven hundred dollars."

We both gasped.

"Just for the ceremony?" she asked.

He nodded. "That includes the organist and flowers for the pews."

"I can't believe it," she whimpered.

"And you must bear in mind that we're booked solid, that's three weddings per Saturday, through October."

I thought Hannah was going to cry. *Again.*

We thanked him for his time and I led her out to the car. "What now?" I asked.

"I guess we'll have to find another church." She sniffled. "You know, it was almost like he didn't *want* us to get married there."

"Yeah, *almost,*" I said, aiming for sincerity as I buckled my seat belt. "Hey, would you mind if we stopped by the Galley for a minute? I promised Dean I'd keep an eye on the place while he's out of town." It wasn't that I didn't trust Katie, I just wanted to see things for myself.

"Sure," Hannah said. "As long as you score me some free fries."

When we arrived at the restaurant, my timing couldn't have been better, or worse. I didn't know whether the senior center was closed, or Dean was advertising a retiree special, but the place was packed with white hair and pastel leisure suits. I directed Hannah toward the counter and grabbed Katie's arm as she raced past me.

"What's going on around here?"

"Fuck if I know," she said, shaking her head and hurrying into the kitchen.

I caught Todd at the counter and asked where the crowd had sprung from.

"Did you see the tour bus outside?"

I shook my head, amazed I hadn't noticed. *A tour bus?* In Bent Harbor? "Where are they going?"

"They're on their way back to Seattle. It's some kind of arts and crafts tour."

At that very moment, I saw a woman pull a painted ladybug from her purse and nearly choked with disbelief.

"Excuse me," I said, tapping her shoulder. "Where did you get that?"

"At a craft fair in the next town over. What was that place called, Joyce?" she asked a shrunken woman next to her.

"Filletville, or something." She shrugged and continued to search the menu.

"Fillington?"

"That's the place. It was an absolute bargain. Only nine ninety-five."

"Nine ninety-five?" I asked.

"Yup. Real stone, too. Made by a local artist."

My mother, the local artist. No wonder she was whipping off three dozen at a time.

I started toward the counter, but the woman grabbed my sleeve. "Miss? Do you know if this place serves cod?"

"No, ma'am. Only halibut."

Disappointed looks spread like a wave from one wrinkled face to the next. I left them to complain among themselves and placed a fry order for Hannah.

"Is everything okay?" I asked Paige as she bolted past me with a fishburger with potato salad in one hand and a bowl of chowder in the other.

"What do you think?" She nodded toward the crowd of oldies. "We're *swamped.*"

"I can stay for a while and help you guys out."

"Thanks, Jode. Just until we're out of the weeds, if you don't mind."

I reached behind the counter for an apron, tying it on as I walked toward Hannah, who was twisting on a stool next to Max and Jaundice.

"It looks like I'm going to be here for a while," I told her, secretly relieved I wouldn't have to hear her plead another case in a church.

"But I thought we were going to book the ceremony today," she whined.

"There's nothing I can do."

"Well, I guess I can take care of that part myself." She paused to sip her Coke. "But you still have to meet with the caterer later in the week, and go to Fillington so I can register for gifts."

Was I the only friend she had?

I nodded assent and turned to my favorite regulars. "How are you guys doing?"

"Not so hot," Max said.

"More service complaints? You could cut the girls some slack, Max. It's damn busy in here."

"No, it's P.J.," Max responded.

"He was having some problems yesterday," Jaundice said. "Left hockey players entirely."

It didn't look like either of them had touched their coffees, so something was definitely wrong. "What do you mean? He's onto a different sport?"

"He stopped talking altogether," Max said.

"Dead quiet." Jaundice nodded, his expression bleak.

I couldn't imagine a silent P.J. Hardison. The sound of his voice was like elevator music when he was near, not exactly pleasant, but constant. P.J. unplugged was like Max minus the bitching.

"What's wrong with him?" I asked.

"Damned if I know." Max shrugged. "Usually Whispering Pines gets him back on track, but this time . . ." His unfocused gaze settled on my shoulder.

"This time, something really wasn't right," Jaundice finished for him.

"Why don't you take him back up there and find out what's bothering him? That seems like the most logical step."

"We *did,*" Max snapped. "After he started listing the newer players, we took him back up there. Now he's a goddamn mute. It's our fault."

"You were just trying to help," I said. "You were being good friends."

"Good friends, my ass." Max took a swipe at his suddenly teary eyes with the back of his hand. "I gotta go."

He slid from his stool and Jaundice followed with a nod in my direction. The odd pair slumped out of the restaurant and into bright sunlight.

My concern for Lucas and his treatment at Whispering Pines overpowered my desire for Justin to make the first move. I swallowed my pride and dialed the home number, but got no response. I called the cellular, and had no luck there, either.

Frustrated, I threw myself into the task at hand, taking over three of Paige's tables, and four of Katie's. Between the three of us, regaining control of the Galley was possible. I refilled water glasses, cleared dishes, listed specials, and patiently explained to every senior in the place that we did *not* serve cod.

Within half an hour, the crowd was happily eating their meals, and two hours later, the place was empty again. Even Hannah had left, without saying goodbye, so Katie and I shared a booth and a chef salad.

"So, have you found a new job?" she asked, brushing dark bangs from her eyes and swallowing her lettuce.

"Not exactly."

"Do you miss being here?" She wiped her mouth with a napkin and stabbed a chunk of tomato with her fork.

"As much as I hate to admit it, I really do."

"We miss you, too."

It killed me that I couldn't warn her that the Galley would soon be a thing of the past, but I had to keep my promise to Dean.

I glanced around the restaurant, my gaze stopping at the infamous corner booth. "Have you seen Marty McDade lately?"

"I think he was here yesterday morning, but it might have been the day before. Why?"

"I don't know." I thought of my strangely civil last encounter with him. "Did he seem weird to you?"

"He's *always* weird, Jody. He's a total perv."

"No, I mean, was he acting differently?"

"Actually, he was pretty quiet. And he was alone. I guess Tony and Ed had lunch somewhere else."

As much as I loathed the way Marty had treated me in the past, I was starting to worry about him, too.

I had the sinking feeling that if the McDade family was going down, they were taking me with them.

twenty-two

I didn't hear from Dean, so I continued to cover for him, going in early to place supply orders and leaving late, after hours of cleaning, clearing, serving, scheduling, and problem solving. I felt like I *owned* the place, and rather enjoyed the responsibility. When Dean finally returned with his niece in tow, he was impressed by my handling of things.

"You're the only person I've left to run the show in thirteen years, and you pulled it off."

"It was fun," I told him. "Hard work, but fun." I was hesitant to leave when he no longer needed me.

In those same three days, I heard *nothing* from Justin. I'd tried calling him several times, for Lucas's sake, but also for my own. At first, I tried to convince myself that something had come up, and there was no way he could get in touch with me, but it didn't take long for anger to rise and shove the speculation aside.

Bent Harbor was small enough that I knew I'd run into him at the grocery store, or walking home from work, but somehow I never did. I *thought* I saw him everywhere, however, which meant my heart careened around my rib cage like a loose pinball several times a day. Early on, before anger took hold, I even raced over to talk to him in the post office one morning, hesitating behind him for a split second before leaning close to his ear and whispering my offer of a sexual rematch. As it turned out, the familiar shoulders belonged not to Justin, but Sam Richards, a kid I used to *babysit.* He'd just celebrated his eighteenth birthday, and his eagerness to take me up on my offer wasn't as flattering as he might have hoped. In fact, it gave me the creeps.

I wanted to talk to Erin about my situation, not necessarily for the horrible relationship advice she was guaranteed to blurt, but to have someone sit back, listen, and tell me everything was going to be fine, that there had to be a reasonable explanation for Justin's disappearance from the face of the earth, or at least from my life.

Unfortunately, once Erin returned from Portland, she and I were operating on different schedules, communicating with cryptic notes and phone messages.

On my first day off from the Galley, Hannah Baxter appeared on the doorstep without warning, as usual.

"Ready?" she asked, jiggling her car keys.

"For what?"

"The *caterers,* Jody. Don't you remember?"

In all honesty, I didn't. She had so many fucking wedding errands I couldn't keep them straight.

I should have turned her down and plotted the next phase of my job hunt, but I'd just deposited a check from Dean and financial ruin seemed a little more distant than it had mere days earlier. I nodded with false interest and followed her to the car.

"How's the shower coming along?" she asked, once we were buckled in.

"The shower?"

"My *bridal* shower. You're hosting it."

"Oh, right." I'd forgotten about that, too. "It's coming along."

We drove to a bakery owned by Hannah's Aunt Clare (called "E-Clare's," of course), to sample wedding cake. Clare was a big woman, a baking recommendation in itself, with pale, doughy skin and Cupid's bow lips. It was a wonder all the food it took to bulk her up had passed through that tiny painted mouth.

She gripped Hannah in a bear hug, transferring flour smudges from her kitchen whites to her niece's black pullover. Hannah winced at the force of the embrace, but managed a stiff smile once released.

"Let's get down to business," Clare said, offering me a surprisingly limp handshake, more like a dead fish than her thick fingers suggested.

She pulled a photograph album out from under the counter and the three of us sat at a corner table, leafing through photos. Granted, I was no expert, but it soon became apparent that we were looking at hundreds of shots of the same four-layer, square cake. The icing flowers may have been different colors, and they may have been created months and years apart, but it was the same goddamn cake, over and over again. I was speechless when Hannah said she was having a hard time choosing, finally narrowing it down to her top three.

"Which one do you think, Jody?"

"I think any of them would do."

"Come on. I need to pick."

"Okay, what about this one?" I asked, pointing at the photo closest to me.

"Oh, that's my least favorite." She chewed on the end of her ponytail. "Which of the other two do you think is better?"

"That one." I pointed to the photo on the left.

"No, I think it's going to be this one," she said, smiling at the remaining picture.

"What the hell did you ask me for?" I muttered.

"What flavor do you want?" Aunt Clare asked.

"I don't know. Coconut?"

"I'm not sure that everyone likes coconut," I said. *I* certainly didn't.

"But I love it, and it's *my* wedding."

"What about carrot?" Clare asked.

"Blech."

"I could do chocolate."

"I'll have brown crud between my teeth in all the pictures."

"What about a white cake, with raspberry?" Clare looked agitated.

"Have you got a sample?" Hannah asked hopefully.

The next thing I knew, we were surrounded by over a dozen slivers of various cakes. "Pick one and let me know," Clare said, leaving us with a jug of cold milk and a couple of glasses.

We dug in immediately, sampling rich chocolate and faint vanilla, hazelnut, carrot, and coconut, cleansing our palates between flavors. It could have been the sugar, or the sheer fun of sampling, but soon we were giggling like a couple of five-year-olds, forgetting about everything but cream filling and raspberry puree, sandwiched between layers of lemon cake. I licked buttery frosting from my fingers, knowing life couldn't get any better.

We finally decided on two layers of chocolate with raspberry filling, and two of white cake with lemon custard. Showing taste I hadn't thought she possessed, Hannah chose to drape the cake with fresh flowers instead of icing petals.

When the imaginary bill was settled with a wink and a nod, we were on our way.

"That was incredible!" I said, buckling my seat belt.

"I was thinking we could stop by another bakery for round two," Hannah said, licking the last of the frosting from her lips.

"But you already ordered the cake."

"I know." She laughed wickedly and drove to La Patisserie on Woodland.

We looked through another book of photographs, and Hannah sweetly requested samples of their most unusual flavors, some variety for our overstimulated taste buds. The head pastry chef was determined to sell us a pale green pistachio cake, but Hannah wasn't interested. I thought it was delicious, but of course, as she was quick to remind me, *I* wasn't the bride. We worked our way through another six slices, from pineapple, to pumpkin spice, with some coffee cheesecake in between.

When we'd demolished the samples in greedy forkfuls, Hannah blithely remarked that we would think about what we'd tasted and let the chef know if we were interested.

We stumbled out to the car, wired with sugar.

"Okay," Hannah said, laughing, "now for the real food."

She had an appointment with the first caterer on her list, so the manager was ready to feed us as soon as we were seated. It was a trip down memory lane. Hank's Place was firmly ensconced in the old-school traditions of meatballs stabbed with frilled toothpicks, sausage rolls that left grease shadows on the fingertips, and cheese balls, covered in either crushed walnuts or paper-thin almond slices.

We were left alone with a platter of food and a pot of coffee, the last thing we needed.

As I nibbled, I was reminded of parties my parents had thrown when I was a kid. I'd been in charge of piling overcoats on their bed and passing hors d'oeuvres to increasingly drunk guests, watching as the combination of conversation and body heat covered the windows with a film of steam. I'd refill my glass with pop, slurping until my head spun with music, laughter, sweet pickles, and white dinner rolls smeared with pats of real butter. Mom forgot my bedtime and it would be eight-thirty, nine, and even ten o'clock before I was hustled away to my room.

"What do you think?" Hannah asked, lifting a paprika-covered deviled egg toward her waiting lips.

"All that's missing is a fondue pot and a wooden bowl of party mix," I said, muffling my laughter.

"Don't forget the cheese spread." She choked on the egg.

"Ah, *cheese spread.* It's all in the wrist, you know."

"All about the presentation." Hannah nodded, lifting an item from the plate with a twinkle in her eye. "Cocktail weenie?"

By the time we left Hank's my stomach was shifting and adjusting to the rather rowdy preservative party it was hosting, but the food frenzy wasn't over yet.

Our next stop was a very expensive-looking shop, managed by a young woman with copper curls and an expression of constant delight. She brought us doily-lined trays of snacks and a carafe of red wine, which Hannah declined, due to her pregnancy. I ended up drinking most of the booze myself.

We ate seafood-stuffed mushroom caps, grinning as they crumpled between our fingers, leaking warm crab juice into our cupped palms. We filled our mouths with salmon canapés, stuffed camembert, hot artichoke dip, and antipasto.

"Oh, my God, this is *so* good," I managed between bites.

"I think I've found my caterer."

"Who did you use before?"

"Let's see. Mom cooked for the first one, a place in Fillington did the third, and I can't remember the second."

The redhead reappeared. "I assume you'll want caviar," she said, flashing small jars with big price tags. They weren't open for our sampling pleasure.

"I don't think so," Hannah said.

"But it's a *wedding,* isn't it?" the woman wheedled.

"Yeah. *Her fourth.*" I put out that fire.

"Oh, my." She frowned, and I wondered how often Hannah's plans inspired that look.

I ate a little bit of everything and by the end of our visit, my stomach was doing backflips. Hannah placed her order and left a hefty deposit, courtesy of her mother.

"I guess we'd better head back," she said, once we'd climbed, wincing, into the car. "I've got to pick up my dress at the dry cleaner's."

"Hot date tonight?" I asked, wishing I had one of my own.

"Hello?" She laughed. "I'm going to the reunion, Jody."

Somehow, I'd forgotten about it. "Oh . . . have fun."

"You're really not going?" she gasped, almost steering us off the road.

"No way."

"Come on. It'll be great."

"How could it possibly be great?"

"You know, seeing how fat everybody got, who lost their hair . . ."

I almost mentioned "who was divorced," but remembered who I was talking to in the nick of time. "It's just not something I want to do."

"You'll regret it, Jody," she sang. "You'll be sitting at home, watching TV and wondering how everybody turned out."

"With my luck, it'll be success central."

"You never know."

"I already ran into Chloe Patterson and Sara Temple."

"I didn't know Chloe was in town," Hannah murmured. "She didn't RSVP."

"Well, she's back."

"I can't believe she didn't call me." Her face was flushed. "My number was right on the invitation."

"I wouldn't worry about it."

She turned onto Erin's street. "Will you *please* come, Jody?"

"No."

"Will you at least think about it? I'll make sure there's a nametag for you."

"No."

"Jody." She obviously wasn't going to give up.

"Okay. I'll think about it." *And decide against it.*

"Wonderful. Oh, and remember, we have a dress fitting tomorrow at ten o'clock."

I thanked her for the entertaining day and climbed Erin's steps, regretting every morsel I'd shoved down my throat.

"You're back!" Erin shrieked, as I stepped across the threshold. "Where the hell have you been?"

"I could ask you the same thing. I haven't seen you for days."

"Yeah, yeah. I've been working my ass off at the nursery. So, what were you up to? I saw someone drop you off."

"That was Hannah. We were checking out caterers."

"Sounds like a regular laugh riot." She rolled her eyes.

"Actually, we had fun." I shook my head. "Amazing but true."

"No shit?"

"I'm beginning to think this wedding could be a good time. Aside from the dresses, of course."

"Is that right?"

"Yeah. You know, she kind of loosened up today. We both did, actually."

"Yippee-skippee," she said, groaning.

"I'm serious. She's really not as bad as I thought, and it was kind of nice to spend the day with her instead of moping around the house."

"I'm glad to hear it." Her tone said something else entirely.

"This will sound crazy, but I may actually be looking forward to the wedding now."

"Great." She sneered.

Is she jealous?

"Erin, I—"

"I picked a reunion outfit for you."

"I'm not going."

"What?"

"I haven't heard from Justin in days."

"So?" She lit a cigarette.

"So, he was going to take me."

"Call him."

"I've tried, and now it just feels awkward."

"Why does it . . . oh!" She gasped. *"You did it!"*

"I don't really want to talk about—"

"You got it on!" she crowed.

"Erin, I don't—"

"Did you?" she demanded, inhaling deeply.

"Erin."

"Confirm or deny, Jody."

"Yes."

"*Yahoo!* Back in the saddle again!" She started coughing and I slapped her back until the sputtering ceased. "Wait a second. He never *called* you?"

"No."

"That fucking bastard!"

It was one thing for me to think it, but quite another to hear her say the words. I jumped to his defense. "He's been really busy, I think—"

"Come on, Jody."

"It could be true. There's probably a very good reason he hasn't called."

"Yeah, he's a shithead."

"Okay, support is the key element here, Erin."

"Fuck! He seemed like a good guy." She took another drag and exhaled slowly. "Listen, you and I'll just go together. Michael has to work, so I don't have a date, either."

"The last thing I need is—"

"To see that all the assholes who intimidated you in high school have turned into a bunch of pathetic losers?" She smiled. "I think it's *exactly* what you need."

"I have nothing going for me right now." I sighed. "What am I going to tell people?"

"Lie." She shrugged.

"I'm not going to *lie.*"

"Then *embellish.*"

"What?" I asked, prickling with annoyance. "You think my life is so bad I have to fake it?"

"No," she said quietly. "You do."

We were silent for a moment. "I just wish things were better for me right now."

"They could be worse. You still have your health, you know." Her flicker of a smile turned into a laugh.

"After the gorging I did today, I'm not so sure," I said, taking her cue and chuckling softly.

"So, will you go with me?"

"Only if I can choose my own clothing."

"That's fair." She nodded.

"And only if we can leave when it gets uncomfortable."

"As long as you at least walk through the door."

"Okay."

"And talk to at least five people before calling it a night."

"Okay."

"Not including me."

"I *said* okay."

"Good." She smiled. "I think we're going to have a great time tonight."

I shrugged, knowing better than to expect a miracle.

twenty-three

I spent over an hour testing the fashion waters with one reluctant toe. I didn't want to wear anything too sexy, crazy, revealing, or bizarre, so I settled on a pair of loose black pants and a pale green, shimmery blouse. Erin talked me into leaving my hair down and used some kind of industrial-strength mousse to defrizz it, making it thick and wavy instead. I borrowed some faux-emerald earrings from Gammy's clip-on collection and Erin sprayed me with a shower of perfume.

"If I know you, you'll be sweating up a storm in there," she said, returning to the task of dressing herself.

"Thanks."

"Am I lying?"

"Well . . . no." I sighed.

While I was making every attempt to appear casual and unconcerned about the opinions of my former classmates, Erin looked as if she were on her way to a restricted-access club, where breaking through the bouncers boiled down to sex appeal.

She wore a red mandarin-style dress, fitted to every curve her body had to offer above the knee, where it abruptly ended, leaving her long legs to stand on their own in black heels. The dress was slit from hem to mid-thigh on one side, thanks to Erin's handiwork with a pair of scissors, and I was sure she wouldn't be able to sit down without exposing even more than she intended.

When we stood in front of the mirror for a final assessment, I glanced at Erin's hair, cascading down her back in a long, dark ripple, and the glossy red lips she was unconsciously puckering. I took a closer look at the subdued shades I'd used on my eyes, the pink of my cheeks the result of a quick pinch of the flesh with my fingers.

"I look like a suburban housewife," I muttered.

"Why don't you wear—"

"It's fine. I'm comfortable, and you'll be cursing your heels within the hour"

We arrived at the Bent Harbor Inn a deliberate half hour late and found the registration table in front of the main conference room. A pounding rhythm came from inside, along with the loud hum of conversation.

Hannah and David Baxter sat on folding chairs behind the table, which was decorated in streamers of blue and white, our school colors. Several people were ahead of us in line, which gave me the opportunity to observe the bride- and groom-to-be.

David wore his old football jersey, a glaring reminder that his life had peaked during those quarterback days. He still had a mullet, trimmed to a buzz on top while the stringy sides and back hung almost to his shoulders. One hand rested against Hannah's back and the other gripped a beer.

His bride looked like a beauty queen, albeit a pregnant one, in a rose-colored satin dress and shawl. Her hair was woven into an elaborate, braided bun with a few long, blond tendrils flowing free. If I was looking at the two of them through the eyes of a stranger, I'd think she was a movie star and he was her thug bodyguard.

The banner on the wall behind Hannah's careful coif read WELCOME BENT HARBOR ALUMNI! SEA HOW FAR YOU'VE COME!

"What's that supposed to mean?" I asked, nudging Erin.

"I have no fucking idea," she muttered.

"If what I've seen so far is any indication of what's inside, this is going to be a long night."

When we finally reached the front of the line, Hannah grinned at me. "I *knew* you couldn't resist!"

She set to work locating our nametags while David's eyes traced Erin's body from head to toe, then returned to her breasts.

"So, the wedding's right around the corner," I said, embarrassed for Hannah.

"Huh?" David turned his hooded eyes toward me.

"Your *wedding.* It's coming up," I snarled, shooting him a dirty look.

"Yeah." His gaze returned to Erin, who pretended not to notice him as she arched her back and accentuated the obvious. She never was one to turn down an appraisal, even if it came from a Neanderthal like David Baxter.

"Here we go!" Hannah said, presenting me with a laminated badge.

It was my graduation picture, one of the worst ever taken. The camera had caught me in mid-blink and my mortarboard was too small for my mound of curls, so the photographer had pinned it just off center. I looked loaded, like the poster girl for the annual campaign against drinking and driving that took place every spring.

Sighing, I secured the nametag to my shirt pocket, branding myself a big loser for the evening, and waited for Erin. When she was ready, we thanked Hannah and moved away from the table.

"Damn, look at this picture," Erin said, frowning.

I leaned over and saw exactly what I remembered, a photo that looked like it came from a teen magazine. "What are you complaining about? You looked great."

"That's the problem." She glanced at my photo. "Everyone's going to tell *you* how much better you look, but this is what *I* have to live up to."

"Uh, thanks a lot."

"I wasn't trying to insult you."

"Then your natural skill is astounding."

"Lighten up. It's a *party,* for Christ's sake."

She led me through a glittering blue and white curtain just as Chloe Patterson reached the registration table.

David Baxter almost fell out of his chair in a frantic move to greet her, clearly thrilled she'd arrived.

"Oh, God, they're using a smoke machine." I groaned, stepping into a cloud of white.

I waved the offensive fumes out of my face and saw two banquet tables, heavily laden with food, a full-sized bar (thank you!), and a dance floor packed with people. Strobe lights flickered through the smoke, making the dancers look robotic as they coughed and choked on the dry mist. A silver disco ball strung from the ceiling added to the dizzying light show, speckling the floor with swirling dots of color.

"Oh, man, there's Rob Moultree," Erin said, pointing at a paunchy guy in a tight suit. He was piling food onto an already crowded plate. "Do you remember when he puked down the heating vent at Samantha Conner's party?"

"Don't remind me. That place reeked like scorched vomit all winter. Is that Karla Novich?" I pointed to a redhead sipping wine next to the bar.

"I think so. Do you want to say hi?"

"Nah, not right now. Maybe I'll talk to her later." I didn't know what to say to anyone, and I already felt uptight and defensive.

"There's Cindy Matheson," Erin said, pointing to the dance floor.

"Where?" Cindy had been the star of the debating team.

"Right over there."

"I don't see her." I craned my neck, straining for a better view.

"Follow my finger," Erin ordered impatiently.

"I am. I still don't see her."

"She's dancing with Paul Atkins."

"Who?"

"*Paul Atkins.* You know, he was on the badminton team."

"Not exactly a spectator sport."

"We were in twelfth-grade biology together."

"I wasn't in that class."

"Well, he's the guy dancing with Cindy."

"I give up." I rolled my eyes. "Want a drink?"

I didn't have to ask twice, and walked over to the bar for a couple of rum and Cokes, thankful to have something to do.

"Jody?" Karla Novich asked, smiling.

"Yeah. How are you doing, Karla?"

"Not bad. Surprised I'm here, I guess."

"Me, too. I don't even recognize some of these people."

"I know. Have you seen Patty Davidson? She must weigh seventy pounds."

"Anorexic?"

"No doubt." She sipped her wine. "Did you see David Baxter at the front door? He is such a jackass."

"Tell me about it. Hannah's marrying him again this summer."

"You're kidding!" She gasped.

"I'm the maid of honor," I couldn't help bragging.

We talked for several minutes, reminiscing over art-class

hijinks and cafeteria food. As it turned out, she had a degree in anthropology, but worked in a cafe, which made me feel better about my own situation. I gave her a brief overview of my past ten years and we had some laughs.

I'd forgotten that, in addition to the thick-necked jocks who still clung together as if they were in a mid-game huddle, and the snotty cheerleaders with matching hairdos, who were arguing at the punch bowl over whose kid was the best soccer player, drummer, or speller, there were people I actually *liked* in high school.

I exchanged phone numbers with Karla and tracked Erin down. She was chatting with Stuart Last-name-forgotten and Pam Hendricks.

"Jody, there you are!" Erin pulled me forward and grabbed her drink. "I was just telling these guys that we need to find Trevor Singh right away."

I was confused until I saw the desperation in her eyes for me to play along.

"I found him," I announced. "He's waiting for us by the chip dip."

We hurried away from Stuart and Pam, Erin hissing, "What took you so long? Those two were driving me *nuts*."

We wafted through the crowd, recognizing most but not all of the faces. Some had been improved by plastic surgery and others were aged beyond our years through excessive tanning, or distorted by weight fluctuations. I would have had better luck guessing who some of my classmates were if I'd looked at them in a fun-house mirror, or through the bottom of a beer glass.

As we stopped and chatted, we heard about who had kids and how many, who was in jail, in grad school, in Malaysia, in a homosexual love triangle, in training for marathons, and in debt. We were handed business cards, patted on the back, and hugged with excessive force. The experience was proving to be more like a family reunion than anything, especially when I saw Chris in the doorway.

"Shit! I can't believe he's here." I pointed for Erin's benefit.

"He's got balls," she agreed. "Where's Beth?"

"She was a year behind us."

"But she fucked half our class. Shouldn't that make her an honorary member?" Erin snickered.

"So you've reverted to 'fuck.' "

"In certain instances, yes."

"Do you think Chris knows about her and Russell McAllister?"

"Doubt it."

"I almost feel sorry for him," I murmured.

"You've *got* to be shitting me!"

"I said *almost*."

"Are you going to talk to him?"

"If he approaches me," I told her. "I'm not walking over there."

As it happened, Chris didn't see me, and I watched him fall in with members of the basketball team before I lost sight of him.

After my third drink, the music was turned down and our class president, Jamie Phillips, appeared at the microphone and thanked everyone for coming. He mentioned the accomplishments of some of our most successful peers and we all clapped enthusiastically, not out of pride, but the potential to tell others, "I knew them when . . ."

Jamie made several announcements, none of which were important to me, and the music returned to full volume, the dance floor crowded with bad outfits and worse moves.

"Let's mix and mingle some more," Erin suggested, leading me toward the bar. "But first, another drink."

"I guess I'm driving," I muttered.

"Well, I drove here, so you can drive home."

"Oh, *that*'s fair." I ordered a Coke.

"Jody?"

I turned to see Chris standing behind me, wearing a crooked smile.

"Oh, hi." I was momentarily thrown, but tried not to show it. Why did he have to be so cute? More important, why did Justin have to disappoint me by being a rat bastard?

Chris tucked his hands into the pockets of his jeans and rocked his weight from one foot to the other. "How are you?"

"Fine." I sniffed.

"Having a good time?"

"I was."

Erin saw us talking and made a surprisingly subtle departure from the area.

"I was hoping we could talk civilly."

"This isn't civil? I think I'm being a wonderful sport, considering. No Beth tonight?"

"Uh, no. Things aren't really working out the way I'd hoped."

"Is that so?"

"She's kind of . . . bitchy."

"Hmm . . . *interesting*. You didn't suspect anything when she was sleeping with her own cousin's boyfriend?"

"I thought things would be different."

"Too bad," I snapped.

"She's moving out."

"Tough shit."

"If you could just look past what happened between us, Jody . . ." His eyes were hopeful.

"Look past it?" I choked.

"I was wondering if there was a chance . . ."

He wouldn't dare to ask me back, *would he*?

"I mean, even the slightest chance—"

Pitiful! I was ready to shred him into a thousand pieces.

"—that you could move back into my place."

My jaw dropped. "You've *got* to be kidding! You actually think I want anything to do with you? Chris, I wouldn't take you back if my life depended on it! I've been through so much shit since we broke up that I've realized I don't need you, or any man. I'm starting a new life and the last thing I need is to fall back into bed with you!"

"I'm not asking you to."

"You just asked me to move back in, you idiot."

"As a *friend,*" he explained. "A roommate."

"What?"

"Purely platonic. We got along so well before, I thought we could do it again, without the relationship."

"Are you brain-dead?"

"Jody, I'm going to lose the house. I can't afford to pay the rent alone."

"Fuck you," I said, through gritted teeth, and turned away.

As I pushed past the crowd to find Erin, disgusted that I'd ever been involved with such an asshole, I stumbled across none other than Mrs. Corbett.

"Excuse me," I said, hoping to brush past without being recognized.

"Get me another drink." Her words slurred together and I tried to keep walking, but she grabbed my sleeve. "I *said* I need another drink." She sighed, then belched loudly.

"That's the last thing you need." I guided her toward a seat. She leaned against me with all of her weight and it was a struggle to stay upright.

"I used to work at Bent Harbor High School," she mumbled, exhaling pure alcohol.

"You were a guidance counselor," I said, parking her on a stool.

"I was a goddamn guidance counselor!" she barked, in a sudden rush of energy.

"Yes, you were." I looked for an easy escape route.

"I came here tonight." She paused to belch again. "To see if anyone here appreciated a damn thing I did for them. I went to bat for these little bastards, and they won't even give me the time of day." Her head bobbed pathetically. "I don't want to go back to high school."

"You don't have to," I assured her.

"I never wanted to go back, but now . . . oh, shit."

She was barely coherent and unable to balance on the stool, so I tried to prop her up against the wall.

"Don't ever go into business for yourself, kid."

"Why's that?" I asked, with no interest in the answer.

"*Liability*. You're liable for every little thing that goes wrong."

"I guess you're right," I said, looking for help.

"I *know* I'm right. I'm the one *telling* you I'm gonna lose it all."

"Lose what?"

"Aren't you *listening*? Lose my business. Where's my drink?"

"Hold on a second." I stared at her. "Why are you losing your business?"

"I told you already. *Liability*. Get me a drink, would ya?"

"I don't understand."

"I mean I need a drink. Do I need to whisper it in your ear? Whisper, whisper, whispering . . . goddamn, fucking Whispering Pines."

"Did you say 'Whispering Pines'?"

"If there's a lawsuit, it'll kill me." Her head bobbed again, but she was able to lift it herself. "That little shit told me she'd taken *classes*. Said she'd worked in a hospital before." She moaned, and closed her eyes. "I never checked. Goddammit, I never checked."

twenty-four

Once I'd found a ride home for Erin, and given her none of the details I'd heard, I drove her car directly to Justin's house. Lucas's health was more important than my ego, and I knew Justin wouldn't want his brother to spend another night at Whispering Pines. I raced through town, wondering what Mrs. Corbett's employee had done wrong.

I pulled onto Justin's street and the house was completely dark. It was only nine-thirty, but I crossed my fingers and hoped he was in bed. I knocked on the door, then pounded on it, ringing the doorbell every couple of seconds. "Where are you?" I whispered.

"Will you keep it down?" a woman called from an upstairs window next door.

"Where's Justin?" I asked.

"Who?"

"Justin McDade!"

"That's Bev Saunder's house."

I gritted my teeth. "I'm looking for the guy who's living here."

"The renter?"

"Yes! The renter!"

"Hasn't been around for a few days, not that I spy on him, or anything. He goes to work pretty darn early."

"Thank you." I started toward the car.

"Wakes me up most mornings, if you must know."

"Thank you for your help."

"I thought about filing a complaint!" she called after me.

I climbed into the car and headed for Whispering Pines, following the curves of Old Marine Highway, more worried about answers than my safety.

When I pulled up to the gate, the hospital looked dark and foreboding, like some evil beast rising from the depths of the earth. I scanned the front lawns in search of activity, but saw nothing but the flickering blue lights of a couple of TV screens. I wasn't sure what I'd expected. Police cars and ambulances? Orderlies sneaking across the grounds to dispose of bodies? And if I'd seen anything, what would I have done? *Made a citizen's arrest?*

I was kidding myself. There was nothing I could do but go home.

Fifteen minutes later, I was eyeing the flashing red light on Erin's answering machine, and hoping against hope for word from Justin. There were two messages, the first from my mom, the second from Dean.

Disappointment struck again. Why did I bother getting my hopes up? There was no relationship between us, and I was wasting my time thinking that was going to change.

I dialed Mom's number as I put on the kettle for tea, hoping it would calm my nerves.

"Hello?" Josh answered on the third ring.

"Hi, it's me. What are you doing there?"

"Do you want to talk to Mom?"

"Sure, but . . ." I heard him drop the receiver and call my mother to the phone.

"Hi, honey," she said, after a short wait.

"Hi. You called earlier?"

"Yes." She paused. "I did."

"And?" I waited. "What's going on?"

"Well, we had a bit of bad news tonight."

Bad news only meant one thing in my family. *Death.* I felt my stomach clench as I ran through the potential losses. Uncle Albert? He'd already had a triple bypass and the recovery wasn't going as well as expected. Grannie Rogers? She was nearing ninety, but tougher than algebra. Was it someone else? A car accident? Fire?

"It's your brother, Jody." She sighed.

"I just talked to him. He's not sick, is he?"

"What? No, he's just had a bit of a setback. He lost his job."

"Thank God," I said, breathing a sigh of relief.

"Jody! How can you say that?"

"I thought something was seriously wrong," I explained.

"It is. Your brother *lost his job.*"

"Big deal. He'll find another one," I assured her.

"Like you have?"

"Thanks a lot."

"You know what I mean. It's a bad economy."

"It'll get better. Don't worry, Mom."

"He won't be able to afford his apartment."

I thought of the dump where I'd visited him and figured that was a good thing. "So, we're both homeless." I laughed. "What a pair of losers."

"Your father and I are thinking about letting him stay here for a while, just until he gets organized."

"Good one," I said, laughing harder.

"I'm serious."

I could tell from her tone that she was. "I can't believe it! Mom, you wouldn't let *me* stay there."

"I know, honey, but you always seem to bounce back better than he does."

"You've got to be kidding!"

"He just needs a little extra help."

"Only because you coddle him!"

"Jody," she warned.

"Was he laid off, or fired?"

"Oh, I'm not really sure." Her tone was awfully squirrelly.

"Mom?"

"Fired." She sighed.

"For what?"

"I don't know all the details."

"I think you do."

She sighed again before answering. "It was the reefer."

"Pot? He was smoking pot at work?"

"Not exactly," she hedged.

"Then what, exactly?"

"He was . . . um, selling it."

"At Video Nook?"

"Yes."

So, Muffin Zone Amy was right, after all. "And you're letting him stay with you?"

"I said we're thinking about it."

"But he's there now, right?"

"He had dinner with us. Honey, we fed you when you left Chris."

"Yeah, a last meal before you kicked me out into the street."

"That's not how it happened, and you know it."

"So, you boot him out of your place for *growing* pot, he gets fired from his job for *selling* it, and now you're letting him move back in because you're worried he won't *bounce back*?"

"Honey."

"Why don't you just let him use your new studio to grow his

dope, Mom. Then you can drive him around when he delivers it, kind of like a paper route, or Meals on Wheels."

"Jody, please."

"Can I talk to Dad?" Surely my father wouldn't allow Josh to move in!

"Not right now. Try to understand, honey. We thought you were more responsible than Josh is, and when you stormed out of the Galley with no plans for survival, we wanted to teach you a lesson."

"That crime pays?"

"No."

"Is it going to take a felony, or will a mere misdemeanor open your door for me?"

"I have to go," Mom said quietly.

"So do I!" I slammed the receiver into its cradle.

I ran a hot bath and tried to keep from crying. Of course, I couldn't control the tears and strawberry bubbles popped as each salty drop left my chin. I ran through my checklist of disaster. I was *still* unemployed, with no hope in sight, Justin had left me for dead, Mom and Dad were punishing me for no apparent reason, my brother was a bona fide jackass, my only admirer was doing time in a sketchy psychiatric facility, my best friend was steeped in the magical bullshit of love, and I would *never* be able to afford a house on Sitka Point. Oh, yeah, and the Galley, practically the only thing I cared about, was going to be demolished.

I soaked until the bubbles had almost disappeared, then added more hot water. If I was going to get through the disappointments and get on with my life, I had to consider the positive side. I reclined against the padded cushion in the back of the tub and racked my brain. It took some time, but I managed to grab hold of a few silver linings.

I couldn't be unemployed *forever,* I supposed. I'd been out of work for ten days, not a huge length of time in the scheme of things, and I had survived. There was a slim possibility that Justin's lack of communication had nothing to do with me, and I was grateful for that glimmer of hope. My parents may not have acted the way I wanted them to, but I had to believe that their intention was to help me. And they had, really. If I'd stayed with them, I would have spent even more time moping on the couch while Mom baked brownies and took care of my laundry. I'd learned how to stand up for myself when I quit my job, and handled the responsibility of running the Galley in Dean's absence without a hitch. I'd given Chris a piece of my mind, and I had Hannah's wedding to look forward to. Lastly, if I never lived on Sitka Point, I'd find a nice little place in town to call my own. It wasn't the end of the world. It really wasn't.

I climbed out of the tub just as the doorbell rang.

"Who is it?" I called, cinching the belt on my robe.

"Justin."

I unbolted the door, and there he was. It had only been a matter of days, but it felt like forever.

"Hi," I said, afraid to show any emotion until I knew where I stood.

"Hi." His voice was soft and low. "Can I come in?"

I moved to one side so he could pass, smelling his aftershave as he brushed past me and into the living room.

"I'm sorry I haven't called."

"That's okay." I couldn't meet his eyes.

"No, it isn't."

"You're damn right it isn't!" I blurted, then caught myself. "Uh . . . go on," I said, as calmly as I could.

"Thank you." There was a smile in his voice. "It's not okay, but I *do* have an explanation."

"So, explain," I challenged, hoping he would convince me to give him another chance, but more importantly, hoping he *wanted* one.

He sat on the edge of the couch. "I'm totally fried," he said, rubbing his eyes. "But here goes. Lucas admitted himself into Whispering Pines."

"That much, I know."

"Right. So I tried to visit him, and the nurses wouldn't let me."

"Same here! And Justin, something's going on up there. Tonight I—"

"Hold on just a second, okay? I tried to contact his doctors and couldn't get through to anyone. Apparently, my name is nowhere in his files."

"Maybe your dad could—"

"I don't know where he is. I've spent the last few days running back and forth to his place, staging a one-man sit-in at Whispering Pines to get access to Lucas, trying to reach my mom on vacation in Milan, and mowing every fucking lawn in Fillington." He glanced at me. "Sorry."

"Believe me, I'm familiar with the f-word."

"Well, mowing lawns is the only thing I've actually been able to do. God only knows where my dad is."

"I don't want to freak you out, but I heard something about Whispering Pines at the reunion tonight."

"Shit! The reunion. I was supposed to take you."

"Don't worry about it," I said, then told him all about P.J. Hardison's odd behavior and my exchange with Mrs. Corbett.

"Jesus," he groaned when I was finished. "What am I going to do about Lucas?"

"I don't know. If they aren't letting you see him—"

"Do you know anyone who works at Whispering Pines?"

"Not a soul." I bit my lip. "Can't you just demand that he be released? I mean, he signed himself in, so surely you can take him out."

"Nope." He shook his head, his expression bleak.

"Shit."

"No kidding." He rested his head in his hands. "I am so goddamn *tired*."

I invited him to stay the night. I didn't expect him to be game for anything physical, but soon discovered that all of the tension and emotion of the past few days made both of us very eager for some kind of release. We shared an intense session of clutching, kissing, and gasping that shadowed anything I'd ever experienced.

"You have no idea how glad I am that you're here," I murmured, as we lay in each other's arms. "I thought whatever we had was over."

He kissed my temple. "Whatever we have is just getting started."

We fell asleep, exhausted, and I never heard Erin come home.

In the morning, I awoke to the sound of Justin's slow, steady breathing and smiled. I crawled out from under his arm and made my way to the bathroom for a shower.

I soaked in the steady stream of hot water for a few minutes before I got down to the business of cleaning, and by the time I turned off the water, the room was full of steam. I dressed, wondering how long Justin would sleep if I didn't wake him. I peered into my room and saw that he was in deep slumber, so I quietly closed the door.

Hearing activity in the kitchen, I decided to share my Justin news with Erin, but when I reached the doorway I saw not her standing in front of the coffeemaker, but a man.

"Michael?" I heard her call from the bedroom. "Can you put on some coffee?"

"I'm doing it right now," he replied.

That was Michael? The mystery man finally revealed?

Batman stood, hunched over the counter, scraping stray grounds into his cupped palm. The first thing I noticed was that he wore the kind of white cotton underwear I associated with little boys who didn't know any better, and chiseled men in unnatural poses, featured in Sears catalogs. Tighty-whities. BVDs. Didn't he understand the aesthetic appeal, the clean-cut mystery that boxers guaranteed?

He was even slimmer than I remembered from our naked encounter, slight and pale with a collection of freckles across his back, much like my own. His straight, blond hair was almost shoulder length, and he had a small bat tattoo on his left shoulder blade.

I stood in awed silence, amazed and incredulous that this young man of modest build, who had by then moved to the sink to fill the coffeepot with water, was responsible for the orgasmic merrymaking I'd been hearing night after night. It was nothing short of *incredible* to me that the woman who had chosen bulk over brains for most of her life had become a swooning, lovestruck ninny over the slender creature whistling before me.

"Thanks for starting the coffee," Erin said, breezing into the room. Thankfully, she was dressed. "Morning, Jode."

Michael turned to greet me, and I didn't know where to look. Apparently, the mere sight of Erin was enough to delight him, and a certain body part strained against the confines of his undies.

"I know *you.*" He smiled. "Good morning."

He had pleasant face and nice green eyes, but apart from that and his anxious organ, he was remarkably *un*remarkable. That was more shocking to me than two heads.

"Morning," I said, wishing he'd put on some pants.

"Nice to see you clothed." He had an unthreatening twinkle in his eye.

"You, too."

"I'm Michael."

"I know. It's nice to meet you, after all I've heard . . ." I paused, thinking of the sexual cacophony he'd generated. "All I've, uh, heard about you."

"Morning," Justin said, resting his chin on my shoulder.

"Good morning!" Erin shrieked. "I didn't know *you* were here. Have a seat in the dining room."

Michael slipped into the bedroom for some clothing and Erin pointed Justin toward the table. He was still within earshot, but that didn't stop her from grinning and whispering, a touch too loudly, "Way to go, Jody!"

I winced in response and joined Justin once Erin had insisted on making breakfast for everyone.

"Way to go, Jody?" He wiggled his eyebrows suggestively. "What's that all about?"

"You know exactly what she meant." I blushed. "You. Me. Us."

"I see." He laughed.

"She's not exactly subtle."

"Much like her friend in the skivvies. I don't think breakfast is his top priority at the moment."

When the four of us were seated at the table, passing toast and spreading jam, Erin asked where Justin had been for the past few days. He outlined Lucas's history and our curiosity about what was going on at Whispering Pines. "I can't imagine trying to barge in. I mean, there are cameras *everywhere,* but I don't know what else to do."

"If only we knew someone who worked there," I muttered, adding sugar to my coffee. "Can you think of anyone, Erin?"

"Yeah, I can."

"Who?" Justin and I asked, in unison.

"Me," Michael said, smiling.

Perhaps he was a superhero, after all.

twenty-five

Over a long breakfast, Michael, a cook in Whispering Pines' main cafeteria, told us that the hospital was a breeding ground for gossip. Any comment made by an administrator to a staff member at eight in the morning reached the doctors by nine, the nursing trenches by their first coffee break, the kitchen heard it during the lunch rush, and it was buzzing in the ears of the groundskeepers by the end of the day.

"I'll keep my ears pricked," he told us as he left for work. "I'm bound to hear something."

"I appreciate it." Justin rose and shook his hand before heading into the shower.

Erin and I waited for the water to start running before she told me Mrs. Corbett passed out before last call and had to be removed from the Bent Harbor Inn by two uniformed policemen.

"So, what about you, Jode? I was surprised to see your little friend here this morning."

"He showed up last night, right after I came to grips with the fact that nothing is as bad as it seems."

"The power of positive thinking," Erin said dryly and smiled. "I'm glad he had a good explanation for the disappearing act."

"So am I." I slurped my coffee. "Michael seems like a good guy."

"We're getting pretty serious."

"I know."

"I want him to move in."

My heart stopped for a second. *Is she kicking me out?* I tried to slow my racing thoughts. Obviously, I wasn't planning to live with Erin *forever,* and I needed my own place. Surely I could find someone to room with if I needed help with rent.

I have to get serious about my new positive attitude.

"I think that's a great idea," I told her.

"I don't want you to feel like you have to leave, Jode."

"I should, though. If you could just give me a few days . . ."

"No problem. Take as much time as you need. I'm a bit nervous about the whole thing, anyway. It's a big step for me."

"You'll be fine."

"Oh, shit. After the surprise of our full house this morning, I forgot to tell you that Dean called twice while you were in the shower. He wants you to call him back."

"I'll get in touch with him later."

The water stopped and I heard Justin clattering around in the bathroom before he appeared in the doorway. "I'm going to the hospital to give it another shot. Might as well keep badgering them, I guess. Want to come?"

"I'm supposed to be meeting Hannah for a dress fitting." I was glad I'd remembered, for once. I was looking forward to getting some of her ideas for the bridal shower, and I already had some of my own brewing. It was amazing what one fun afternoon with Hannah had done for my attitude. "I'll call you this afternoon to see how it went."

He walked over to my chair and thoroughly kissed me before heading to the front door.

"Nice seeing you, Justin," Erin teased.

"You too, Erin," he sang in response.

* * *

Sprinklers were already out in full force and lawns sparkled with moisture in the morning sun as I walked toward Hannah's house. I finally felt at peace with myself, and vowed that from that day forward I'd be the kind of person who went with the flow and let the chips fall where they might. I'd be so laid-back, I wouldn't even vacuum them up.

When I reached the Baxter home, I took in the sight of rusty bikes propped on their kickstands, unhinged gutter pipes, a cracked kiddie pool on the front lawn, and two children standing on the front step, wearing hooded sweatshirts and no pants. At least the little one was wearing a diaper, although it was visibly full.

"Where's your mom?" I asked, as I approached them. Both kids stared at me blankly until I repeated the question and the bigger one opened the door for me.

I stepped into the house, which smelled like a comforting mixture of oatmeal and coffee. The floors were surprisingly clean, given the appearance of the home's exterior, and everything seemed to have its place, folded, stacked, or tucked into toy chests.

"Hannah?" I called.

"In the kitchen," she replied.

I followed my nose to the end of the hallway and Hannah smiled when she saw me. She was dressed to the nines in a well-cut plum maternity dress and heels.

"I hope I'm not late," I said, checking my watch. It was only a couple of minutes past ten.

"Late?" she asked, turning to the dishwasher.

"For the dress fitting." Had *she* forgotten?

"The dress fitting," she repeated absently. "Want a cup of coffee?"

"If we're okay for time," I said, sitting at the round table, still damp from cleaning.

She brought me a steaming mug and sat down.

"So, I was thinking about silver shoes," I told her. "But I guess black would look nice too, wouldn't it?" I'd spent so much time and energy dreading the event, it felt good to look forward to it. *The power of positive thinking.*

"I need to talk to you, Jody."

"Is something wrong?" Whatever it was, I'd do my best to cheer her up. "Are you and David fighting?"

"No, we're fine." She took a small sip of her coffee.

"I'm glad to hear it, considering the invitations are at the printers." I laughed.

"Jody?"

"Yes?"

"You aren't going to be my maid of honor."

I was momentarily stunned. "What?"

"Chloe Patterson was at the reunion last night, and we got to talking. We used to be pretty good friends."

"And?" *What does that have to do with me?*

"I asked her to be maid of honor."

"But you already have one." I pointed at myself.

"I hoped you would understand."

Be positive.

"So, I get bumped down to the rank of regular old bridesmaid." I shrugged. "That's no big deal."

"Actually, I'm keeping the other bridesmaids."

She didn't seem remotely uncomfortable breaking the news. I was finally looking forward to the goddamn wedding, and now I wasn't even part of it? She could have at least had the decency to be apologetic.

"I don't know what to say." I took another sip of coffee.

Hannah checked her watch. "Oh, dear, I'm going to be late for the fitting. Don't worry, Jody, I'll give you back what you paid for the fabric."

The next thing I knew, I was standing on the street outside her house, watching Hannah drive away with her carload of kids.

I walked back to Erin's and told her the news, trying to hide my disappointment.

"That girl is such a flake!" Erin groaned as she laced her work boots. "You'd be a way better bridesmaid than Chloe fucking Patterson."

"Maid of honor," I reminded her.

"Whatever."

"At least I'll be able to watch them walk down the aisle in their shiny robot dresses."

"You'll be thanking your lucky stars." Erin snickered. "Oh, hey. Dean called while you were gone."

"*Again?* Did he say what he wanted?"

"Nope."

"He probably needs me to cover a shift or something. Shit, I should have called him back earlier."

"Give him a call," she said, standing to leave. "I'll see you later."

Before I had a chance to pick up the phone, the damn thing was ringing. It was Josh.

"Are you at Mom and Dad's?" I asked.

"Yeah, I stayed here last night."

"I figured as much." I *knew* they couldn't give us equal treatment.

"They're driving me nuts, Jode. Dad woke me up at six this morning to help him with yard work, then clean the gutters. Do you have any idea how much crap was in there? Never mind the fact that I can't stand heights."

A smile began to form as I listened.

"Then we had to go to the hardware store because he's suddenly decided they need new light fixtures, and you *know* there's nothing wrong with the old ones. He actually expects me to fix the downstairs toilet, like I know anything about plumbing! When we got home, Mom made me clean out both bathtubs and mop the kitchen floor. It's only ten-thirty and I'm exhausted, Jode!"

Maybe my parents know what they're doing, after all.

"Just slow down for a second," I said, trying to contain a snort of laughter.

"I'm going mental over here," he whined.

"Listen, I've got a couple of things to organize first, but I'm planning to move out of Erin's and get my own place."

"Thanks for rubbing my nose in it."

"If you'd let me finish, I'd appreciate it."

"Go ahead." He sighed.

"If you find another job, stay away from dope, and I mean *completely away* from buying, selling, and smoking it . . ." I took a deep breath, hoping I wasn't making a dreadful mistake. "You can move in with me."

Gratified hysteria ensued, and it was all I could do to get him off the phone.

I called Dean and apologized for not getting in touch with him sooner. He asked me to meet him at the restaurant at two o'clock, but wouldn't tell me why.

To thank Erin for her hospitality, I cleaned the house from top to bottom. I vacuumed, mopped, and even dusted the windowsills, shelves, and bookcases before scrubbing the kitchen counters and cleaning out the fridge. The work felt good. Hell, *everything* felt good.

When Justin called, it was almost one o'clock.

"Did you see Lucas?"

"Nope."

"Shit."

"Well, they can't hold me off forever."

"I suppose," I murmured.

"In the meantime, Michael discovered there was a girl from a certain temp agency working at Whispering Pines."

"*Temp*tations."

"You got it. Apparently, she didn't know what she was doing and damaged some of the equipment. I didn't get the whole story, but it had something to do with electric therapy."

"Was someone hurt?"

"I'm not sure, but I'm kind of wondering about that guy you told me about."

"P.J. Hardison. I'm wondering the same thing. I'll be at the Galley this afternoon. If Max and Jaundice are there, I'll run it by them."

I thanked Justin for telling me what was going on, and wished him luck with his father. As I said goodbye and pulled the receiver away from my ear to hang up, I heard him whisper, "I love you." I bit my bottom lip and pretended I hadn't heard him, hanging up the phone instead of responding. I wasn't quite ready.

I left the house with the unread Ziggy album tucked under my arm and walked to the Galley, my head buzzing with a million thoughts. He *loved* me. Could it happen that fast? I concentrated on other things, trying to imagine why Dean wanted to meet, wondering what Michael's information would mean to Max and Jaundice, envisioning the day I had enough money for a place to call my own. *Justin loved me.* I was uncertain about where life was taking me, but knew I could get through it one step at a time.

Think Positively.

As I turned the corner and saw the Galley, my heart lurched

and I stopped dead in my tracks as if I were seeing the building for the first time. I stared for a good ten minutes, a terrific idea slowly forming.

When I stepped into the restaurant, the lunch crowd was gone and the wait staff was setting up for dinner. I was twenty minutes early for my meeting with Dean and beelined toward Max and Jaundice when I saw them at the counter.

"Well, well, well," Max said. "Darkening the doorway again."

"Good afternoon to you, too, Max."

"To what do we owe the honor?"

"I might have some information about P.J. and Whispering Pines."

"Sit down," Jaundice ordered.

I told them what I knew and both men remained silent, nodding as I spoke.

"I'm pretty sure that's what they do to him when he stays there," Jaundice said. "Shock treatment."

"They don't actually call it that anymore. It's—"

"Damn," Max cut me off. "I *knew* we shouldn't have taken him."

"Thanks for filling us in, kid," Jaundice said. "I guess we'll try to take care of it from here."

"It's the least I could do." I smiled and headed for the kitchen.

Dean invited me into the cubby office and closed the door. "I'm glad you could come down. I've been wanting to talk to you for a couple of days."

"I know. I'm sorry I didn't get back to you sooner. Things have been kind of out of control lately."

"Are they better now?"

"Definitely."

"Good. Listen, the buyer is taking forever deciding whether he wants to go through with it, and I'm going to need to go to the city for a couple of days to meet with an accountant and my lawyer."

"Dean?" I said, nerves jangling.

"Yeah?"

"I've been planning to buy a house on Sitka Point forever."

"I know."

"And I've been putting money away to do that."

"The illustrious savings account." He laughed. "I know, Jody."

"I don't have nearly enough to buy that house right now."

"I'm sorry, kid. Keep putting that money away and you'll get there."

"No," I said quietly.

"No, what?" he asked, squinting at me.

"I have an idea. No, a *plan.*" I took a deep breath. *Think Positively.* "You need money and less responsibility here. I have money, and I need something of my own."

"But the house—"

"I want to buy in on the Galley, Dean." I took a breath. "I want to be your partner."

"You're joking," he said, shaking his head.

"Nope. Bent Harbor needs this place. *I* need this place."

"I don't know what to say." His gaze met mine and he was silent for a full minute. "Can I think it over for a couple of days?"

"Sure!" He hadn't shut me down. It wasn't a "yes," but he was willing to consider it!

Over Dean's shoulder, I spotted a Ziggy strip on the wall, ending with a rainbow and the words "Think Positively." I was so excited, I didn't mind sharing a mantra with that little bald twerp.

Life is good. My eyes met Dean's again and I grinned. *Damn good.*

epilogue

I became the co-owner of Dean's Ocean Galley and the first thing I did was insist we re-upholster the booths and give the dining room a fresh coat of paint. I love the feeling I get when I pull my new Honda into the parking lot and see customers sipping coffee and chatting, knowing I'm at least partially responsible for their contentedness. I'm trying to talk Dean into adding cod to the menu, but he's being pretty stubborn. I know I'll wear him down eventually.

I'm renting a bungalow and meeting with Sunny Dandridge whenever she has a new listing. I know what I'm looking for, it's just a matter of holding out until I find it.

Josh lived with me for two unbearable weeks before I kicked his ass out. Mom and Dad let him have his old room back, which came as no surprise, but he's paying for the privilege in sweat. He's working as a fryer at the Donut Hut in Fillington, and retiling Mom and Dad's bathroom at night. Once he's finished with that project, they have at least a thousand more for him.

Mom was profiled in a local magazine as an up-and-coming artist. She is broadening her skills by painting grasshoppers and beetles on her stones. It's not exactly high art, but she makes a killing at craft fairs.

Dad didn't find any *Antiques Roadshow* treasures in his vast collection of junk, but he did find an old boxing dummy. He's been working out in the basement every night and he's managed to shed fifteen pounds. It would have been twenty if he could stay away from Josh's day-old chocolate doughnuts.

Hannah and David Baxter did *not* get married for the fourth time. David ran off with my maid of honor replacement, Chloe Patterson, shortly before the ceremony, *which I wasn't even invited to.*

After his relationship with Beth ended, Chris met the girl of his dreams during a weekend trip to Olympia. Unfortunately, her dreams were of other girls.

Max and Jaundice visit the Galley every afternoon to give me updates on the trial. As it turned out, the *Temp*tations employee wasn't qualified for the job, but she also wasn't responsible for injuring any patients. The equipment, manufactured by Wallace Enterprises, was faulty. Max and Jaundice filed a suit on P.J.'s behalf, and the families of other patients joined them. P.J. is still living at Whispering Pines for the time being, and may have to stay there permanently. My two favorite regulars are hoping for the best. They plan to take P.J. to the first live NHL game of his life if and when he's ready to travel.

It turned out that the reason Justin couldn't see his brother at Whispering Pines was because Lucas was no longer there. Marty picked him up one morning and the two men met with the former Mrs. McDade to figure out where to go from there. Lucas lives in Fillington now, and meets with a therapist a couple of times a week. He's too smitten with his new girlfriend to care that Justin and I are an item, and from what I've seen in her coy smile and fluttering eyelashes, the feeling is mutual.

Justin is very busy with landscaping, and he bought a street salter to guarantee work in the winter months. He says that since we met, he hasn't had the slightest desire to leave Bent Harbor, or my side. I am absolutely, wholeheartedly in love with him, but haven't quite managed to tell him yet. I'm sure he already knows, but I'm still a bit shy about saying it out loud.

It'll come.

Just like everything else in my life, those words will fall into place.